THE HARPY AND THE DRAGON

MARIE LIPSCOMB

Karen Ubel
2022

ISBN 978-1-957313-07-8

Cover: Najla Qamber of Qamber Designs and Media

Editing: Lauriel Masson-Oakden of LMO Editing

Formatting: Jack Harbon

To new beginnings.
And for anyone who has ever been told to smile more.

CONTENT NOTES

The main characters of this story are definitely on the darker gray end of the morality scale, and the book includes potentially triggering scenes of violence, blood, death, and one instance of the heroine being whipped with a riding crop.

For a portion of the story, the hero intends to ride out to meet his death and has thoughts of the world being better off without him. However, he does not go through with the plan. There are also scenes with characters eating food, drinking alcohol, and using bad language.

There are multiple explicit scenes of vaginal, oral, and anal sex (in all instances of anal sex, the hero is enthusiastically receiving and the heroine is eagerly giving.)

This story ends with a childfree happily ever after.

A SUMMARY

* A SUMMARY OF EVENTS FROM PREVIOUS BOOKS. *

After twelve years of petitioning the Champion's Guild, Lady Natalie Blackmere was beyond excited to host the champions' Grand Tourney. Known for being the strongest and most skilled fighters in all Aldland, the champions were her heroes. Determined to meet them as a commoner and not as a noblewoman, Natalie disguised herself as a barmaid. After hearing reports of bandits on nearby roads, she dispatched the entirety of her castle's guard to deal with the problem and ensure her people's safety, and spent the night serving drinks to the champions. There she met Brandon the Bear, once the greatest champion who ever lived, and that is where their love story began.

But among the champions was Henry Percille, the most recent winner of the Grand Tourney; handsome, skilled, and a firm believer in his own fame. Seeking to win favor with the noblewoman and further his reputation, he paid bandits to attack the village, with the aim of fighting them off and becoming a hero. His plan failed when the bandits betrayed him, seeing an opportunity to take the town and its castle for themselves after finding it unguarded.

One of the few surviving champions after the attack, Henry fled into Blackmere's woods alongside Brandon, another champion named Genevieve, and a barmaid from the tavern. There he attempted to rectify the situation, pleading with Lady Blackmere's allies in the hopes that his mess could be fixed. When the barmaid was revealed to be none other than the noblewoman herself, Henry saw an opportunity to not only gain riches, but to be free of the Champion's Guild which would no doubt punish him when word of his betrayal reached the Guild Master.

Henry proposed to Lady Blackmere, offering to fight for her in exchange for her hand in marriage, but when she refused, he fled, knowing the likelihood that the bandits would reveal it was he who had hired them.

Returning to the Champion's Guild, Henry set to work convincing the Guild Master that he had done no wrong, so that when Brandon the Bear returned to the Guild, the groundwork would be laid on which he would build the case for his innocence.

So began a fraught year at the Champion's Guild, with Lady Natalie Blackmere acting as a squire to Brandon the Bear while continuing their forbidden relationship in secret. If they were to be discovered, Brandon would be stripped of his titles and cast out of the Guild. Knowing this, Henry used it as leverage to ensure Brandon and Natalie would not have him expelled from the Guild.

When the time came for the Midsummer Melee, Henry was determined to win, his ambition consuming him to the point where he purposefully injured a fellow champion, Darius, and when—to Henry's horror—Brandon the Bear was revealed to be back at the top of his game and defeated the younger champion, Henry attacked the moment Brandon let his guard down.

Arrested in Westgarden, Henry was dragged back to the Champion's Guild, where he was whipped without mercy by the Guild Master. After publicly declaring their love for one another at Midsummer Melee, Natalie and Brandon became highly sought after, and when Lord Caine of Caer Duloon was announced as the host for the next Grand Tourney, he specifically requested that they compete.

Tasked with training Lady Natalie Blackmere as penance for his wrongdoings, Henry seemed to have been cured of his hubris. He worked closely with her, teaching her to fight like a champion, and secretly hoping that one day he might fill the role of Guild Master, and raise the champions to their former glory. But when the Guild Master died, Brandon was named as the Guild's new leader and together he and Natalie set about abolishing the centuries old position.

After losing in the final round of the tourney, Henry was broken. Not only had his rival been named Guild Master and made sure the role would never pass down to Henry, but he had repeatedly broken the traditions of the Guild, flaunted his forbidden relationship publicly, and been forgiven all his transgressions while Henry was beaten, whipped, and punished.

In a moment of rage, the young champion took a sharpened blade out into the ring, intending to kill Brandon when the time came for them to fight. Realizing his plans, Natalie charged in and thwarted Henry's plans, using the moves he had taught her to fight him off.

Had Henry stopped there he might not have lost a third of his life to a dark, lonely cell.

He plunged his blade into Natalie's belly, almost killing her. But, by the grace of the Goddess, she survived to sentence him to life in a dungeon.

THE HARPY AND THE DRAGON

ONE

Annora clung to the stones of the dungeon walls by her fingertips, heart thundering as she kicked out at her captors.

"Let go of me!" she shrieked to the two guards gripping her arms and dragging her down the stairs. "The Goddess as my witness, you'll pay for this."

Her frantic heart lunged against her ribs, desperate to escape confinement as her blood boiled in her veins. But it was hopeless. They pried her from the algae-slicked granite, lifted her legs from the stairs, and hauled her down into the dungeon. Down into the dark.

The chambermaid filled her lungs with fetid air and screamed, powerless against the guards. No matter how hard she fought and beat her fists against her captors, the dungeon swallowed her down. The light at the top of the stairs shrank smaller and smaller.

Regret and rot wept from the walls, the steady drip

constant throughout the seasons; the stench as familiar to the prisoners of Caer Duloon as fresh air had once been.

Though Annora had never set foot this deep into the bowels of the castle, she knew that reek of decay well. It permeated the lower levels of the fortress where she and the other maids had spent most of their days, a grim reminder of what awaited them if they did not comply with their lord and master's wishes. Now it was to be all she knew; the dark, the smell, the iron bars, and the prisoners.

"This'll teach you to strike a nobleman," one of the guards grunted as they reached the bottom of the staircase.

"He deserved to be struck," she hissed back.

Finally, her feet touched the ground and she was allowed to stand upright, though her hands were pinned behind her back by one of the guards. The other glared at her.

In the dim light of the dungeon, his dark blue uniform appeared almost black. Torchlight flickered on his steel breastplate. He was lean and bald; tall, and hard-eyed. She knew him—not by name, of course—but they had passed each other in the corridor and muttered their good mornings more than once.

She refused to be intimidated by him. "You saw what Lord Caine did to that boy"

"Aye," the guard said. "I saw what he did, and he had every right to do it. Lord Caine is a nobleman who gave a clumsy squire a crack around the ears for spilling his wine. It was over in a moment, until you intervened—"

"The squire was bleeding!"

"And now so is Lord Caine—in front of his party guests, no less."

"I don't give a shit—"

"And on his order, you'll spend the rest of your life in a cell. Be thankful we're not dragging you to the headsman."

The final word rendered her silent. Every breath was like swallowing molten glass as the man leaned toward her and sliced the ties of her apron at her hips with a curved knife.

"Don't want you cutting your own sentence short," he growled, pulling the garment away and casting it aside.

"I wouldn't give you the satisfaction." Annora's skin bristled in the cold, her full, curvaceous figure clad only in a plain, white wool dress, the tanned leather slippers on her feet barely keeping out the chill which seeped from the stone floor. Her honey blonde hair trailed in loose waves over her shoulders, pulled from her braid sometime during the fight.

Her captors' teeth chattered as they stared her down, but Annora locked her lips together so they would not quiver, in case they mistook her shivers for frightened trembling. Instead, she turned her attention to the cells on the other side of the dungeon.

The few torches dotted around the walls cast dim light over their iron bars, though the fires were more for the benefit of the guards than to give any sort of cheer and warmth.

Lord Caine did not keep prisoners for long, and for now, that was a mercy. Most of the cells were empty, but for one. A large man sat with his back to them, so silent and still

3

he could have been dead already and frozen stiff. His long black hair sat in tangled waves about his broad, slumped shoulders, which were shrouded in a filthy gray wolf pelt.

"Do I need to put you in irons, or will you get into the cell?" the guard asked, snapping Annora's attention back to him.

Panic clawed at her chest, and the dungeon seemed to tilt as the hopelessness of the situation pressed down on her, suffocating, and snuffing the fight from her heart. She could not overpower the two of them; her struggle from the banquet hall to the cells had proven that.

But perhaps, if she earned their trust, she could outsmart them. Annora was approaching her fortieth spring, and had learned through years of servitude that sometimes it was better to comply and wait for the opportune moment.

"I'll go to my cell," she said as submissively as she could manage. "What other choice do I have?"

"None," the guard said, before giving a curt nod to the man at her back. He stepped back, raking his gaze along the length of her body. "You know, if you smiled a bit more, perhaps the lord wouldn't have been so harsh."

Coiling her fists and clenching her jaw, she kept her eyes level with his and her expression neutral. She rarely smiled, and certainly not by request. She would sooner die than smile for a man holding her captive.

The second guard tired of her first and shoved her hard in the direction of the cells, past black iron shackles and chains which rattled in the breeze as she passed. She would not fall prey to them. If her hands were bound it would be hopeless, and she might never escape.

As she passed by the only occupied cell, the prisoner turned his head to watch her, and enough that she caught a glimpse of his face. He was not dead. Far from it.

Filth clung to him, embedded in every crease of his pale skin. His beard and hair were long and unkempt, his clothes tattered, and though he sat huddled beneath the wolf pelt he still shivered. But his piercing blue eyes shone even in the dungeon darkness. If not for the light in those eyes, Annora would have thought him broken by his captivity. But they were burning, mesmerizing, and the only sky she was guaranteed for a long time.

"We brought you a friend," the guard at her back chuckled, nudging the bars of the man's cage with the toe of his boot. "Bet it's a long time since you saw a woman, eh?"

Dutifully the prisoner stood to his full height, towering half a head above the guards. He was a large man, solidly built and dressed in a tattered black wool tunic which stretched tight over the soft mound of his stomach.

"No," the prisoner said, in a smooth, dark voice. Smoke and spiced honey. "You had a beggar woman in here not two weeks ago—"

"Quiet," the guard growled. "Or it'll be the pail for you again."

It seemed impossible for the prisoner's eyes to burn brighter, but he glowered at the guard as though he could melt the iron in the bars by touch alone. It was as though the cage surrounding him was merely a suggestion of captivity.

His large, strong hands curled to fists at his sides, and every muscle in Annora's body tensed in response.

The man had not spoken one word to her and yet she

knew without doubt he was dangerous. Instinct told her to stay away from him, yet curiosity pulled her closer. However long he had been left in the cell, it had not yet broken him, and that resilience could be useful. Besides, he was to be her only companion unless she found a way out.

"Why are you locking her away?" the captive asked. "Did she steal a turnip from a stall like the beggar?"

Annora turned her head to face him as the guard's keys jangled in the lock in the empty cell opposite. "No. I hit Lord Caine."

The prisoner's lips pulled into a slow, confident grin which told her that beneath the grime and unkempt beard, was a man who knew how handsome he was. In the years before he was caged, it would have been a smile which stole hearts, a smile which would tempt anyone he wanted to follow him to his bed.

"Is he hurt?" he asked.

She found herself mirroring his mirth, at least internally. Outwardly she remained as stone-faced as ever. "Aye, I think his nose is broken. He was bleeding when they took me, but I didn't get much time to be sure."

"Shut up," the guard growled, the clear threat of violence sharpening his voice.

The prisoner chuckled, flashing that disarming smile once more. "Excellent. May I ask your name?"

"Annora." She had no idea why she was answering him, only that her lips would not allow silence.

"Annora."

Her name was silk on his tongue sending a shiver down her spine.

She did not allow her gaze to falter. "And yours?"

"Henry. Henry Percille. Tell me, Annora, did he cry?"

"Bring the pail," the bald guard barked at the other. In an instant, the man was gone from sight, and the sound of sloshing water came from the back of the dungeon.

Calmly, Henry took a step toward the bars, wrapping his hands around them. He braced himself as the guard reappeared with an overflowing wooden bucket and handed it to the bald one. With a sneer, the man stepped back toward her cell, drew back the pail and flung water over the prisoner. Icy drops tingled against Annora's forearms as Henry gasped and wiped his face.

Droplets fell from his hair and beard and ran like rivers over his burly frame. And Annora's gaze traced each one, down over the hills and valleys of his body. She swallowed against the barricade in her throat.

"Yes, Caine cried," she said. "He sobbed in front of all his dinner guests—" A pained gasp burst from her lips as a blunt force between her shoulder blades rammed her forward into the cell. Iron bars clanged shut behind her.

"Quiet, both of you, or I'll have both of you frozen solid before the night is out," the second guard snarled.

There was much Annora still wanted to say; why she hit Lord Caine, that she would do it again given half the chance, that she hoped the guards' beds were filled with venomous spiders when they got home that night. But she needed them. If she was to escape, her best hope was to give her captors cause to trust her.

"Forgive me," she said, loud enough for the retreating guards to hear. "Today has been...trying."

"It can get a lot worse," the bald guard warned before walking from sight.

Their boots clattered on the stairs as they ascended, and the heavy oak door groaned and slammed closed. Annora and the prisoner were alone.

The erratic drip of water somewhere in the dungeon filled the empty seconds. Annora fought her instinct to panic, breathing through the terror of confinement. It was temporary, nothing more than an inconvenience she told herself. She would be free before the night was out.

But the dungeon reeked of filth and decay, the suffocating air powdered with mold and already unbearable.

Her burgeoning panic stalled as Henry let out a gasping breath and pulled his black hair back behind his shoulders, squeezing out all the freezing water he could. He shivered as he lifted his dripping tunic over the top of his head, and stood in his cell naked from the waist up.

Though the tight tunic had done little to hide the shape of his figure, now he was without it she could map it faithfully. Pale sun-starved skin dusted with dark hair on his broad chest and round, softened stomach. Long scars covered every part of his torso, left no doubt by a whip or blade. Whoever this man was, he had known suffering.

Perhaps he even deserved it.

He was the largest man she had ever laid eyes on, strong and powerfully built, but fed well and left to sit idle in his small cell. The sight of him alone was enough to make her thighs clench.

"I can't imagine how good it must have felt to hit that bastard," Henry said as he wrung the water from his tunic and let it splash upon the stone floor. "I'd give anything for the chance."

Chest aching, Annora sucked in a breath, realizing she had not drawn one since before he removed his tunic. "Aye, and I'd do it again—"

"Truly?" A low chuckle sounded in the opposite cell as Henry's scarred shoulders shook. "Even knowing you would have to spend your life in a cell?"

"Aye, well..." She turned, glancing behind her at her new living quarters. Like her room upstairs, there was a simple cot for her to sleep upon, a chamber pot stashed beneath it, and little else. But at least her room upstairs had a threadbare rug on the stones to keep out some of the cold. Then again, her former neighbors were not quite so dangerously handsome. "The view's nicer down here, at least."

Henry paused a moment, his tunic twisted between his large hands as water droplets fell from the wool. He arched an eyebrow and continued his task.

Curiosity burned in Annora's chest, desperate to break loose. Henry was not at all what she imagined when she first saw him sitting on the floor of his cell. She had expected a ruffian, all snarls and vulgarity, but Henry was altogether more quietly intimidating. If he was to be her only companion, she should know what sort of man he was.

She cleared her throat. "How long have you been down here?"

"Has midwinter come?"

"Just last week."

His eyebrows lifted a moment in silent surprise. "Almost ten years. A third of my life."

The answer chilled her blood. Ten years of darkness while the world above went on without him. Ten years without human contact save for the guards' brutality. Forgotten, left in the dark while his fellow prisoners were dragged to the executioner. And yet, he outlived them all.

Whoever he was, he was worth keeping.

A fear prickled in the back of her mind, that perhaps he was a nobleman too; a leech, a parasite feeding off the labor of commoners. Prisoners were not cheap to hold, but Lord Caine had gone to great expense to keep this man not only alive, but well-fed.

"What did you do?" she asked.

"Hm," Henry chuckled as he untwisted the black wool in his hands. "Should I list my crimes alphabetically, by date, or in order of severity?"

That made her chuckle. "Oh aye? Are you so terrible?"

"The very worst," Henry said with a weary sigh, squeezing his damp tunic back over his body. It clung even tighter. "My crimes are far beyond hitting a lord."

Annora's breath caught. Yes, for the foreseeable future, she was to be locked in a cage, but at least she was locked away with a man who piqued her curiosity. She may as well be entertained while she thought out an escape plan. Crossing her cell, she sat on the edge of her cot. "Start at the beginning. Tell me everything."

CHAPTER

TWO

enry was tired, an exhaustion which had long since settled into his marrow and could not be relieved by sleep. He had been that way for years, confined to a cell with little to do but fester. His only comfort was the fur—a wolf pelt given to him by Lady Natalie Blackmere, the noble who had callously sentenced him to languish and rot in the dungeon for the rest of his life.

No, that was wrong.

Natalie was a woman who had forgiven him time and time again, who had almost become a friend. A woman he had betrayed and stabbed in the gut when she stopped him from lashing out in anger against the man she loved.

And, soft-hearted as they were, Natalie and Brandon had made sure that Henry at least had a wolf fur to keep him warm, even after he had tried to kill them.

But now he found himself tossing his only comfort

across to the opposite cell, to a chambermaid, who shivered from the cold.

"Take it," he told her, nodding toward where it rested on the ground between their cells.

"It's yours."

"Yes, I'm well aware, but your teeth are chattering."

She eyed him and the pelt suspiciously, and he could not blame her. He could not fathom why he was doing it either. Henry was many things but he was not soft. Not for anyone.

"You're keeping me awake," he added. "You can give it back when you've warmed up."

Annora crouched and reached between the bars, retrieving the fur from the stone floor. He tried to turn away from her, tried not to glance across as the tops of her breasts spilled over the neckline of her dress, but he failed. A kick, low in his belly, told him he was not yet completely drained of all feeling.

She was pretty, undeniably so; all ample curves and—apparently—fiery temper. If she had been a tavern maid and he was still a champion, he'd have charmed her with a smile and had her pinned against the wall in some dark corner by now.

"Thank you," she said, wrapping the gray fur around her shoulders, dipping her head to cover her nose.

Henry clenched his fists so she might not see him shiver. "Better?"

"Aye," she nodded, and yet she grimaced. "It stinks though."

"Give it back then."

Without a word, she returned to her cot and sat cross-legged, tucking her feet beneath her knees. "How can you stand it down here?"

A laugh shook his chest. "Well, I asked them for a nicer room, one with a window, a roaring fireplace, and a steaming bath, but the service in this establishment is appalling." His heart lifted as she chuckled at his jest.

"Well, we should complain to the owner in the morning."

"I wouldn't bother. The landlord doesn't give a shit."

Annora laughed again.

She was a curiosity. Ordinarily people wept when they were thrown into the dungeons, even for a short time. Sometimes they screamed throughout the night, throwing themselves at the bars of their cell, trying to shake loose the iron with their white-knuckled fists until they passed out from exhaustion. But not Annora.

"Aren't you afraid?" he asked.

"Of you?"

Well, that thought had not occurred to him, but since she mentioned it... "You probably should be."

She shrugged beneath the fur. "There are noblemen sat up there in the banquet hall who I'm sure have done far worse than you have. One of the worst among them is the lord of this castle, and I've served him for more than twenty years. As far as I'm concerned those are the people who should be removed from society."

That he could not argue with. "Well, you're awfully calm for someone who found out moments ago that they have to spend the rest of their life down here."

Another shrug. "I told you, the fair view softens the blow."

The fur slipped from her shoulders revealing a slither of her pale skin and Henry's chest ached at the sight of it. More than ten years had passed since he had lain with anyone, and almost as long since he thought himself fair. He pulled in a breath, fighting to drag the air past the fluttering barrier in his chest.

"Anyway, you were going to tell me about your crimes," she said. "We have a lot of time to kill and I'm fond of a good story."

"Alright." He backed away from the bars and settled on the end of his own cot. "What do you want to know?"

"Who were you before?"

"A champion." The words winded him every time, leeching a little more of the fight from him. He had been a champion, one of the very best champions... but never good enough. Never as good as Brandon the Bear.

"Ah," Annora rolled her eyes. "I might have known."

"You recognize me?"

Her laughter rang around the dungeon. "No? Why would I?"

Indignation furrowed his brow. How could she not know him? One of the worst of his crimes had been committed in that very same city before an audience of thousands. "I'm Henry Percille..." He waited for a reaction but remained wanting. "The Dragon?"

The revelation only made her laugh again. She tilted her head to the side with a strange sort of affection. She wasn't only ridiculing him, she *pitied* him, and that heated his blood.

"How can you not—?"

"Henry, I come from the Marshlands, far, far north. Up there we don't call you champions."

"What do you call us?"

A grin curled the corners of her lips. "Posers, mostly. That's when we want to be nice. Sometimes it's less flattering."

His face heated. "I—"

"You live in castles and have make-believe fights against your friends with blunted swords. As far as we're concerned, you're no different from the nobles upstairs. Aye, I lied. I've heard your name. I've heard the songs about you, the mighty Dragon and all your conquests. I've yet to be impressed."

"How dare you," he snarled as he stood from his cot and crossed the cell in a stride, wrapping his hands around the iron bars as though he could crumble them like burned bread. "And what exactly have you achieved in your miserable little life?"

"Nothing, but I don't claim to."

"I'm *nothing* like the nobles."

She only shook her head and let her eyes trail the length of his body. "You might be a bit more intimidating if we weren't both caged."

"Give me back my fur."

She chuckled quietly before standing and crossing her own cell. "The world is filled with men drunk on their own self-importance, Henry Percille."

"There are no men like me."

"Tell me then, before you were sent down here to rot, did you ever have to empty your own piss pot?"

Henry frowned; his arm still outstretched awaiting his fur. His life before the cell seemed a distant dream, but he remembered parts of it. He would awaken each dawn to a feast, surrounded by people who spoke of his prowess and potential. And when his belly was filled, he would go out to the courtyard and show them how right they were. After a hard day in the list, his bed was always prepared, his chamber pot not only emptied but scrubbed clean by unseen servants. He would trade all his remaining days but the last one, if it meant he could spend it like that. "What does that have to do with anything?"

"I take it that means, no?"

"We had servants *who were paid—*"

"Well," she said, tossing the fur across to him. He snatched it from the air. "I'm one of the servants who cleans up after men like you, and believe me, one chamber pot is the same as the next. None of you smell of roses, none of you shit golden eggs. Nobleman or champion, makes no difference to me. You spend your life standing on the backs of others. Or you would, if you weren't caged and declawed." She laughed scornfully. "Dragon indeed. You're nothing more than a worm."

His blood burned, and his heart lunged against his ribs. He could barely stand to look at that foul woman. She was beautiful, yes, but already a thorn in his side, and he was possibly condemned to spend the rest of his life with her, unless fate smiled upon him and either one of them was bound for the executioner's block.

And yet, just as her praise had stirred his interest in her, so too did her ridicule. Try as he might, he could not look away, and curse it all he could not stop talking. The need to prove himself to her, to prove he was unlike any of those men upstairs sitting at Lord Caine's tables, burned at the core of him.

"*Declawed*? I betrayed the champions," he said as she turned her back on him and stooped to slide the red clay chamber pot from beneath her bed. He averted his eyes in case she meant to use it. "I paid bandits to overtake Blackmere castle so that I could fight them off. But they double-crossed me and I got my friend killed."

She laughed, approaching the bars, and once more drawing his gaze. "Is that supposed to impress me? Sounds more like foolishness and incompetence than anything."

"And I stabbed Lady Blackmere."

"Good," she sighed, pushing the pot sideways through a gap in the bars. When it went through, she gave a contented sigh. "I recommend everyone get at least one good hit on a noble at some point in their life. It does wonders for the heart."

He stepped back, holding the fur to his chest. It still held the warmth from her body, and above the usual foul stench of it, the soft scent of her wafted over him. He despised how intoxicated he was by her, how desperately he wished there were no bars between them. Whether he would silence her with a kiss, or with his hand clamped over her mouth he was unsure.

He turned his back on her, willing the strength of his resolve to hold out as she continued her strange ritual with the chamber pot. "It's more impressive than just hitting a lord," he muttered.

"Oh, aye, I'm sure."

The old fire of battle flickered in the depths of his dormant heart. He would prove her wrong, prove he was more than she could possibly imagine. "You have some nerve, chambermaid!" His voice echoed around the dungeon. "I know that without these bars between us, you wouldn't be half so bold."

Her reply was quiet and frustratingly calm, "Without these bars between us, I wouldn't spend a single second in your company. I've no interest in rich little boys who chase their friends about with wooden swords."

"By the Goddess, I hope they hang you!"

"*Oi!*" A voice called from the top of the stairs. It was a voice he was all too familiar with. "What's going on down there, scum?"

The steady clunk of boots on the stone steps echoed around the dungeon, announcing the arrival of Henry's more detested tormentor. Across the way, Annora pulled the chamber pot back into her cell and concealed it behind her skirt. She stood to attention, her chin raised and lips clamped shut.

The guard appeared between them, a pail of ice-cold water already sloshing beside him, but his eyes were not on Annora. Weak torchlight gleamed on his bald head as he sneered at Henry. "Why are you shouting, *Dragon*?"

"Because she—" He stopped himself, keeping his

temper in check. He would be drenched either way, but if he was quiet, it might only be once. "I apologize."

"We can hear you upstairs, you know. Lord Caine isn't very happy with you. He's trying to salvage what remains of his banquet."

Lord Caine's name clawed at the back of his mind. There were many people Henry hated, but none so much as the coward who held him prisoner for a decade without even once coming down to the depths of the dungeon. He breathed slowly through his nose as his muscles coiled, preparing for the cold water.

"He told me to give you this," the guard snarled, stepping back in preparation to throw.

Henry closed his eyes and gripped the iron bars, preparing to be drenched. The sound of shattering pottery filled the dungeon as cold water sloshed over Henry's boots. His eyes darted open in shock, in time to see the guard stumble toward him and collapse onto the stones at the front of his cell, surrounded by broken shards of Annora's chamber pot. The woman stood wide-eyed, staring at the unconscious man on the ground.

"Oh," she breathed, color draining from her cheeks.

He followed her line of vision, to the belt at the guard's hip, and the cell keys hanging there. Lying within easy reach of Henry.

THREE

E verything had gone according to plan. Henry was as easy to rile as she suspected, the guard as cruel as she anticipated. He had stepped back the same as before, and she had struck him with desperate ferocity. Annora had planned for everything but one inevitable twist of fate.

The guard had not fallen at her feet, but had stumbled toward Henry before he crumpled to the ground,

"Henry..."

A wicked smile curled his lips as he retrieved the keys from the guard's belt and turned it in his own lock. The sharp *clunk* of freedom turned that wicked smile ecstatic. "Well, I suppose I should thank you."

"You could thank me by setting me free." The treacherous quiver in her voice brought tears to her eyes. "Please."

The door of his cell groaned as it opened, the hinges old and hardly ever used. His lips parted as he stepped through it, no doubt the furthest he had ventured in a decade. "What was it you called me? A worm?"

"I wanted the guard to come down. I needed to make you angry."

"Ah." His eyebrows raised as he stepped toward her cell. "So, insulting me was all part of your plan?"

"Yes."

"You couldn't have told me to shout?"

"I didn't know whether I could trust you."

He was close, so close the heat of his body pressed against her through the iron bars. Without his confines he was somehow even larger, his blue eyes even more striking.

She was breathless as he reached between the bars, tilting her chin with a crooked finger.

"You can't," he whispered.

Icy fear seeped into her bones but she could not look away. "Don't leave me here alone."

"Oh, I wouldn't worry about that," he said, stroking a hand down her cheek. "I doubt you'll be here for long once they find him lying on the floor like this."

"Set me free."

"Make me."

She swallowed the lump in her throat even as she found herself leaning into his touch. He was at once the most toxic poison and the most alluring, thirst-sating elixir. "I'll tell them you did it."

He chuckled. "Ah, but my pot is still in my cell, and yours..." he glanced down, to the shards of blood-red clay littering the dungeon floor and cringed in mock sympathy. "I don't think they'll believe you. Such a shame to know this lovely, cunning head of yours will soon be on a spike outside Lord Caine's bedroom window."

Her heart thundered as he stepped back, the smile on his face never faltering. "Henry... please don't leave me."

"Farewell, Annora." He dipped his chin in lieu of a bow and prepared to bolt.

In the next heartbeat she pulled in a breath as a scream gathered force inside her chest. She was a dead woman either way, but at least she could take him down with her. No sooner had her lips parted that his hand clamped over her mouth.

"Quiet," he hissed, eyes wide as he snaked his other arm around her waist, pulling her to him through the bars. "They'll hear you."

"Then let me go!" she cried, the words stifled against his palm. Even with the cold bars between them, his body was hot and heavy against hers, a sturdy wall of scarred flesh and untold strength. Intimidating. Intoxicating.

All her life she had heard stories of the champions, of their skill and prowess. And, of course, there were few in Aldland who had not heard tales of the champions' lust when they were finally permitted to leave their fortress to compete. It seemed every town in Aldland was filled with people who had shared a bed with one of the legendary fighters. Despite her fear, a shiver coursed through her at the thought of the unsated needs of a champion held captive for a decade.

His breath blew hot against her cheek as he waited, listening. The beat of her heart drowned out any merriment above. Henry had the strength and size to break her neck like it was nothing. It would take a flick of his wrist to dash her skull against the bars, but he simply held her, the rise and fall of his broad chest measuring the passage of time.

"Alright..." His throat pulsed above her as he swallowed. "I'll let you out but you have to be silent, understand?"

She nodded, relief almost bringing tears to her eyes. Gently, he pulled his palm from her lips, a hair's breadth at first, then more as she remained silent.

"Good," he whispered and the keys jingled in his hand. "I'll let you out."

Her breath came back to her in hurried bursts as he unlocked her cell and opened the door, stepping aside to let her pass. She no more trusted him than she did a viper coiled and ready to strike, but he was her only hope of freedom.

"We need to hurry," he said, turning on his heel toward the dungeon stairs. "They'll send someone looking for him."

Instinctively, she reached out, gripping the damp wool of his tunic at his elbow. "Aye, and they'll see two prisoners escaping the dungeon when they come this way."

Realization dawned across his features as his eyes darted around the gloomy dungeon and settled on the man lying at their feet. The uniform would be too small for a man such as Henry, but if he could squeeze into the dark blue surcoat and steel breastplate, it would serve as enough of a disguise to get them out of the castle.

Without a word, Henry dropped to his knees and set to work stripping the man of his uniform.

"Is he alive?" Annora asked.

"I don't care," Henry muttered as he unbuckled the

breastplate. He glanced back up at her, his eyes searching her face a moment before his brow softened. "I think so. Just sleeping."

"Pity."

Henry's eyes narrowed before a grin broke across his face.

While he dressed, Annora found her apron, the ties cut by the guards. She made do with what little was left, creating a tight, unsightly knot at her hip, and hoped it would not be too obvious at first glance. She smoothed her hand over the fabric as Henry dragged the guard into his cell.

"It should make him a little harder to discover," he grunted as he lugged the man across the stones. When he was in place Henry closed the cell door and slipped the keys onto the belt at his own waist. He looked the part from the neck down, the long dark blue surcoat coming down to his thighs, skimming over the shape of his body. Thick thighs strained against the pale cloth of his breeches, which seemed to be held together by nothing more than the will of the Goddess. Annora averted her eyes from the sight of them, and silently scolded herself for wishing the seams would burst apart.

A short sword and crossbow hung beside the keys at his hip. The breastplate could barely contain him either, but there was little they could do about it. Certainly, she would not spend what could be her last remaining minutes alive wishing the seams would fail and the clothes drop off him. Certainly not.

She forced herself to focus above his neck, where he was undeniably wild.

"Will I do?" he asked, throwing the gray wolf pelt over his shoulders.

"You're taking that?"

"Yes." His answer came hard and certain.

"The guards don't wear wolf pelts—"

"This one does."

It was futile arguing with him. As well as being built like he wrestled oxen for fun, she was quickly learning he was also as stubborn as the beasts.

"Your hair, then," she said, stepping toward him. "We need to do something about it at least. Here, kneel for a moment."

"We haven't time—"

"If they see you, they'll never believe you're a guard with hair like that. On your knees."

With a resigned sigh he did as she instructed, dropping to one knee on the stones before her. Even kneeling, he was only a head shorter than her.

"Sword," she said.

"Why?" His eyes widened a little. "You're not cutting my hair, are you?"

"Hurry, just give me the sword."

"How do I know you won't slit my throat?"

"You don't."

Her blood simmered. He was the most exasperating man she had ever met, but inconveniently, he was also the most handsome. Half of her longed to hit him, as she had Lord Caine, but the other half, the half she tried her best to

25

drown out, relished the knowledge that if she tried it, he could so easily overpower her. And she would let him. Goddess save her, she would love it.

He pressed the hilt of the blade to her palm, his throat twitching as his eyes never faltered from hers. "Do what you must."

"So, you trust me?"

The corner of his mouth curved. "No."

If they died right there, she would be content that the last thing she saw before she was beckoned to the Goddess's side was his face and those eyes gazing up at her, his pupils spreading like spilled ink in azure waters. She forced herself to breathe, to move quickly as she swept back his hair with her fingertips and gathered it at the nape of his neck.

A thrill of pleasure jolted her as his fingers skated along the outsides of her thighs, quickening her pulse, and sending heat flooding to her cheeks. Even through the wool of her dress their strength was unmistakable, as was their bridled brutality. And, despite her indignation, some part of her longed to feel that same touch between her thighs. It pulled at her like a thread connected to the very core of her.

"What are you doing?" she heard herself say.

"Do you want me to stop?"

The answer pressing at her lips scared her, so she said nothing.

Henry winced as she wrapped his long hair around her fist and pulled it tight, tilting back his head and exposing his throat. His lips parted in anticipation as she placed the blade at the nape of his neck and sliced upward, cutting away the long, black curls of hair, and letting them fall to the stones.

"Happy?" he growled.

As his breath blew against the exposed skin above her breast, she was anything but.

His beard was still long and disheveled, but there was nothing she could do about that. The blade would only make it worse, so she ran her fingers through it, smoothing what she could. All the while his hands trailed the lengths of her thighs, stoking a deep almost painful urge.

"Come on," she muttered when she was done making him look as domesticated as possible. "We need to hurry."

She turned on her heel and marched toward the stairs, hoping her cheeks were not blazing quite so bright as they felt.

CHAPTER

FOUR

P lunging his face into the barrel of icy water at the foot of the staircase, Henry held his breath a moment, hoping it might quell the fire burning in his chest. Desire called to him, taunting him. The desire to throw Annora down on the cold stone steps and release ten years of frustration and lust between the soft pillows of her generous thighs. She was sturdy, unbearable, almost unwavering, and Goddess, he wanted her desperately.

He had no idea what color her eyes were, only that they regarded him with disdain and genuine curiosity, and he loved her a little for that. The dungeon was still dark, but without the bars separating them, he could make out a few dark freckles on her round cheeks and petulant brow.

But now was not the time to stop and admire them, and he was certainly not risking his life for anyone else. Especially not the woman who had insulted him a hundred times already. He had lied to her about the guard simply sleeping to protect her conscience, but that would be the full extent of his affection for her. Not that she needed him to. Savage little creature that she was.

Gasping, he pulled his face from the water and shook his head, smoothing his hair back. The dungeon grime still clung to him. It would take several long soaks in a scalding tub to even permeate beneath the layers and begin to remove the stench of that wretched place from his body. But first, they needed to escape.

"Are you done preening?" Annora asked, already halfway up the stairs.

He glared in response and followed her. The short climb up the steps should not have drained him as much as it did. Not him. Not the champion, the warrior who once fought and won six straight melee rounds in the Blackmere Tourney. But as he climbed the dungeon stairs his calves burned, his thighs ached, and the sight of Annora's rounded backside ahead of him made it even harder to catch his breath.

"Hurry," she hissed over her shoulder.

Henry's fingers curled around the hilt of his blade as they reached the top of the stairs. His heart pounded against his ribs, as eager to break free as the rest of him. The promise of the world awaiting him was as terrifying as it was enticing, his freedom so close that the warmth of the sun was already beating against his back. He was not about to let anything, or anyone, risk that.

Annora was spirited, but she was also unarmed and likely untrained in combat. She could no more fight off the guards than he could lift a mountain.

"This is where our alliance ends," he told her, his voice

little more than a hoarse whisper. "Beyond this door it's each for themselves."

Her eyebrows knitted together. "Oh, so you know your way about the castle?"

His jaw tightened as he forced out a breath. "No."

She folded her arms across her chest. The silence as she waited for his admission was broken only by their shaking breaths.

"Fine," he muttered. "We stick together, for now. But if you hold me back, I'll not wait for you. And if you get into trouble, I will not stop and fight to protect you. Do you understand?"

She nodded. "The same to you. We stick together but I have no intention of dying for you."

The ridiculousness of her statement almost made him choke. The mere suggestion that a chambermaid could fight trained guards when Henry could not, was laughable. But he needed her for directions, and she, unarmed and help-less, needed him to fight.

Her eyes bore into his, her pupils almost entirely swal-lowing her irises. Her lips parted as her gaze dropped to his mouth. "Are you ready?" she asked.

Unhooking the keys from his belt, he found the largest, and placed it in the lock of the door. "You first. If there are guards posted outside, you can't be on the stairs when I throw them down."

She nodded, her breath stuttering as she smoothed her hands over her apron. "It's a right turn, then down the corridor to the door by the crossed blades. That'll take you to the kitchen entrance. You can escape there. There's a small gate in the castle wall as soon as you get out. They bring the supplies in there each week and it's in need of repair. The hinges are naught but rust. You should be able to break it down easy enough."

Her words sent a shiver down his spine. Part of her did not expect to make it out of the castle. She was giving him his freedom.

"Annora," he whispered, raising his hand to brush an errant strand of golden hair over her shoulder. Her eyelids fluttered shut at his touch. Brave Annora. Beautiful Annora. Vicious Annora.

If he did not make it out of the castle, he could content himself with only ever seeing the golden sunlight locked in her hair, or the infinite night sky in her pupils as she gazed up at him. He unhooked the crossbow and a set of bolts from his belt and placed them in her palm. "If they're to take us, let us fight till the end."

The shift in him was uncomfortable, gripping his chest tighter and making it ache more than any pail of ice water could. Henry Percille was not that sort of man. He did not surrender his weapon to anyone, certainly not when it lowered his chances of survival.

Perhaps it would be better to remain in the dungeon after all, so that news of his weakness did not reach the ears of those who would relish his downfall.

His skin tingled as she placed her hand upon his, and guided it toward the key in the lock.

"Let's go," she whispered.

One last glance at her. One last breath to draw the scent of her into him.

He twisted the key and pushed open the door.

Annora was out like a kitchen rat scurrying from a cook, free from the dungeon before the guard posted at the door even knew what was happening.

Henry silently thanked the Goddess there was only one man to fight. Ten years of confinement had ravaged his skill and his strength, but the heat of the fight coursed through him.

The muscles in his arms screamed as he pulled the witless guard back and shoved him with all his might down the stone steps, slamming the dungeon door closed before he even hit the bottom.

He turned the key in the lock and hooked it to his belt, gripping Annora by the crook of her elbow.

"By the Goddess," she hissed between panicked breaths. "Is he dead?"

"I'm certain he's fine," Henry lied. "He'll be beating his fists on the door in no time though, we have to hurry."

With the fire of battle flowing through his veins, lending him strength which felt simultaneously familiar and unknown, he turned to the right and attempted to drag her down the corridor to freedom.

"Wait... wait," she hissed, pressing her heels to the floor to slow him. "It's left."

He frowned. "You said right."

"I lied. I needed a weapon." She tightened her grip on the crossbow and turned on her heel.

"Goddess, I hate you," he sighed, following her.

"Oh, believe me the feeling is entirely mutual," she said,

quickening her pace as much as her short, sturdy legs would allow.

Like a faithful hound, he followed at her heels.

They marched down the hallway, surrounded by luxury and comfort Henry had not seen for so long. Though the walls were still built from the same gray stone which had surrounded him for almost a third of his life, there was a torch in every sconce, narrow windows revealing the darkness outside. Light and space, fresh air, freedom, the perfume of Annora's hair, the sway of her hips. All of it called to him.

Raucous music sounded from above, bringing Henry to a halt, face lifted to the gray stone ceiling.

"Henry," Annora hissed, tugging at his forearm. "We must hurry."

Lord Caine's banquet continued upstairs, his noble guests dancing, their jaunty steps pounding on the floorboards in time with the tune.

Henry swallowed the knot in his throat. "Who was invited to the party?"

"I don't know... it was noble men and women from all over."

His pulse quickened. It was a noblewoman who had sentenced him to his fate. Before he had been sent to the dungeon, he had learned that Lady Natalie Blackmere and Brandon the Bear were betrothed. Brandon was to be the new Lord of Blackmere. A nobleman. That the pair of them could be at the party above was an opportunity he might never be presented with again.

Revenge beckoned him.

"Do you remember any of the names?" Henry asked.

"The guests?" In the periphery of his vision, Annora shook her head. "No. It was all Lord This and Lady That."

"Were any of them Blackmere?"

"I..." She shook her head. "I don't know. I didn't care to learn them."

A low growl of frustration rolled through Henry's chest. "How easy is it to get up there?"

"Are you out of your senses?" Annora wrapped both hands around his wrist and pulled. "We're almost free, Henry."

He did not tear his eyes from the ceiling. The image of them up there, parading about with the other nobles, believing he sat festering while they danced and feasted, tormented him. A thousand potential scenarios played through his mind, a thousand outcomes. Perhaps the guests were so inebriated he could slip in unnoticed and find them.

A firm grip on the neck of his surcoat brought his attention back down, to the woman who glared at him as though she could turn him to dust with her eyes. She twisted her fist in the dark blue fabric, pulling him down toward her.

"Whatever you're thinking, stop," she spat. "If you go up there, you'll be caught and killed, as will I."

"What's going on here?" A man's voice at Henry's back turned them both to stone.

He spun around to see a guard, dressed identically to him patrolling the hallway. The sword at Henry's hip called to him as his heart beat a storm inside his chest.

A smile curved the guard's lips as he scratched at his pale blond beard. "Lover's quarrel, is it?"

"Aye," Annora said, stepping out from behind Henry. "Your guardsman is being an ass, *as usual.* I'm trying to get him to come away with me for a minute, but he's too duty-bound to his post."

Clever, cunning Annora. Tension ebbed from Henry's muscles as she stood by his side.

The guard's eyes scanned the pair of them before he laughed, shaking his head at Henry. "Where are you posted?"

"Back there, outside the dungeon," Henry said.

Annora nodded, tilting her chin. "Mind it for him a minute, would you?"

The guard cringed sympathetically, "I have to patrol."

"We'll be quick..." Annora begged, wrapping her arm around Henry's waist. "I'll only take a minute."

Pressed tightly against him she was warm and soft, and far stronger than she looked. The sensation of her body flush against his heated his blood and set his pulse racing. She placed a hand beneath his breastplate, resting it on the curve of his stomach.

"Likely less than that," Henry added. "It's been a while."

The guardsman laughed again. "Aye, go on then, be as quick as you can. There are already three guards rutting in the stable so you might want to head out to the surplus food store."

"You're a king among men," Annora said with a curtsey.

"Ah, there it is," the guard chuckled. "You're far prettier when you smile."

Henry's back bristled in annoyance as the instinct to cut

the guard down curled in his gut. But Annora's arm was tight around him as she ushered him around and down the hallway, away from the unsuspecting guard.

Her false smile faded as they reached the door by a pair of crossed broadswords. "You're a fool," she whispered, shoving the door with her hip and storming through it.

He had no defense. His hesitation had almost gotten them both caught, but he would be damned before he accepted the blame aloud. "So, to the surplus food shed then? Or shall we see if those rutting guards have room for a fourth and fifth?"

"You're despicable," Annora said, but she was unable to fully hide the curve at the corner of her lips. She did a far better job than he at hiding her amusement.

They entered the kitchen, immediately swallowed by the din of working cooks and maids scrubbing dishes and cooking-pots clean. Bracing himself for more questioning, Henry raised his chin to give off the impression of confidence. These people were Annora's comrades, and surely they would question where she was going with one of the guardsmen while they worked.

Annora's hand grasped his, pulling him through the bustling kitchen as he ducked beneath wooden beams, low hanging herbs, and smoked meats. But the workers paid them little attention, perhaps worn out and desperate to simply get their tasks finished so they could go to bed. Then again, there was every chance they knew what an odious shrew she was, and avoided her altogether. He decided on the latter.

They passed through and reached the back door without so much as a glance cast their way.

Henry's heart leapt to his throat as Annora braced her elbow on the door, still clutching the crossbow in her hand. A blast of freezing air tore toward them, lifting the hair from her shoulders and bringing tears to Henry's eyes.

And it was the cold which tightened his throat. It was. Not the endless night sky, nor the clarity of the wide-open world, welcoming him back with starlight and sparkling frost. Every inch of his skin pebbled as lightning bristled through his veins. Freedom.

He took a step forward and another and another, each step further than he had ever dared to dream he would get.

Someone behind called for them to close the door, so Annora did, her breath coiling through the air in puffs of silver. For a moment, Henry wondered why his own breath did not plume the same way, before realizing he had not yet drawn one. Perhaps tomorrow he would return for revenge and search for Natalie and Brandon but, for now, he intended to savor every moment of freedom he could cling to.

"Just a little further," Annora gasped, bounding down two short steps and onto the castle courtyard, desperately, fruitlessly pulling him. "Come on."

She was right, of course. They were still within the castle walls, and the guard he had sent to mind the dungeon door might be alerted to their escape at any moment. His freedom was an illusion for as long as they hunted him.

But the illusion was enough.

"Henry..."

His gaze fell to their joined hands, their tightly laced fingers. If not for Annora, he would never have gotten even that far. Still, he could not allow himself to grow dependent on her company. Wrenching his hand from hers, he set his jaw. "Alright," he said. "Let's be rid of this place and of each other."

FIVE

Annora stood back as Henry kicked the castle gate, flinging it open like it were made of parchment and string instead of oak and iron. For all his faults—of which there were many—the man was certainly physically impressive.

"Quickly," he barked, fleeing through the gaping portcullis before anyone had a chance to investigate the noise. She followed as fast as her legs could carry her, and when she began to fall behind, he reached back a hand and pulled her along with him.

Together they ran until their lungs gave out and they could do nothing but stumble across the frostbitten land as frozen, yellow grass crunched beneath their feet. The icy wind lashed against them, piercing her skin and biting deep into her bones. But the cold was a small price to pay as the castle faded to a distant silhouetted menace against the milky indigo sky.

"It's almost dawn," Annora wheezed as she stumbled to a halt, resting her hands on her thigh. Every muscle in her body burned, every breath was like swallowing gravel. "Can we rest a minute?"

"You may rest all you want," Henry muttered. His cheeks were red above the dark shadow of his beard. "We said we'd part ways once we left the castle."

"Aye," Annora nodded, even as their hands remained joined. "Very well, off with you then."

Henry's blue eyes scanned the horizon at her back, his broad chest rising and falling rapidly as he fought to catch his breath. "I'll go in a moment."

"Are they behind us?" she asked.

He shook his head. "I don't think so. I don't see any riders."

"Good." She wiped her mouth on the back of her sleeve. "How does freedom feel after ten years?"

"Cold." His brief smile dissolved almost as soon as it appeared before he raised his eyes to the sky. "I'd forgotten how big it all is. But now you're free too. How is it for you?"

Annora nodded. "I've worked in the castle near twenty years. I don't know what's beyond it. But I'll never go back to serving. Never."

"Then what?"

"Perhaps I'll go back north to Marshdown... maybe there's work there."

"Work?" Henry said disdainfully. "Well, if that's what you want then you'd be better off coming with me further south."

"South?" She grimaced. "Nothing good ever came from the south."

His eyebrows stitched together. "The Champion's Guild is in the south. *I* came from the south."

"Aye, exactly."

Exhausted, Annora released her grip on his hand and crumpled to the ground, landing heavily on her backside and setting the crossbow down. With a grunt she flopped back, lying on the frozen grass. The bones in her spine cracked and popped as she stretched.

"You can go," she told him. "I need to rest. Not all of us have the stamina of champions."

"I'm leaving," he said. "I need a moment."

She closed her eyes, as he sat down beside her. Even his big body was sapped of its warmth by the brutal winter air. But as irritating as Henry was, there was also a strange sort of comfort in his presence. A familiarity if nothing else. At least for the time being, she was not so completely alone.

"Why did you hesitate?" she asked.

"Hm?"

"In the castle, you wanted to go upstairs to the banquet hall to find someone. You asked if I remembered their name. Who was it?"

The darkness behind her eyelids threatened to smother her as she waited for his response. When it finally came her heart quickened, jolting her from the onset of sleep.

"No one of any importance."

It was a lie. She barely knew the man but she knew that much. "If you say so."

41

"I do."

"Well, it was a fool thing to do. You could have got us both killed."

He chuckled. "Not at all. I would have thrown you to the guard and escaped while he dealt with you."

With a huff, Annora rolled onto her side and away from him. "I was right, you are a worm."

She awaited his response, vaguely disappointed when none came. Her worn wool dress did little to keep out the chill, and it was not long before she began to shiver. Soon her lips were trembling from the cold, her arms pressing tight around her body as she drew up her knees.

Her muscles clenched at the sensation of something soft and heavy thrown over her body, and the familiar dungeon stench came with it. The fear she had dreamed it all, that she was still on her cot in that forsaken hole sent her heart racing. Opening her eyes, she found the sky above to be a pale gray and dazzling. And Henry's stinking wolf pelt was covering her body.

Somehow, she had been turned around and was facing him once more. He sat still by her side, gazing out across the horizon. One of his hands rested on the ground close to her cheek, the other lay loose across his bended knees. Silver morning light illuminated his features; his bewitching eyes, which had been alight with the thrill of escape the previous night, now soft and peaceful.

His back was to the castle as he looked out over the land ahead of them. In her exhaustion, Annora had not realized they had stopped atop a hill, the rolling plains south west of

Caer Duloon stretching out forever beneath their resting place.

"Good morning," Henry grumbled.

Annora frowned. "How long was I lay here?"

"Long enough for my feet to turn numb."

She sighed. "Did you sleep?"

"No. Somebody needed to keep watch." He turned his head slightly to frown at her. "And you snore."

The thought of him watching over her while she slept churned like curdled milk in her belly. With a groan, she stood, shaking the cold from her aching limbs. The soles of her feet stung, tender after a long night of running. "Well, you're facing the wrong way. If the guards were coming, they would've come from behind." Placing the wolf pelt back over his broad shoulders, she put her hands on her hips and stretched out her back.

"I'm not worried about them coming from the castle. No doubt Lord Caine is glad to be rid of the financial burden," he said, raising himself to stand beside her and held out a hand toward the steep drop below. "I'm watching *them*."

She followed his gesture to a road snaking beneath them, and to a cart making slow progress up the hill, pulled by two black horses. At the sight of the sigil of Caer Duloon fluttering from a banner atop the cart, Annora's heart plummeted to her stomach. There were three guards; two walking beside it, and one steering the horses.

"You fool, we need to run," Annora hissed.

"No," Henry said calmly, lifting the crossbow from the ground and affixing it to his belt. "You need to run *toward* them, make as much of a scene as you can, and I'll get the horses."

"The horses?" She could hardly breathe as her chest grew tight, not yet fully awake and already filled with terror.

"I trust you know what a horse is?"

She narrowed her eyes.

"Good," he smiled, smoothing her hair back over her shoulders and gripping her upper arms. The sensation of his hands on her cut through the cold and the fear, anchoring her to the world. "Do not give them a reason to draw their weapons. There are three guards and I need them unarmed if I'm to stand a chance of fighting them off."

Annora nodded, still trying to piece together what was happening. She was about to walk into danger and risk her life, for no reason other than he had asked her to.

"Can you do it?" he asked.

"Aye," she nodded again, doubting herself even as the word left her throat.

"Good, I'm counting on you." He turned her about and released her. "Go. Now."

Each step was agony as she walked down the hill, mind whirring with questions, insults, ideas, and curses. The thought crossed her mind to let him take down the guards and then take both horses for herself. She would ride far, far north to where neither Lord Caine nor Henry Percille would ever dare to set foot, lest they get a splash of mud on their boots. Either way, whether for him or herself, she needed the horses.

As she reached the bottom of the hill, she lifted her

skirts so she did not trip and quickened her pace, calling out to the guards. "Thank the Goddess I found you! Help me!"

The three men turned toward her, eyes widening at the sight of a bedraggled woman running toward them so far from the city. One of the guards sat atop the cart, and pulled back on the horses' reins, bringing them to a halt.

"Who goes there?" he called. "State your business."

"My daughter," Annora called, the lie rolling from her tongue with ease as she reminded herself these men would likely send her to her death if they were coming from the castle, rather than heading toward it. "She's missing. Will you help me look?"

The two guards on foot looked to the other for guidance as he sighed deeply. "How old is she?"

"Not yet three. She'll be so scared out here by herself."

The guard stood, scanning the area immediately around them. Wherever Henry was, she hoped he could conceal himself well. "Aye, we'll help for a minute. Arthur, keep an eye on the supplies."

"Oh, thank you," she called, hoping she sounded every bit as pitiful as she needed to.

"What's her name?"

"Hen—rietta. Henrietta."

Curse her tongue, and its tendency to run faster than her mind.

The men began to call to the imaginary child, two of them walking away from the cart and climbing up the hill she had run down from. Annora eyed them nervously, willing that, at any moment, Henry would appear as he had promised.

Then again, he could have sent her to her death for calling him a worm and then apparently snoring through the night. He had freely admitted that he had betrayed the champions he had known all his life. She hardly knew the man and had no idea the depths he would slither to.

A chill coursed through her veins as she remembered what he had confessed; that he had been willing to throw her to the patrolling watchman to aid his own escape the previous night.

And she, foolishly, had believed he would keep her safe from harm now that it was morning.

"You have to help me," she called over her shoulder to the remaining guard by the cart. "There's a dangerous man out there, a prisoner who wants to—"

As she turned, the guard fell, and Henry's smile greeted her from beside the horses. "Wants to what, Annora? Tell me, what do I want?"

Her words turned to ice in her throat as Henry climbed onto one of the horses, and severed their harness with his blade, detaching them from the cart. The two remaining guards had disappeared up the hill, hidden from view, still calling out for a child who did not exist.

"Henry..." Relief tangled with regret as she stepped toward the champion. Again, she had underestimated him, refused him the trust he deserved. "Thank the Goddess, I was afraid you'd left me."

The man narrowed his eyes, cocking his head to the side with a disappointed sigh. "You truly think so little of me after all we've been through?"

As soon as the words left his lips, he kicked his heels to

the horse's flank, spurring it into a trot as he led the other by the reins. Leading it away from her.

The guards on the hill called out in alarm, their armor rattling as they hurried down the slope, blades drawn.

"Stop him!" the head guard ordered his second. "Kill them both!"

Annora's eyes widened as her demise closed in. "Henry!"

"Good luck, my cunning Annora," he called over his shoulder, twisting in his seat to aim his crossbow. The dart whistled past her, landing in the grass beside the guard. "Shit." Henry sighed and aimed again. The second bolt landed with a sickening thud in the closest guard's chest. A third bolt took down the second guard, the men's lives snuffed as if they were nothing.

Annora could only stand, mouth agape as Henry rode away, the horses breaking into a gallop as he disappeared down the road.

"Goddess curse you!" Her voice echoed around the empty plain, answered only by the howling wind.

She drew a deep breath and checked the guard's bodies for anything of use before looting the cart. Her efforts were rewarded by a few coins, two smoked sausages, and a skin of water. The rest of their cargo was nothing but blocks of gray stone.

Her best hope was the road, travelers who might exchange the coin for warmer clothing or if they were feeling generous, a ride on their own cart. So she walked and hoped.

The day passed slowly and painfully, but spite proved

an excellent motivator. She would not lie on the roadside and give up; Henry would no doubt enjoy that, and she would not give him the satisfaction. She walked until her feet blistered and those blisters broke. She walked until the sun began to sink and the threat of night loomed above her.

Defeat crept in with the dusk, tormenting her with the knowledge that there would be no Henry to watch over her while she slept, no stinking wolf pelt shielding her from the frost. The strength in her legs was failing, and already half her supplies were gone.

She had been made to join Lord Caine's household staff at eighteen years of age, and now, more than double that, she finally had the freedom she had craved for so long. It did her little good.

For years she had dreamed of running away, away from the noblemen who saw her as something to touch and belittle, away from their chamber pots and stained sheets. As a girl she had dreamed of living in a castle, but once she was there, all she wanted was a cottage like the one she was raised in; small, built from stone, and far from everyone else. A place where she could surround herself with comforts and simply be left alone.

But the world beyond the castle was harsher than she ever remembered.

Tears sprang to her eyes as tiny lights gleamed in the distance, a small settlement at the foot of the mountains, her only hope of salvation. Hope spurred her on as she limped and shivered down the road.

"Oh, thank the Goddess," she whispered, relieved

laughter bubbling in her chest as she approached a cozy looking tavern.

Two horses stood in the stable, tended by a wiry stableboy. Two black horses.

He was there. The bastard was inside, comfortable and warm while she froze and starved.

Annora's limp turned to a march as her relief turned to fury.

CHAPTER

SIX

Apples had never tasted so sweet. Back in the dungeons Henry's captors fed him plentifully, but they had fed him whatever Lord Caine did not eat. Stale bread, meat on the verge of turning rancid, cheeses with spots of green mold which something had already nibbled.

Every meal was a punchline, an insult, letting him know he was no longer considered worthy of humane treatment and nothing more than a burden to the lord of the castle.

As the years passed, he had grown hard-pressed to contradict them, but for now he enjoyed his apple, the crisp freshness of the fruit drawing a sigh from between his lips. He slid his thumb over the firm red skin and tried to ignore the tiniest twinge of guilt which itched in his chest, relentless like a bothersome gnat. Perhaps leaving Annora alone on the plain was a little crueler than necessary, but she was beginning to seep beneath the surface of him. Like the dungeon filth. That would not do.

Henry was alone, as he needed to be. After all, that night might be his last one, and if the Goddess saw fit to let him live after he returned to Caer Duloon and confronted Lord Caine, he had much to accomplish thereafter. Annora was not part of that.

He pressed a knife into the flesh of another apple, cutting out a thick wedge of the fruit and eating it straight from the blade. At least his last night would be a comfortable one. The guard he had stolen clothes from had a full purse, and Henry had every intention on spending all of it at the tavern.

And he was already beginning to recognize himself. The innkeeper had been so good as to lend him a pair of shears to trim his beard to a neater state and had spent the evening heating water at Henry's request.

"Will that be all?" the innkeeper asked. He was a small, rosy-cheeked man with vivid copper hair.

Henry contemplated while he chewed. "A bottle of honeyed wine too, and cake if you have any."

"Aye. That I can do."

"Is my bathwater scalding?"

"Hot enough to strip flesh from bone, sir."

It would still not be hot enough to wash every trace of that vile dungeon from Henry's body, but it was a start. "Thank you."

The innkeeper nodded, failing to disguise the crinkle in the bridge of his nose. "Long ride?"

There was no doubt in Henry's mind that he reeked. Ten years in that dank hole would hardly leave him smelling of roses. "Something like—"

A loud crash cut Henry off as the tavern's door was flung open, and the sight of the woman in the doorway silenced him entirely.

Annora's honey blonde hair was windswept, her pale complexion now flushed scarlet. But her eyes; those were entirely transformed. Ordinarily so large and soft, framed by blonde-tipped lashes which fluttered against her rounded cheeks while she slept, they were now alight with furious indignation.

"You!" She stormed across toward him as his blade bit into the apple once more.

"Ah, you made it," Henry said, pushing the wooden chair opposite out from under the table with the toe of his boot. "You really are quite tenacious."

She collapsed into the seat, reaching across to snatch the wedge of apple from his knife. "You're the most odious, self-ish, vile prick I've ever met."

He tilted his head. "Thank you."

"I hope lice eat your cock."

People rarely impressed him. He had spent much of his life surrounded by champions who were stronger and more accomplished than anyone else, and the bar was set high. But Annora... her assets came not through years of training, nor by being born larger and stronger than everyone else. Annora was quick and cunning; determined, and vicious. She was a chambermaid, and yet in every significant way, he was certain she could best him. Annora interested him far more than anyone else ever had, and only part of that interest was because of the way she looked.

A smile pulled at his lips as she took the knife and apple

from his hands and began to carve the peel from the fruit. Clear, bubbling juice trickled over her thumb as she worked. Her hands, though small, were surprisingly strong after decades of labor; calloused and tipped by short, stubby nails.

He pulled in a breath and tore his gaze from her hands.

She sniffed. "I'm furious with you."

"I can tell."

"You left me to die."

"No, I left you to make your own way. I told you I was heading south and you opposed the idea. I didn't know you meant to follow me."

"You took both horses!"

"I needed a spare. How was I to know how tired they would be? I didn't know there was an inn so close."

He could hardly conceal his smile as she cut a slice, the stab of the knife exaggerated as if she imagined the apple to be his heart. Piece by piece, she would consume him. He had half a mind to let her.

Between mouthfuls she glanced up at the innkeeper, who was doing his best to blend in with the furniture. "Do you have any rooms available for the night?"

"I already have a room," Henry told her.

Her eyes slid to him. "You truly think I would want to share a room with you after today?"

Triumph bloomed in his chest. "But yesterday you might've considered it?"

"I considered a lot of things yesterday. Not all of them as charitable as sharing your bed." She stood and addressed the innkeeper again. "Which room is he in?"

"Uh..." the poor man glanced toward Henry. With a slight nod, Henry gave his permission. "Up the stairs to the first door on the right."

"Goddess curse you, Henry Percille," she huffed, placing the apple core on the table and skewering it with the knife.

"I think she already has." Henry bit down a grin as she stamped her way up the stairs.

"I hope you trip on these stairs and smash open your skull." Her footsteps continued to thump on the boards above before the slam of a door shook the tavern.

The innkeeper audibly exhaled, shaking his head. "She's a cheery one."

"Yes, well, pray for me," Henry chuckled as he handed over five silver pieces he had requisitioned from the guard's body in the dungeon.

"I doubt the Goddess herself could save you," the man muttered. "Fortunately, I've no other guests for you two to disturb."

"Pity. I'll still take the cake and wine. You may leave it outside the door."

"Very good," the innkeeper said.

Following her path up the stairs, Henry's heart began to flutter. He placed his hand over his chest and scowled. In his days with the Champion's Guild, he had no shortage of lovers whose faces had long since faded from his memory, but they had never made his heart race so. Whether it was excitement or terror, he was unsure. Perhaps both.

He silently told himself it was simply the anticipation of the unknown, that Annora might very well spring out from behind his door and crack him over the head with a chamber pot as she had done to the guard. Savage beast that she was.

Perhaps that would not be the worst thing in the world.

Perhaps it would be better if he died at the hand of a beautiful woman there in the tavern with a belly full of good food, than on the floor of Lord Caine's chambers if his plan failed. As certain as he was about what he needed to do in the morning, some part of him did not want to go.

Pausing outside his rented room, he held his breath and pressed his ear to the door. The bubbling sound of water sloshed within, accompanied by a long sigh. Indignation brewed in his chest. She was in his bath, the luxury and comfort he had dreamed of for years.

Yes, he had abandoned her on that frostbitten, forsaken wasteland, but she had gone too far for revenge. Pushing open the door, admonishments swelled in his throat, but at the sight of her they died on his tongue.

Annora sat in the large copper tub, arms spread across the rim, her breasts flushed pink and only half-submerged in the milky water. His cock ached at the sight of her, yearning for release. Wet, blonde hair clung to her shoulders in tendrils, trailing down over her chest, but his gaze was drawn upward to the challenge which burned in her eyes, at odds with her relaxed pose. If he stepped across the threshold, he risked everything; his plan, his freedom, his heart.

Everything.

The fire in the hearth popped and crackled, illuminating the room with golden light as he forced himself to breathe, to swallow, to appear as anything other than the desperate, dying man he was.

"Am I forgiven?" he asked, stepping into the room and closing the door.

"No. Never." She drew her knees up to her chest. "Tell me, have you ever done a single unselfish thing in your life?"

"No. Nor do I intend to."

Her eyes followed him as he strode across to the fireplace and crouched to throw more wood on the already blazing fire. His back bristled in the silence, but the cantering rhythm of his heart never slowed.

The urge to pull off the guard's clothes and throw them into the flames called to him. He longed to incinerate every visible trace of Lord Caine which still clung to his body, but he would need the clothes in the morning. If he was to sneak undetected back to the castle, the guard's uniform was his only hope.

"Annora—"

"Just shut up," she muttered, flicking the water with her index finger. "You left me for dead."

"I did not. I killed the guards for you before I left." Standing, he pulled off the surcoat and the shirt beneath.

When he stood naked from the waist up, Annora turned her head by a fraction. "You are truly despicable."

"And yet here you are in my room." He worked open the lace of his breeches. "Naked, and redder than a ripe cherry just begging to be plucked."

A derisive chuckle shook her chest. "Maybe so, but that doesn't mean I want it to be you who does the plucking." She rolled over in the water so that she turned to face him, folding her arms on the rim of the tub and resting her chin upon them. "In fact, I'd sooner pluck myself."

The blushing pink hills of her backside bobbed atop the water, causing an ache in his chest.

Her eyes betrayed her, following the descent of his breeches as he pushed them down, releasing his straining cock.

"I thought champions were castrated," she said.

"Cut," he corrected her as he stepped out of the breeches and walked toward the bathtub. She rolled over once more, unwilling to take her eyes from him. "They cut us inside so we can't bear children."

He lifted a leg to step into the bath, closing his eyes as the hot water caressed his skin. The inn was far simpler and less luxurious than any he had visited as a champion, but at least the bath was large enough to fit them both. The water rose to the lip of the tub as he lowered himself in, sitting opposite her, letting his legs rest exactly where they wanted to, even though it meant laying on top of hers. It was *his* bath after all, and no amount of eye-rolling or huffing from Annora would stop him from enjoying it.

Cupping water in his hands, he leaned forward and began the arduous task of scrubbing away the dungeon grime. The sensation of his shortened hair, severed by the blade, was still strange to the touch after so many years, and his fingers grasped at empty air where the hair had once been. Once he was satisfied he was clean, he leaned back against the wall of the tub as Annora sighed.

"Well now the bath may as well be a swamp," she grumbled. "You're filthy."

"I'll remind you this was supposed to be *my* bathwater."

"And I'll remind you every day for the rest of your life that you left me to walk alone across a frozen shithole while you were here in the tavern filling your belly." She dipped her finger into the bathwater once more and flicked it at his chest.

That time, he caught her hand and dragged her toward him, heart pounding as her soft body pressed to his. Her breasts brushing against his chest, her thighs, straddling his even as she scowled and tried to wrench her hand from his grip. Henry's body burned with sensation; her body so soft and slippery against him, the rush of hot blood coursing beneath the surface of his skin, hardening his cock and heating his face.

Ten years of starvation sated in an instant by her touch.

Her breaths came in shattering gasps as he traced the fingertips of his empty hand down the center of her back, following the path of her spine. Back in the dungeon he had been able to make out a few dark freckles on her cheeks, but when she was bathed in firelight it was obvious how wildly he had underestimated their number. Every inch of her skin was speckled by the sun's gentle kisses, some dark rich brown, others pinkish red, burnt orange, golden yellow. It would take a lifetime to kiss every one of them.

A lifetime exquisitely spent, though no doubt accompanied by a long stream of profanities.

Slowly, she reached out to touch his chest, her fingers tracking the blushing flesh surrounding his nipple. It took all his composure not to surrender to her there and then.

Even after all those years of stagnation and lifelessness,

even with his days of glory and youth so far behind him, she desired him as much as he craved her.

In the morning he would ride out to Caer Duloon. He would find Lord Caine and run his blade through his heart and when the bastard lay dead, he would search the castle for Lady Natalie Blackmere and Brandon the Bear if they remained after the party.

And if he survived—oh, then the world was his. He would ride down to the Champion's Guild and take back everything he had lost. By force, if necessary. It would be glorious, the vengeance he would reap. They would bow to him whether they wanted to or not.

In his heart he knew it was unlikely. Henry would not make it out of Caer Duloon alive a second time. He would die while those who detested him relished his final breath. But he would take Lord Caine with him. On that he would not budge.

But before then, he had every intention of filling his remaining hours with as much pleasure as he could. He would fill his last night with Annora.

CHAPTER
SEVEN

Annora hated the man. She despised the brute and his mournful winter-sky eyes, ferocious strength, and hair as black as nightshade. Black like his rotten little heart.

It beat against hers as he held her to him, the warmth of his big, cruelly beautiful body threatening to burn her to a husk as they lay together in the bath, so close his breath fluttered against her lips. His hand trailed lower, his palm cupping her backside.

"If you want me to stop then tell me," Henry said, his chest rumbling beneath her breasts.

She could not. Every protest was born and died in the same heartbeat, laid to rest on her tongue. She ached for him, deliciously punishing twinges pulsing between her thighs as his hand skated back up her spine. In turn, she traced the thin, puckered line of a scar from the top of his shoulder diagonally down to his nipple. He shivered beneath her touch.

"Who did this to you?"

His shoulders rose as he drew a long breath. "The Guild Master."

"Why?"

"To punish me for what happened at Westgarden. I stabbed one champion here." He traced a finger along her underarm, making her flinch and draw back. A grin curved his lips as she pressed herself close to him once more. Smug bastard. "And then, when I lost the fight, I attacked Brandon the Bear while he was unarmed and distracted. So I was whipped."

"And did the punishment work?"

"For a time."

"And then?"

"I did it again."

His nonchalance amused her, but that quickly faded as he began to trace the silver scars streaking her back.

"And what about you?" he said. "Who did this to you?"

"Who do you think?"

"One more reason to be glad of your escape."

Her treacherous hands trailed down the center of his torso, between the valley of his chest, down to the soft hill of his stomach. She tried to imagine him at the height of his glory days with the champions; stronger, leaner, his handsome face not yet etched with the lines of time. He was rather more beautiful now, she decided, if still an odious shit.

Henry was the largest and most beautiful man she had ever seen. His only flaw was simply everything that he was.

Color flooded his cheeks as he lifted his hips, trying to press the head of his cock between her thighs.

"By the Goddess, look at you," she whispered. "Keen to get it in so soon."

"Annora, it's been ten years." He sucked in a breath through gritted teeth. "I need release. I need it now."

She chuckled, relishing his agony. "Aye, I can imagine. But you're not getting it until I've had mine."

Henry released her wrist with a groan and threw back his head. "Fine. If you must, frig yourself until you're ready. You said you'd prefer that anyway."

Indignant, she swatted his chest, before pulling his hand towards the water. "I don't care how long you've been locked away for. If you want release, you'll earn it. My pleasure is as important as yours and after this morning you owe me that much."

A muscle in his cheek danced as his blue eyes watched her hand lead his down beneath the water. He did not resist, nor try to pull away. He simply watched, curious and somehow simultaneously unimpressed. The initial shock of pleasure as he cupped her cunt in his palm faded as he held it completely still.

"Changed your mind?" she asked "Or have you forgotten what to do?".

His lips pressed to a firm line as his eyebrows dipped. "I've never learned."

"But—" She mirrored his frown. "The songs about all the women you've bedded—"

He sighed heavily, withdrawing his hand. "The songs

62

are all exaggerated, but the few ruts I've had were quick instances."

"Even quick can be pleasurable—"

"Annora... the man I was ten years ago simply didn't care about it. We were permitted to leave the Champion's Guild for tournaments but had to return when they were done and spend our days training. Relationships between champions were forbidden and we were sworn to chastity within the Guild's walls. So, when the time came for us to visit the taverns and meet people outside the Guild... I just chased my own pleasure. Ofttimes I was too drunk to even know who I was sharing a bed with."

Her lips parted around half thought out questions. Finally, she settled on, "So after all this you mean to tell me that the legendary Henry Percille is terrible in bed?"

"I wouldn't say terrible. I spent every time."

The sincerity in his voice and the ridiculousness of what he was saying pulled her lips into an incredulous smile. For all his posturing and confidence, he was a sheltered man, locked away most of his life behind stone walls.

"How did you get people to lay with you if you didn't care about their pleasure?"

"Because I had titles, a reputation, a lot of coin, and a pretty face." Regret drew across his features. "Now I have none of it."

Annora bit her tongue, unwilling to contradict him, no matter how vehemently her body would argue against the latter part of it. "Would you like me to teach you then?"

His cheeks were ablaze, the redness glowing from them spreading down his throat and to his chest. A war raged in his eyes; the selfish part of him caring only for his own pleasure, but something else stirred within him. Inquisitiveness, maybe. His throat pulsed as she ran her fingernails along the length of his thigh beneath the water.

"Annora..."

"Have you ever kissed a woman... down there?"

"Where?"

"Between her legs."

His eyes narrowed. "Now why would I do that?"

Her eyebrows stitched together. "Oh, Henry. To make the woman feel good; there's nothing like it." She drew a circle around his nipple, her fingertips rising and falling along with the streaking scars. "Most enjoy doing it too—most I've known."

His gaze darted about her face, as though expecting her to tell him it was a trick she was playing on him. "Other men have done that for you?"

"Aye. Women too."

His throat flexed, and the possibility he was jealous sent a thrill through her. "How does it feel?"

"Like... Goddess, Henry, I don't know. It's wonderful. It's like nothing else in the world." She sucked her lower lip as his cock twitched against her belly. He was curious at least. "Would you like to try?"

How could such a large and intimidating man—a brute who had ended the lives of men as easily as swatting a fly— look so afraid of her? His lips parted as he drew a shaking breath and gave a barely perceptible nod.

The air in her lungs solidified as she untangled her limbs from his and stood, the water churning beneath her, lapping against the walls of the tub and his big, brutal body like the waves before a storm. She placed one foot on the edge of the bath by his shoulder, exposing herself to him.

His breath stuttered as his hands curled around her calves, sliding across her wet skin. Reaching between her thighs, she pressed her fingertips to her clitoris, stroking herself as he watched. Her breath grew shallow. "Here's where it feels the best but the rest feels good too. You can use your lips and tongue."

"Hard or soft?"

"Soft first." Anticipation crackled beneath the surface of her skin as his hands slid higher to her thighs. His breath tickled against her skin. He was hers to teach, to mold. "I'll tell you when to do it hard—" Pleasure darted through her at the first gentle swipe of his tongue joining her fingers. "*Oh...*"

He pulled back to glance up at her. "Like so?"

She nodded, stroking her hand back through his hair, gently pulling him to her. And Goddess, when he licked her again, her legs almost buckled.

Each tentative stroke of his tongue ripped the air from her lungs, leaving nothing but the whisper of his name on her lips. There was no Aldland, no Caer Duloon.

For Annora, standing there, face turned to the ceiling as he pleasured her, there was only him, the rasp of his beard against the tender skin of her thighs, the strength of his hands squeezing her backside, binding her to him.

With her gasps came his boldness. He slipped his tongue between her folds, exploring her, deeper, tasting her, slowly, gently, until she found herself tangling her hands in his hair, thrusting her hips against his mouth. He was quick to learn, eager, greedy for her, his sole purpose her pleasure.

She bore down on him, spurred by the relief and adrenaline of escape; the residual anger she felt toward that beautiful man with his wicked tongue; and the pure bliss of being there, alone with him. If Lord Caine stormed into the room with a hundred of his guards, she would not stop, and from the deep, fervent pace of Henry's licks, she suspected neither would he.

As she tightened her grip on his hair and ground her quim against his tongue, a groan sounded from Henry's throat. Hot blasts of air caressed her skin as he cried out against her, ecstasy making his legs tremble beneath the water. Drawing back once more, lips glistening with her arousal as he gazed up at her, the rapid rise and fall of his chest ebbing to a languid rhythm.

Annora's lips parted with the dawning realization. Heat flooded her cheeks. "You spent without me even touching you?"

He gave a broken sigh, leaning back against the wall of the tub, leaving her only half-satisfied. "Goddess, Annora, you taste like nothing I've ever known. I couldn't stop it." Reaching down he gripped his cock in his fist, stroking out the final pearly beads of his spend and letting them slide into the water. He chuckled at the thinly-veiled disappointment on her face. "That doesn't mean I want to stop. This is what I want to do tonight. All night. Just you and I."

Heat crept along her throat as he leaned forward and kissed her thigh. "All night?"

He held the lip of the tub as he stood, sending the bathwater spilling over the edge. He paid it no mind. When he was standing, towering over her, he ran his fingertips over her scalp.

His cheeks were rosy, his eyes dark and flooded with desire. "Yes. Until dawn. Until my name is the only thing you can remember. Until the sensation of my tongue on your cunt is all you know. If this is my last night and I die tomorrow, I want you haunted by the memory of my mouth on you."

A thrill of excitement coursed through her body as she stared up at him. He truly was a beautiful man, powerfully built; a wall of softness and strength and scars.

But there was something else there, tucked away beneath the bravado, the man behind the callous grin. Vanity. Pain. Loneliness. Vulnerability. That was it. She saw him just for a moment, as his blue eyes pleaded with her to play along.

"You terrible man," she whispered, her lips trembling as he pressed his thumb to their plump pillow.

He smiled. "Did you doubt that before?"

She took his thumb between her teeth, biting down on the pad as his lips curled and he hissed, never taking his eyes from her. Arousal still coursed through her body, unsated, still yearning. Longing for the man she should despise.

"No", she said. "I've known what you were from the beginning."

"And yet here you are."

"And yet here I am." She closed her lips, sucking the tip of his thumb and swirling her tongue around it as he groaned. There was no doubt in her mind that he was a beast, dangerous and capable of cruelty, but he was also a man, a champion turned prisoner turned fugitive, who wanted more than anything to convince the world he was untouchable.

No one had stirred her desire like he had for a long time, and if that made her weak and wicked then so be it. She would be weak and wicked with a handsome brute's face between her thighs.

Carefully, Annora stepped out of the bath, glancing over her shoulder as Henry's gaze traced the curves of her body. "Come on," she said. "I'll show you how to live up to your songs."

He followed her, his skin flushed pink and gleaming as water cascaded from him, leaving a spotted trail on the floor. There was a chest to store blankets at the foot of the bed, so she sat atop it, parting her thighs.

"On your knees," she told him.

"That's the second time you've demanded that of me since we've met." A grin titled his lips. "I'm beginning to think you rather enjoy seeing me submit to you."

"You catch on quickly." Her chest rose as she pulled in a labored breath, her body burning with the need for his touch.

As he knelt on the rug at the foot of the bed, she braced herself for his mouth on her, but it did not come. Instead, he kissed her breasts, slowly, deeply, his tongue sending darts of pleasure straight to her core as he traced the bumps and ridges of her nipples, first one, then the other.

"What are you doing?" she gasped, her back arching involuntarily as he pinched her nipple between his teeth.

"Does it feel good?" Even as he grumbled, he caressed her breast with the tip of his nose.

She sighed, her eyes closing for a moment, before she realized she could not bear to look away from him. "Aye."

"Then stop complaining." His hands traced the soft fold of her stomach, squeezing it gently, tracing the creases and lines of her body with his fingertips before following their path with his lips. He sighed like a man besotted with the love of his life.

Trailing her hand through his wet, black hair, she smiled as he groaned, placing a hand beneath the back of her knee, and lifting her leg to place it on his broad, scarred shoulder. Desire clawed at her from within, desperate for release, craving more. And as he kissed a slow, gentle line down the soft, sensitive skin of her inner thigh, she was certain she would burn up like parchment in embers.

"Henry..."

He laughed darkly. "Patience. Do you know how long it has been since I've seen a woman in all her glory?"

"You think I'm glorious?"

"Amongst other things." He nipped the skin of her inner thigh with his teeth, making her gasp. "Not all of them so flattering. But for now, I'm content just to bask in your glow."

He had a pretty tongue to match his face, both of which she longed to ride, but if she demanded it of him again, that would mean he had won. Instead, she leaned back, bracing her elbows on the foot of the bed, watching him as his long, dark eyelashes fluttered against his cheeks. He pressed forward, bending her knee along with his body as he kissed her stomach, flicking his tongue against the rim of her navel before biting the fold at the curve of her hip.

There was not a part of her he did not seem fascinated with, and there was little she could do but lie back and remember to draw breath. For all his insistence that he did not know how to pleasure a woman, he was entranced by her body. He was dedicated to it, each caress an ode to her shape, each bite and lick a playful reminder that he cruelly relished her desperation for release. She burned, the blood coursing through her veins, flooding her cheeks and chest with color.

"I only have tonight," he whispered. "And I want to fill it with you."

"And tomorrow?"

He grinned, pulling her other leg onto his shoulder. "Tomorrow I will be the best mistake of your life. Tomorrow I'll be nothing more than a memory for you to touch yourself to."

"You think highly of yourself."

"Don't worry, my glorious Annora," he whispered, his breath cool and agonizingly light against her aching core. "I'll earn the honor."

At last, he pressed his face between her thighs, drawing a gasping breath from her. Somehow, in the short span of time between the first and second time, her body had grown addicted to him, and now he had returned to her, she wanted nothing more. And she would never let him go. Gripping the hair at the back of his head, she held him to her, tilting her hips toward him. She brought her other palm to her brow, consumed by the sensation of his tongue sliding around her clitoris, ravenous, relentless, groaning softly as he cupped her left breast in one hand and stroked her nipple with the rough pad of his thumb.

He was no man, she was certain, but a wild beast molded into the shape of one, devouring her with wanton moans and gasping breaths, seeming to take as much pleasure from it as she. She answered his call with her own, crying out his name as he licked and licked, his tongue seeking out her taste, her pleasure, driving her back so she reclined on the foot of the bed, back arched, cheeks burning, heels digging into the soft cushion of his hips. A coil tightened inside her, tighter, tighter, until her orgasm broke loose, rendering her silent and tense, her toes curling as her legs trembled against his shoulders.

When she opened her eyes, he was grinning. That smug bastard. His dark beard was drenched, his lips coated with her. Some spiteful part of her hated that he did it so well, that he looked so lovely covered in her.

"And?" he asked, placing his hands on her calves and pinning them to his shoulders as his chest rose and fell. "Your verdict."

Annora shrugged her shoulders, placing her hand over her heaving breasts. "You did quite well."

"Only quite?" His eyebrow arched.

"Aye, for a novice." She bit down on the inside of her cheek as he glared, letting her legs slide off him. "I was only bored once or twice."

"Perhaps you're simply difficult to please."

She sat, scraping back her wet hair and crossing one leg over the other, letting her toes brush the fur on his belly. "Hm," she pondered. "I don't think it's that."

He stood, bringing his semi-hard cock to eye level. "Fine," he muttered, bending down to scoop her into his arms.

Annora held back a laugh as he jolted her up into his arms, carrying her the few steps to the bed before throwing her down on the mattress. He wiped his beard off with his palm and turned, snarling, to stride toward the door. He pulled it open and bent to pick something up.

When he returned, he was carrying a plate and a bottle.

"What is that?" she asked.

"It's my cake and wine, and I intend to enjoy it before I ravish you again." He set it on the bed and sat beside her.

"Are you going to share?"

"Of course," Henry said, closing his eyes. "You may enjoy the sight of it, and I shall enjoy the taste."

Annora sighed. Her belly was empty, and her thirst for him subsided. And with it, her tolerance. "You are, without a doubt, the worst man alive."

"Yes," he smiled, taking a bite of the cake and sighing. "But not for long."

That should not have hurt her as much as it did.

EIGHT

Of course Henry would share, though he did not fully understand why. It was against his nature. Ordinarily he would have feasted without a single thought for onlookers, but then again, no one he had ever shared a bed with had remained as long as Annora had.

Still, he teased her a moment, groaning with pleasure as he took a bite of cake, letting the sweetness of honey and apple roll across his tongue. The cake was coated in a syrupy glaze which left his fingers sticky. He sucked each one in turn as she watched, silently seething.

Back in the Champion's Guild he had eaten many fine meals, but none of them had ever tasted as good as anything he had eaten that night.

"I hope you choke on it," she sighed, lying back against the pillows, her naked body as soft and lovely as before he had sated his lust.

"Fine. If it'll keep you quiet and salve your temper.

Open your mouth," he told her. His chest ached as she did as he asked, her big, dark eyes gazing into his. Carefully, he placed a piece of the cake on her tongue, letting his thumb drag over the cushion of her lower lip. "Satisfied?"

"No," she said, chewing slowly. "Far from it."

"You weren't caged as long as I. Perhaps freedom doesn't taste as sweet to you."

She rolled onto her side, propping herself on her elbow. "Mealy cake made with rotten apples and a smidge of honey served by the biggest prick to ever plague Aldland doesn't taste sweet to me."

Despite himself, he laughed. "Annora, my dear harpy."

She was so delightfully grumpy, her world-weariness surpassing even his own. Even her navel was a frowning arc in the center of her soft belly. She glowered and took the wine bottle from beside him, pulling out the cork before taking a long swig. Her throat pulsed as she swallowed, mesmerizing, begging to be kissed.

He moistened his lips with the tip of his tongue. "Would you like me to order a second bottle?"

She shook her head before pulling the bottle from her lips. "How are you paying for this?"

"I stole money from the guard. The one you hit with the chamber pot."

Her eyebrows dipped. "And you meant to keep it all for yourself?"

"Am I not sharing it with you now?"

"But had I not found you here you would've ridden away with two horses and a full purse, and I with nothing, despite giving you your freedom." She gave a bitter chuckle. "And that's why the cake tastes sour."

Henry sat in silence, watching her. The steady rise and fall of her chest, the way she traced the neck of the bottle with her fingertips. She had touched him that way in the bath; gently exploring his shape, wanting him even then, even after ten years in a cell had taken away what youth had graced him with. Silently, he broke off another piece of cake and touched it to her lips. Her eyes burned into his as she opened her mouth and accepted his offering.

Had he known she wished to come with him, he might have waited, but then, upon his return to Caer Duloon, it would have been necessary to bid her farewell regardless. The list of terrible deeds which had led him to that cell was already long enough, he would not add to it by leading Annora to her death.

But tonight, he was hers, and Lord Caine's blade was not yet through his heart.

In place of an apology, he took another piece of cake and placed it on the soft, supple mound of her breast, bowing his head to eat it from her. His tongue lapped at the honey glaze left behind on her nipple as she swatted at him, her hand slapping against his shoulder, then trailing down his arm to squeeze his bicep.

She sighed loudly. "What are you doing, you strange man?"

"Whatever I want, as I always have."

He took another piece, this time crumbling it onto her as she huffed and rolled her eyes. Raising onto his hands and knees, he set to work finding every miniscule crumb, licking her breasts, her stomach, tracing the curves he had already memorized by heart, inventing invisible crumbs where he could not find any. Her body was more intoxicating to him than anything he had ever known.

Annora raised her arm, resting it on the pillow above her head as she set the bottle on the floor. Even as her breaths grew heavier and her body bowed to his touch, she complained. "Well, now I'll need another bath."

"I'll have the innkeeper bring you more water in the morning after I leave." He settled back between her thighs, rubbing the tip of his nose against her clitoris as she sighed, tilting her face toward the ceiling. "Until then there's little point."

"Why's that?"

"Because I fully intend for you to be my last meal, and I want you to get very messy."

Perhaps she was only teasing when she said he had done "quite well," but if it was to be his last night, he would make certain he left his mark. Henry had never settled for mediocrity in anything he had attempted, and he was not about to start with her.

He would leave her breathless, boneless, gasping and sobbing his name, and he would do it out of sheer spite. Nothing more. Absolutely nothing more.

He would prove himself to that foul-tempered harpy if it was the last thing he ever achieved.

But his chest ached at the taste of her, a fluttering sensation billowing beneath his ribs as her body undulated and a sigh escaped her lips. She was exquisite.

He had often heard Brandon and the other champions

talk of pleasuring their partners that way, but he had never even thought to try it. In the days long since passed, once his cock was satisfied, he had little interest in the continuation or elaboration of sex, but Annora... Goddess, whatever spell she had cast over him, he had no intention of breaking it before sunrise. If Lord Caine did not end him in the morning, he would gladly ride back to the inn and spend the rest of his long life between her thighs.

She whimpered his name as her fingers tangled his hair, her quim hot and wet beneath his tongue. What a fool he had been in his life before the dungeon. So preoccupied with chasing glory in the arena and seeking riches, when he could have poured his passion into simpler pleasures. Simpler but no less life-affirming.

"Am I doing better this time?" he asked, raising onto his elbows.

"I swear if you stop, I'll beat you over the head," she growled, pushing him back down, tilting her hips to grind against his tongue, drawing back the hood of her clitoris, demanding more. Goddess, how he loved that; to be conquered, used for her pleasure. He relished it, relished her, licking and sucking and fucking her with his tongue.

When she came, she was not silent like the first time, but feral, releasing a loud, breathy cry. And he adored it. He adored her. All of her.

He rested his head on the inside of her thigh, a grin tightening his cheeks as she fought for her breath. "I'll take that as yes."

"You're foul," she sighed, smoothing back his hair. "I can't stand you."

"Do you want me to rent a second room so you can be rid of me?"

"No."

With a satisfied grin, he raised onto his knees before bending to brace his fists at either side of her shoulders. Gazing down at her, his breath snagged in his chest. Her cheeks were pink, her eyes dark and heavy-lidded, her lips parted. His cock was hard again, and from the way she moved her hips beneath him, brushing her belly against it, she knew it was all for her. That harpy.

"Have I earned it yet?" he asked, rolling his hips to stroke his cock against her.

"Already?" she asked, reaching up to stroke the curves of his chest. "You spent in the tub just minutes ago."

"What can I say, Annora?" He sighed as her hands traveled lower. "I spent ten years in a cell and tonight is my last night alive."

Her brow furrowed, a simple gesture which seemed to push all the warmth and giddiness from the room. "Why do you keep saying such things?"

He climbed off her and instead lay beside her, his fingers at once seeking out new parts of her to explore. She pushed away his hand as he stroked a feathery touch along the crease between her stomach and thigh, only to place it higher on her belly.

"I want to enjoy tonight. Tomorrow I'll ride back to Caer Duloon, find Lord Caine, and kill him."

She raised her head, rolling over to face him. "Why?"

Henry stroked his hand along the hills and valleys of her hip and waist, letting his hand dip down to squeeze her backside. He was quite certain he could happily spend a lifetime touching her. But, he reminded himself, he did not have that luxury.

"Back in the Champion's Guild, I had a friend, for a time. Sara. Lord Caine was her father, and her mother—once his servant—was made destitute, forced to give up her baby because Caine wanted to know nothing of her. And I feel in my heart—and I'm sure you can confirm—she was not the only woman he forced into such a fate."

Realization dawned on Annora's features as she released a slow breath. "I never denied he was a shit."

"And beyond that, I have my own reasons. The man kept me locked in a freezing dungeon for ten years, feeding me on moldy bread and rancid meat. I've stabbed friends for less."

Annora's lips twitched but she said nothing as her hand drifted down the center of his chest, resting above his heart as though she could somehow protect it.

"I'm a bad man, Annora," he whispered. "I've done unspeakable things, but that man, that leech, sitting in that grand castle is far worse than I. And if I do one good thing with my life, I want it to be ending his."

"But you're free. You broke out of the cell and you're free to live your life now. You could ride far away where they would never catch you."

"But I would always know he was still out there."

"And if you get killed?"

"I will be," Henry said. "I know I will be. But it doesn't matter."

Her eyes scanned his face, her lips turning down. "I

don't believe you. Men like you are always full of talk of valor and quests and revenge. But that's all it is, talk."

Those words stung, but she was wrong. He had sworn an oath that he would end Caine's life, and for once, he would hold an oath true.

"And what of women like you?" he asked, rolling onto his back. "What are you full of?"

"Weariness and disdain for men," she shrugged. "And cake crumbs."

Despite himself he laughed, and to his surprise, she laughed too. Frustratingly, she was somehow even lovelier.

"Well," she said, placing her palm on his stomach and stroking his dark hair there. "If you are to die, then I suppose it would be a kindness to allow you to bed me."

His heart sank, "Don't say it like that. As though you're performing some act of charity."

"What difference does it make?"

"Because I want you to *crave* me, Annora." He lifted himself onto his elbow, trailing his fingers along the length of her thigh. "I want tonight to be the best night of your life, for you to feel things you've never felt before."

She scoffed. "You'll have to work hard."

"I will. I want to be the memory that keeps you awake at night, the one that brings you close to ecstasy just by thought alone."

"Why?" she said. "I thought you never did anything unselfish."

"I want one person in this world to remember me fondly after I'm gone, even if the rest of them celebrate my demise."

Her eyes scanned his face for a long time, as a maelstrom of emotion churned behind them. There was pity there, and frustration, but she was also tempted. The way her lips parted as his hands slid between her thighs told him as much, as did the slow caress of her fingers over the puckered skin of his scars. She was still wet from his mouth and her own arousal, her folds gliding beneath his fingers as he explored her body.

"You are beautiful, Annora," he whispered, closing his lips as soon as the words escaped. His eyebrows dipped as he averted his gaze, focusing on the scuffed threads of the overworn bedsheets. "Just for tonight... I want you to fuck me as though you love me."

"I could never."

"Pretend then. I'll even pay you for your performance."

Annora sighed deeply, her eyes tracing his features again and again. He could almost see the instinctive refusal crumbling on her tongue. At last, she scowled. "And here I thought I was only worth leaving behind in a frozen wasteland."

The corner of his mouth quirked as she parted her legs, permitting him to see more of her. "You'll never let me forget that, will you?"

"Never," she whispered, placing her hand on the back of his neck. "As long as you live."

"Will you kiss me?" he asked.

"Must I?"

"Am I so hideous?" He knew the answer, and from the flush on her cheeks, so did she, and it annoyed her greatly, which pleased him even more. "I did just spend the past hour with my face in your cunt."

She snorted a laugh. "It was a couple of minutes at that."

"Which would imply that I was good." He flashed her a grin, as some long-forgotten part of him—the part which would stride around the tourney arenas like a freshly preened cockerel—billowed with pride.

"You aren't terrible. That's all I'll say."

"Such flattery. I didn't think you were capable."

She placed her hand on the back of his head and pulled him toward her, stopping when their lips were agonizingly close. Her breath fluttered against him, sending tingles shooting through his body.

"I'm capable of many things," she whispered.

He swallowed hard. "I don't doubt it."

He closed the gap between them, unable to hold back any longer. At the first touch of her lips, the world spun out from beneath him, fading to distant darkness until all that existed for him was her. Her lips, soft and sweet beneath his. Her fingers, tightening as she gripped his hair at the back of his head. Her body, so welcoming and warm, pressed against him. His heart squeezed as her tongue slipped between his lips, and her kiss deepened, until he was no longer certain that he had not in fact died trying to escape the castle.

Surely, he was at the Goddess's side, granted all the bliss his cold little heart could take. If Annora was pretending, she played the part well; so well, in fact, that he almost believed her.

CHAPTER
NINE

Henry kissed like every heartbeat would be his last, and Annora matched his passion. No matter how she tried to convince herself otherwise, her body wanted him, desperately, recklessly. If he were to die in the morning, she would send him to the pyre a happy man, and she would convince him she loved him if it led to her freedom and pleasure. Besides, coin was coin, and if nothing else he was pretty.

Pulling her lips from his, she rolled on top of him, straddling his hips, letting the head of his cock tease her entrance, but he was not a man to back down. When he could not reach her lips he raised his head, body trembling from the effort as he kissed her breasts, her shoulders, not knowing whether to use his tongue, or lips or teeth.

"Do you want it hard or soft?" she asked, a smug smile pulling at her lips as he tried to thrust his hips up toward her.

"Hard," he growled through his clenched jaw. "Goddess, Annora let me have my release."

"Now, now," she chastised him, placing her hand on his chest and pushing him gently down onto the pillows. He obeyed her silent command, jaw twitching and throat flexing as he stared up at her. She undulated her hips, teasing him, drawing a desperate moan from his pretty lips. "If this is your last night alive, we should savor it, shouldn't we? When I love someone, I make sure to take my time."

A muscle in his cheek danced as he let loose a sharp breath. "You'll be the death of me before Lord Caine even gets a chance."

"Aye, maybe," she said, bowing toward his lips once more. "But I'll make it a beautiful death."

Every kiss was honey and heat, pleasure and pain, his teeth sinking into her lip as his tongue stroked hers. It was a powerful feeling, holding so much man between her thighs, denying him everything he wanted yet giving him everything he needed.

He had barely told her a thing about himself, but already she knew he was spoiled in his life before the cell, prone to tantrums if he did not get his own way. He was vain, and rightly so, intelligent yet somehow naïve and unworldly. She would change that.

And those eyes. Blue eyes which were somehow warm as summer skies, yet could turn cold and hard like the deepest frost. They stared at her with an almost disarming intensity. If she did not keep her head, this man could easily make her surrender, and then she would truly be lost.

He groaned as she nipped at his lower lip and traced the

curves of his body with her fingertips. No matter how hard she tried to resist, her hands betrayed her and went to him. Her disloyal lips swore fealty to his. Her will surrendered to the deep, primal craving for him as she positioned her hips so the head of his cock pressed against her entrance.

His hands squeezed her hips, silently pleading, desperately urging her down.

"Annora." His voice was little more than a growl, his cheeks flushed scarlet above the dark stubble of his beard.

She could happily torment him all night, but the sight of him was too tempting to continue denying herself. Slowly, she lowered herself onto him, shivering as he filled her. He moaned as he raised his head from the pillow to watch her take him.

"Oh Goddess," he whispered.

"Is that a prayer?" she asked, rolling her hips against his to make him sigh. "Or a compliment?"

His lips quirked. "Both."

Trailing his hands up the length of her thighs, he brought his fingers between them to stroke her clitoris. Annora raised her face to the ceiling, her breath shaking as she rode him, tendrils of white-hot pleasure coursing through her veins. She set a slow pace, letting her own climax build before she would give him his. Every time he bucked his hips, demanding more, she slowed. Every time he focused on her pleasure, she gave him more.

His primal growls and wanton moans filled the air, obscene and beautiful all at once.

"Goddess," she gasped. "The whole tavern will hear you."

He pressed his head back against the pillow, arching his neck so his throat was exposed to her. "Oh, let them hear."

Annora gasped as his fingers rubbed her harder, faster, her pleasure building higher and higher until her climax rolled through her and heat flooded her body. Her cunt gripped him, pulsing around him. The heavy rise and fall of Henry's broad chest quickened as he drank in the sight of her and his teeth pressed against his plump bottom lip.

"Are you satisfied now?" he asked, breathless. "Have I earned mine?"

"Aye," she nodded, still riding him, raking her fingers back through her damp hair.

She gasped as the world shifted beneath her. With a grunt he turned, rolling over and taking her with him, until he lay on top of her pinning down her hips with his own. He forced the air from her lungs with his first powerful thrust.

His strength was unlike anything she had ever known, driving into her with a wild, desperate ferocity. Ecstasy speared through her as she ran her nails down his back, drawing a hiss from him. He raised himself onto his knees, lifting her legs onto his shoulders, and Goddess, she was certain he would be the end of her. And what an end. Deep, unyielding, unspeakably brutal. His breaths blew hard and fast to match his pace as a sheen coated his big, broad body.

Nothing else mattered. Nothing else existed.

"Tell me you love me," he growled. "Say it."

"I do," she gasped as his thrusts left her breathless. "I. Love. You."

She almost convinced herself.

Lines forked from the outer corners of his eyes as he squeezed them shut. He came with a savage cry, grinding his hips against her as his back arched and his body shuddered. His breathless moans turned to quiet chuckles as he withdrew from her and lay on the bed, facing the ceiling.

Annora lay still, her knees bent where he left them, her heart pounding in her ears. In all her years and in every quick tryst with guards, maids, and footmen, no one had ever rendered her so utterly speechless with the intensity of their passion. It was an injustice that it was he who had achieved it.

Henry rolled onto his side, breaths still strained, and placed his arm across her. "Well?" he asked. "Your verdict?"

"I'll tell you when my spirit returns to my body," she replied, placing her hand on his forearm. It was solid beneath her touch, warm and dusted with hair. His muscles slackened as she stroked it.

He flashed a smug grin and rolled to blot his face on the pillows, edging slightly closer, until his soft stomach pressed against her hip. "Tomorrow I'll go to my death remembering tonight, and their blades will land a little softer."

Annora's eyebrows stitched. His bullish body was well-matched to his foolish, stubborn mind. "Why do you have to go? It's beyond foolish."

"Because Caine doesn't deserve to live."

She rolled onto her side, pressing her soft body to his. "And what about you? Do you deserve to die too?"

A long sigh flared his nostrils. "There are some who would say so."

Concern for him sat heavy in her chest as she pushed

back the tousled strands of hair from his brow. She knew she should hate him, and part of her did, but another, more persistent part was curious about him. Freed from the prisons which had held him all his life, Henry was unbridled potential. Potential which he intended to waste on his ill-advised, suicidal quest. The man frustrated her to no end. "And what of those who would argue otherwise?"

His blue eyes scanned her face, but he said nothing.

She continued, "Instead of giving yourself to your enemy, you could die as an old man, safe and warm in your bed, in the arms of someone who finds your life worthwhile."

He chuckled derisively. "Not I. That sort of death is more suited to bears than dragons."

"You ridiculous, stubborn man," she sighed, rolling away to climb from the bed. "Have it your way, but know I'll remember you as nothing more than that."

"I don't care what you think of me," he laughed. "Just as long as you remember my cock and tongue."

"I won't. I'll remember instead that you *are* a cock, and that your tongue spoke nothing but bullshit and nonsense this entire night."

As she went to stand, his fingers curled around her wrist, tugging her back to him. She gasped as he wrapped his arms around her, so powerful she stood no chance of fighting him off even if she tried. But she found herself unwilling to even try. Instead, she gazed into his eyes, watching his smile fade to a hard line.

"Is that how you want to die?" he asked her. "Old and in your bed?"

"Aye. What person in their right mind doesn't?"

His throat flexed as he leaned forward and kissed her forehead, then her temple, her eyelid, her cheek. His lips were hot, carrying with them the scent of her and the honey from his meal. "Tell me about it. What life do you imagine for yourself now you're free from Caer Duloon?"

"In fantasy, or reality?"

He smiled. "I doubt the two would conflict for you. If someone tried to deny you, you'd simply badger them to death until they gave you whatever your heart desired."

Rasping her fingers through the stubble of his beard, she braced herself for ridicule. "Well, I'll have to find a way to make money, some skill I can offer for coin. Though I'll never serve anyone."

"Hm," his brow creased. "Where will you live?"

"I always dreamed of a woodland cottage, far away from castles and nobles, where I can live freely."

"That sounds awful." Henry closed his eyes, his face a picture of serenity. "Go on..." he said. "Would you live alone?" He was imagining it, she realized, imagining living the life she spoke of.

"Yes. Goddess, yes, I want nothing more. I'd make sure all the local children thought me a witch and everyone would leave me be."

A chuckle shook his chest. "And what of children of your own?"

"I've never wanted them."

He hummed at the back of his throat. "Well, perhaps you'll meet a handsome woodsman who can kiss your quim whenever you ask him to and has a similar disinterest in heirs."

"I don't want one of those either."

"Not even one who came to you only when you beckoned, and then skulked back off into the woods when you were done with him?"

She considered it for a moment. "That might be alright."

A slow smile spread across her lips as the picture formed in the back of her mind; a big, brawny man with rough hands that cared only for her pleasure.

Her smile soon faded as the imaginary woodsman took on Henry's form.

It was out of the question. Henry Percille was a pampered champion and an odious one at that. It mattered not that he was handsome or burly or keen to please her over and over. She cared nothing for him and she certainly would not enjoy a life trapped alone with him in the woods, even if he spent most of his day between her thighs.

Goddess, but he was beautiful.

She placed her hand upon his wrist as it lay cradled in the valley of her waist, and she held it there. Just in case.

CHAPTER
TEN

Henry awoke before dawn, heart pounding and drenched in sweat after only a few minutes of sleep.

Nightmares.

The same nightmares he had endured for a decade clung to him as he fought for his breath. The image of the champion, Robert the Ironclaw, slumped over the tavern table, a crossbow bolt through his skull put there by a man Henry had paid and invited to Blackmere.

It was not simply a dream. It was a memory, one which haunted him.

Ten years in a cell was only part of his punishment; one put upon him. The nightmares were the punishment he inflicted upon himself. It still was not enough.

When he caught his breath and the vision of Robert's body had faded back to the shadows of his mind, he took stock of the room. The fire had dwindled to hissing embers, moonlight glowed on the water of the bathtub, and the chambermaid still slept peacefully beside him.

Even in sleep she scowled, her face a perfect picture of insolence, daring him to wake her and incur her wrath. So he let her sleep on uninterrupted.

Instead, he watched the little window transform slowly from a square of black to indigo, and finally to pale, hazy blue. It was well past the hour by which he had told himself he would leave, and yet, no matter how many times he tried to rouse himself from bed, he could not.

Annora began to wriggle restlessly beside him, her brow creasing as she whispered nonsensical things beneath her breath. She was every bit as lovely as she was strange, and try as he might, he found he could not fight back his smile as he watched her dream.

It was impossible to leave her side as she slept. She was soft and warm, one of her arms wrapped around his waist, the other pushed under the pillows. He had never shared a bed before for more than a minute or two, and it was an unusual, yet comforting feeling having her sleep so close.

And he needed a little comfort, even if he did not deserve it.

Henry was not afraid to die. In fact, he welcomed it. Or rather the idea of it. Death would mean he no longer saw the faces of those he had hurt. He would no longer awaken, panicked from dreams of Blackmere, and of Robert. In death he could finally rest.

But Annora filled his world with something he had never known before, something he wasn't sure he even deserved. He drank it down anyway, breathing in the scent of her and feeling her flood through him.

He closed his eyes, telling himself he would enjoy her a moment longer before he faced the cold and the grim destiny ahead of him. A moment of softness before the sharp agony of steel.

But when he opened his eyes again, Annora was dressed and walking back into the room, carrying a wooden tray in her hands.

Henry bolted upright, blinking away sleep as hard as he could. "What hour is it?"

"Late," she said, a sly smile spreading across her lips. "The innkeeper is grumbling that we didn't come down for breakfast when he cooked it this morning, but I convinced him to make us more."

She set the tray on the bed and sat beside it. The room filled with the savory scent of bread, butter, bacon, and eggs, and the sweet tang of spiced apples.

"How did you pay for it?" Henry asked. "I thought you hadn't any money."

"No, but you do," she said, tossing his sagging coin purse on the bed beside him.

"You robbed me?"

"Aye. Well, you owed me for last night." She shrugged. Her hair was braided over her shoulder, the tip of it curling like a scorpion's sting. It suited her well.

He leaned back against the headboard as she poured a cup from an earthenware jug and offered it to him. He peered down at the cloudy brown liquid. "What is it?"

"Apple," she sighed. "The place is riddled with the

wretched things. Applewood smoked bacon, cooked apples, apple juice, apple cakes. I'm surprised we didn't wake up with one of the rotten things stuffed in our mouths this morning."

Henry chuckled, taking a sip of the sweet, tangy juice. "I suppose there are worse things to be stuffed with."

"Are there?" She grimaced. "I can't stand them."

Leaning forward, Henry took a stiff, overcooked rasher of bacon from the tray and let it crumble between his teeth. The succulent taste of salted meat flooded his mouth, so delicious it almost brought tears to his eyes. After he swallowed, he said, "Apples are too sweet for you, I imagine. Though you didn't seem to mind the taste when you were stealing mine last night."

"I was hungry," she muttered, taking a rasher of bacon for herself and dipping the tip of it into an egg's golden yolk. "I'll eat anything if I'm hungry enough. Not all of us were raised spoiled."

A huff of dismissive laughter burst from Henry, but she paid him no heed. Instead, she simply ate, staring at the little square of blue through the window. Panic and failure gave way to contentment as they sat and feasted together, swaddled in a comfortable silence.

Yes, he had sworn vengeance, but it could wait. Revenge, not bacon, was best served cold after all.

"I notice you're still here," she said at last. "Did you change your mind?"

"No. I intend to leave soon."

Perhaps he was still groggy from sleep, but there was a shift in her. It was barely perceptible, but he could have sworn it was there. Her smile faltered, and her eyebrows sloped downward. If she were anyone else, he might suspect she was disappointed.

Taking a piece of bread from the tray, he buttered it before placing two bacon rashers upon it and folding it in half. Somehow, she had remained unfairly lovely throughout the night, and bathed in soft morning light he wanted her again, desperately, scorpion tail and all. It would not be so terrible to remain in the inn with her a little longer. "Though, you bringing my breakfast does ruin my plans somewhat."

"How so?"

"Well," he said, chewing the bread and bacon as his heart beat harder, sending his heated blood coursing toward his cock. "I had intended that you be my last meal. Now it's this."

"How terrible for you." She chuckled then, a knowing, satisfied laugh as though everything had fallen into place. If not for her insistence that she hated him, he might suspect she had planned for him to remain with her, rather than riding back to face his death. "And terrible for me that I must endure you again this morning."

Henry narrowed his eyes and threw the bread crust at her head. It landed above her ear before tumbling to her shoulder and down her arm, leaving a trail of white crumbs in its wake.

He stifled a laugh, "You harpy."

She whirled around to face him, her eyes wide with outrage as her mouth hung agape. "I... did you... you threw..."

"Yes, I did. And I'd do it again."

She grabbed the crust from the bed and darted toward him, pinning one of his wrists to the mattress with her hand as she attempted to force the crust into his mouth. Henry held his breath, wriggling his head from side to side, refusing to take it, secretly relishing the softness of her body through her clothes, pressed to his bare frame.

"I brought you breakfast," she scolded him. "Now, eat it."

"Ne—er," he grunted, his protest unintelligible through his watertight lips.

She was playfully rough with him, but he could take it; he'd endured far more brutal play fights throughout his life with the champions. But her body against him, her thighs straddling his, her fingertips grazing his lips... they were worth the crumbs on the bedsheets.

As she fought with him, he bucked up his hips, pressing his erection to the warmth between her thighs, making her breath hitch and snatching the smile from her lips.

"Fiend," she whispered as she let go of the crust and let it fall to the floor by the bed.

Henry tsked, disguising his own breathlessness. "Oh, dear Annora, I didn't think you'd cave so easily."

He thrust up again, overbalancing her and rolling on top of her as she yelped and laughed, pinned down by him yet defiant as he snarled down at her. The breakfast tray clattered to the floor but they paid it no attention. There was little he could do to rattle her, and he adored her for it. Fierce, insolent, yet gazing up at him with an uncharacteristic affection.

"What will you do now?" he asked, pressing his hips down onto hers, torturing them both as her hand trailed over his shoulder. He glanced off the edge of the bed at the fallen bread crust. "You've been disarmed and lost your tactical advantage."

"Am I supposed to be afraid?"

He kissed the corner of her mouth as it tilted into a smile, "Very. I told you, I'm a bad man."

His eyes followed the flash of her teeth, pressing to her lower lip as she shifted her hips beneath him, grinding the heat of her core against him. "I've spent my life surrounded by men who claim to be the biggest and the baddest, Henry Percille. Not all of them grew up pampered in castles with an armory at their disposal."

"Well, I'll bet none of them grew up spending every day learning how to fight."

"Aye, you might be better at fighting, but I can defeat you with one finger."

Her bold claim piqued his curiosity. The softness in her eyes turned to resolve as she took the first finger of her left hand and trailed it down the center of his chest, slowly... oh so torturously slow.

His treacherous body quivered at the sensation of her touch, but he fought back, tensing his muscles and denying her the satisfaction. As she brushed her fingertip to his nipple, he clenched his jaw, paying no heed to the tingling pleasure shooting through his body, silencing the urge to gasp, to whimper, to kiss her. When his nipple was a dark, aching peak, her finger traveled lower, to his stomach, tracing the line of hair down the center which had once been unyielding muscle and sun-kissed skin.

He braced himself for the insults and teasing he would have thrown at a man who looked like him—the insults he had relished raining down on Brandon the Bear—but they did not come. There was only tenderness. And it was devastating.

In Henry's mind, he deserved many things—punishment, ridicule, even death, but not that. Not adoration.

"Annora…" He bit down his urge to ask her to stop, even as heat flooded his cheeks.

"What's the matter, mighty Dragon? Do you yield already?"

He shook his head as she traced the curves of his belly. "No."

"Then, what could you possibly have to say to me?"

He was not the man he once was, outwardly, at least. The champion, the Dragon, had been a hard, perfectly sculpted man who wanted nothing more than to be admired, both for his skill in the arena, and for his body. He had also been a vain man, and now he was certainly not that.

"Are you shy?" she asked gently.

There was no ridicule in her voice, nor in her eyes when he finally met them. "Perhaps. A little."

"You needn't be. Your body is one of your few favorable assets," she said, her lips lifting into a smile and drawing his with them.

"I spent my early years longing to be a man like

Brandon the Bear, but I did not mean for it to be quite so literal."

She chuckled. "Well, I don't know who Brandon the Bear is, but I know that despite trying my hardest to despise you, I can't help but find myself wanting you. You're a beautiful man, Henry Percille. I like how you look. I like how you feel pressed against me like this. And I like knowing that your cock is straining, and your breath is sparse because I'm touching you with just one finger."

He found himself chuckling. "Not to dampen your victory, but my cock has been hard all morning. You'll have to do a little better than that."

With a sigh, she brought her hand around his back, trailing her finger up along the edge of his spine before letting it slip over the swell of his shoulder and up his neck and to his lips. His breath shuddered as she traced them, fascinated by him, wanting him despite her reservations. Nothing had ever made him feel so aroused.

No one had ever made him want to supplicate like she did.

He parted his lips, inviting her to draw closer, and the moment her finger was between them he took it into his mouth and sucked. She watched him, that victorious smile playing on her lips as if that was all somehow part of her plan too.

He licked the length of her finger before releasing it from his hold as she raised her head to kiss him, her tongue seeking his with an urgency that left him lightheaded. Annora. She could destroy him, seize him body and spirit, hold him captive between her thighs forever, and he would thank her for it.

The sensation of her finger slipping between the cleft of his backside hardened his lungs, but as she circled his hole, he kissed her deeper. His nerve endings flared, spreading exquisite pleasure throughout his body, curling his toes as he shifted up, giving her easier access. When she penetrated him, pushing her finger inside him, he barked her name. His cock lay flush against her, pressed between their bodies as he thrust his hips in time with her.

"Good," she whispered against his throat, curling her finger inside him, stroking him, coaxing out his pleasure. "I wish you could see how beautiful you look now."

It was too much; her praise, the feeling of her inside him, her teeth grazing the skin of his neck beneath his beard. "Goddess, Annora," he gasped, squeezing his eyes shut as she stroked his prostate. He ground himself against her, seeking release. "Glorious, diabolical harpy."

"Do you yield?"

"Will you stop if I do?"

"Yes, if you tell me to," she said.

"Then never," he gasped. "You'll have to kill me first."

With a grin she tugged her skirt which was rumpled between them, hoisting it over her hips and wrapping her ankles around his thighs. She was wet and hot against his cock and as he pushed inside her, sinking into the soft, exquisite heat of her body, the world around him turned dark for a moment, dangerously close to losing his balance.

When he regained focus, she brought her free hand to his cheek, her eyes wide with concern. "Are you alright?"

He nodded as his body trembled against hers. "Don't stop."

His face burned as he thrust against her, drowning in sensation, gasping for air as she praised him. He gripped the headboard of the bed as his orgasm charged closer, the wood creaking beneath his hands as he held to it, eyes screwed tight, lips parted in blissful agony. The peak of pleasure tore a cry from his lips. He did not care if the landlord heard him. He would not have cared if Lord Caine himself heard the cry while sitting on his carved stone throne.

In fact, he hoped he did.

The pleasure went on, and on, and on, as she drained him, milked him. The headboard snapped and splintered beneath his grip as Annora pressed her lips to his chest.

"Ann... Annora... Goddess..." he gasped as pulse after blissful pulse throbbed through him and tears slipped down his cheeks. He did not care. In that moment nothing in the world mattered beyond her. "You did it, you harpy. I think I'm dying."

She chuckled beneath him, kissing his chest once more. "Your heart still beats."

He nodded, taking an aching hand from the headboard and wiping his tears. Yes, his heart still beat, but the rhythm of it had altered irreparably.

In that moment, it beat for her.

ELEVEN

enry lay beside her, his dark eyelashes resting on his cheeks as the flood of color faded from his face.

A strange sense of pride filled Annora as she watched him gasp for breath, knowing that she had rendered him entirely helpless, given him so much pleasure he had broken the headboard and, she suspected, come dangerously close to fainting.

"Are you recovered?" she asked.

"I doubt I ever truly will be," he muttered. "I'll never be the same again."

The pride ballooned in her chest. "An honorable man might return the favor," she whispered as she smoothed back the tousled strands of his black hair.

Silence followed, and for a moment she assumed he had fallen back to sleep, but then his lips parted. "Whatever have I done to give you the impression that I'm an honorable man?"

Annora sighed as she rolled onto her back and away from him. "Fair point."

He caught her wrist and dragged her back to him, surrounding her in his arms, and throwing a heavy, hairy thigh over her hips.

"Brute," she whispered as she nestled her head beneath his chin, breathing in the salt and warmth of his body. A comfortable, irresistible brute.

His jaw flexed against the top of her head and his chest shook as he chuckled. A frustrating, unjust desire for him burned at her core, but she silenced it, listing his worst qualities in her mind. He was brattish, spoiled, mostly intolerable, and quick to become annoyed. But then, so was she.

Each of his flaws she saw echoed in her. Their origins could not have been more different and yet, they had collided. They had slotted together so perfectly, so intricately, it had to be a cruel trick of the Goddess herself.

The steady gush of Henry's breath slowed as he held her, and his limbs grew heavier, pinning her to him. Quieting her instinct to wriggle free, she sighed. There were far worse places to be trapped than in the arms of a large, handsome, sleeping former champion.

The clatter of approaching horse hooves sounded on the road outside, reminding her that a world existed beyond them. A world she no longer knew her place in.

Her fortieth spring was fast approaching, and employment could be hard to come by, especially if Lord Caine told his noble friends of her and she was recognized. If word reached Marshdown and she returned there, her family would sooner turn her in for a reward than greet her.

That left south, and the brute sleeping atop her was the closest thing she had to hope. For a while it was comforting to pretend her place was with him, and he would not let her come to harm.

She had her freedom, and whether she wanted him or not, she had Henry. That was strangely soothing.

"You need a bath," she grumbled against his chest, before her affection toward him settled too deep inside her.

Henry sucked in a long breath and wound his arms tighter. He kept his eyes closed as he muttered, "That's an excellent idea. Why don't you go downstairs and ask the innkeeper to replenish our water?"

"Why don't you go yourself?"

"Because you're dressed, I'm naked, and you wore me out, you terrible woman."

Even as he grumbled, she could not help but smile. The memory of his ecstasy, the way he had howled and sobbed as he spent, was one which would keep her company for many nights. He would likely have to pay the innkeeper for the damage to the bed, or he would have done, had he been an honorable, honest man.

"Please..." he said as he rolled away, showing her his broad, scarred back, and the round, fuzzy globes of his backside for a moment before he tugged the bedsheets over him. "If you have him draw us a bath, I'll pleasure you in the tub when I'm recovered."

"Alright," she muttered, untangling herself from the sheets. "I'll go."

"I'll lick your sweet cunt as payment."

Annora grinned and forced a sigh. "If you must, I suppose I shall endure it."

The man on the bed turned his head slightly before letting it fall back to the pillow. "Just for that, I'll do it twice."

"A fate worse than death..."

"And bring us some cheese."

"Cheese?" She pressed her fists to her hips and frowned. "Will there be anything else, *my lord?* Shall I rub your feet too?"

"That would be wonderful."

She released a disgusted grunt and turned toward the door. "Of all the men for me to escape a prison cell from, it had to be the very worst of them."

She closed the door on the sound of his laughter and tramped down the wooden staircase to the tavern below. Though it was past midday, the bar was empty, save for the rosy-cheeked innkeeper who refused to meet her eye. She could hardly blame him. Henry was vocal and neither of them were gentle with the furnishings.

"His lordship requests a bath," she said as she leaned on the wooden countertop. "And cheese if you have it."

The innkeeper's hands trembled as he set a cup on a hook above him. "Aye."

His voice was thin, breathless, as though she had found him in the grips of terror. A deep scarlet blush stained his throat and the bottom of his jaw.

Something was wrong.

Even for a tavern on the outskirts of Caer Duloon, it was too quiet. Annora's heart kicked into a cantering rhythm as she stepped back from the bar and searched for the source of his anxiety.

"What is it?" she asked, her eyes scanning the empty tables and chairs, and the tracks of wet boot prints trailing from the door to the center of the tavern, fading as they got closer to the bar.

She opened her mouth to call out to Henry, to warn him, but the guard sprang from behind the counter and slammed her face-down onto it in a heartbeat, forcing out her breath. Confusion, pain, the stench of unwashed bodies that had ridden for days, the residual earthy scent of horse. Fear.

"Annora, is it?" the guard hissed in her ear. "You've left quite a little trail of our brothers' bodies since your escape. I have a knife above your spine. One word and I'll slice it in two. Understand?"

She nodded, her legs trembling beneath her as her mind raced. There were at least three of them, all clad in the same sapphire blue, each of them wielding a blade. She could fight, and the fire burning through her veins begged her to, but she would lose. She was unarmed, untrained, her vision blurred by rage and terror.

Cold air blasted against her back as the tavern door swung open, and slow footsteps fell against the boards. A man chuckled quietly at her back.

"Well now, here we are, at the end of our long journey," the man said. He was well-spoken, quiet, and calm as he approached. She knew him well.

"Caine," she hissed.

"*Lord* Caine," he corrected her. "Show some respect for your betters."

He stepped beside her, his long dove-white hair braided over one shoulder as he removed his riding gloves, finger by finger. She had seen the nobleman many times in the castle — a middle-aged man with a near lipless smile. By the standards of nobles, he was no different than any of them; harsh, demanding, lazy. A purple and yellow bruise stained the narrow bridge of his nose. At least she had left a mark.

"How long did you remain in the cell?" he asked.

Annora tightened her lips, refusing to answer, even as the guard pressed the tip of the blade to the small of her back, sending a spike of sharp pain across the surface of her skin.

"Let's say an hour? Shall we?" Caine said, holding his arm out to request a riding crop from one of the guards. "I could've sworn I'd sentenced you to suffer the rest of your life down in that hole, did I not?"

"You did, my lord," the guard at her back answered for her as he stepped around, exposing her back to Lord Caine but keeping her arms pinned to the bar.

"Well, since the cell couldn't hold you, I'd say we have a lot of time to make up with the crop."

Terror gripped Annora's heart as she realized what was to come. She raised her head to meet the guard's hard eyes, his thin-lipped snarl. "Please don't—"

"Quiet," he snarled, tightening his grip until she felt his fingertips between the bones of her wrist.

Lord Caine chuckled darkly. "You know, all of this could've been avoided, Annora. If only you'd been a little nicer. I don't ask much of my girls, only that they are pleasant, that they smile at me, do as I tell them, and behave in front of my guests. You couldn't do any of that."

Bile rose in Annora's throat as the nobleman took his riding crop and bent it into an arc between his hands. She had felt its bite more than once, but never before had she witnessed quite so much cruelty in the lord's eyes. Nor as much sadistic pleasure.

"You're going to whip her here?" the innkeeper asked. "This inn is my livelihood. If people hear—"

"You'll be compensated," Caine smiled slowly. "But you see, this miserable little bitch has caused me a lot of trouble. She ruined my party, humiliated me in front of my guests, killed my guards and escaped with a prisoner I've been holding captive by the order of the Queen."

Annora's view of the innkeeper blurred behind a veil of unshed tears as she set her jaw. If they were to whip her, punish her there in the tavern she would not give them the satisfaction of weeping. She would let her teeth shatter before she let Caine or the guards know she was afraid of them, or that she was in pain.

"What about the other one... the champion?" one of the guards asked. "Should we go up there and drag him down to watch her die?"

Lord Caine chuckled. "Excellent idea."

"First door on the right," the innkeeper said without hesitation.

Annora's heart plummeted as two of the guards charged up the stairs, blades drawn. Henry was unarmed, and in all likelihood, still naked and sleeping. Every

muscle in her body tensed as she filled her lungs, antici-
pating pain.

She called out, "Henry!"

The crop sliced across her back, savagely cruel. White-
hot pain spread across her body as Lord Caine snarled.
"Silence!"

"HENRY!" she called, louder as the whip came down
again, harder.

Whether from genuine fear for the brute's life, or
simply the fact that calling for him defied Caine, she did not
know. But she poured every shred of spite and fear and pain
into her purpose. Footsteps thundered on the boards above
her and men's voices cried out in surprise, anger, and pain.
She called for him again.

The guard in front of her clamped his hand over her
mouth, so she bit down, his flesh bursting between her teeth
as her mouth flooded with bitter copper and salt. A scream
pierced her ears as she squeezed her eyes shut. He beat his
fist between her shoulder blades, but she did not let go.

"Vicious bitch," Caine roared behind her, cracking the
crop across the backs of her thighs with such force she was
certain for a moment he had severed her legs entirely.

He would not let her live, she knew it in her heart. Her
punishers would not stop until she lay cold and bloodied on
the ground, but she would not go quietly. Kicking back with
all her strength, the heel of her foot connected with soft
flesh and Caine howled in pain.

The riding crop clattered to the floor behind her as she
released the guard's mangled finger from her jaws and stag-
gered back from the bar. Hot blood oozed down her back

and from her lips as she stumbled, vision blurring, ears ringing. A flash of searing pain blinded her as a palm cracked
across her cheek, and a force at her ankles sent her tumbling
to the floor. She blinked as Lord Caine's face came into
view above her. He clamped his eyes shut as he cupped his
crotch, his throat pulsing as he heaved.

She had hated him for twenty years, but now, with the
flesh at her back throbbing and stinging, she despised him.
She wanted him dead.

But the feeling was mutual.

As Caine wiped his lips on his cuff, he kicked the toe of
his boot into her ribs, forcing the air from her lungs.

"I'm going to make sure your death is slow," he hissed,
his face scarlet and the veins in his forehead bulging. "But
I'll have your mouth sewn shut first so you cannot scream.
I'll have the bones in your arms and legs shattered so you
cannot escape. Your remaining days will be agony."

"It will be better than emptying your shit pot," she
gasped.

The inn, which only moments ago was silent and still,
was in chaos. Blood shot from the wailing guard's finger,
dripping over the bar as the innkeeper backed into a corner.
Lord Caine strode over to her, the riding crop now back in
his hand. The pain in Annora's back was overwhelming,
burning, throbbing. She bit down on the urge to cry, to
scream as the powdery, acerbic aftertaste of blood cloyed
her senses, clinging to her tongue.

The next bite from the crop came to her ribs, below her
breast, and the moment it connected her heart threatened to
burst from her chest. Another hit to her side, one across her

stomach. She rolled onto her back, biting into her arm as blow after blow streaked across her flesh.

A cry pierced the air, but it was not her own. It was shrill, male, laced with terror and agony, and it continued as Lord Caine fell to the ground beside her, teeth bared, and fists clenched.

Terror barely had time to sink its barbs into Annora's heart before a pair of strong hands rolled her onto her back, and the will to keep fighting flared through her veins. But the moment Henry's blue eyes met hers, that fire turned to relief.

He was crouched beside her, shielding her body with his, naked and bloodied, with crimson smears streaking across his handsome face, which made his eyes shine all the brighter.

"Can you stand?" he asked, letting his bloodied blade clatter on the floorboards.

"Aye. I think so." Her voice was faint, distant to her own ears.

She turned toward the sudden sound and was met by a river of crimson, pouring from two deep cuts at the backs of Lord Caine's knees. The nobleman sobbed as he dragged himself across the floorboards.

The world spun around Annora as she raised herself onto her elbows, and pain pounded her back like burning hail. The guard she had bitten by the bar was dead, slumped over beside the weeping innkeeper.

"Here, let me help," Henry said, placing his arms around her and hoisting her from the ground.

He walked by her side as she climbed the stairs, stepping over the bodies of the guards in the narrow hallway, and back to their room where only minutes before they had lain in such bliss. And all the while, Lord Caine's screams echoed through the tavern. With a grimace, Henry closed the door.

In the haze of agony, Henry was the only comfort, the only clarity. His face was so close his breath blew against her cheek, the warmth of his body wafting gently against her skin as she pulled the wool dress away from her wounded flesh, exposing it to the cool air. When she was naked, she slumped belly-down on the pillows of the bed.

"It hurts," she whispered, as a tear slid down her cheek.

Henry crouched beside the bed and pressed his forehead to hers. "I know. I know. I've had the same done to me." He kissed her tear away as his large, rough hands cupped her face lightly, as though she were a precious, fragile thing about to shatter. He trembled as he spoke. "Breathe deeply, Annie, try to think of something else. The pain will subside."

Her face pulled into a halfhearted scowl. "Annie?"

He chuckled, his lips grazing her jaw. "You don't like it?"

"I despise it."

He smiled, showering her with gentle kisses on her cheeks, her temple, the tip of her nose. "Good. Well, Annie, I need you to stay here for a little while. You're safe, and I'll be back for you soon."

It was only then that panic struck through her heart. She tightened her grip around his arms. "Don't leave me."

"I'll come back, but Lord Caine yet lives and I can't

have that. Not after what he's done." As he spoke, his kisses landed softly on the aching skin of her cheek like snow on cracked stone, his tenderness at odds with his intentions. "He must suffer, as we both have at his hands, as so many have. The world will be a better place without him."

Annora nodded, still gripping his arms. He was strong enough that it would take nothing to tear himself from her grasp, but he held her and let himself be held, kissed her, assured her the pain was only temporary. Another facet of that impossibly frustrating man.

She let her eyes close. "What will you do to him?"

"You don't need to know," he said, running his fingers through her hair and pushing it back from her brow. "But know that he'll pay for what he's done to you and I. And then I'll come back, and we'll flee. We'll find somewhere."

Her heart pounded against her ribs as she slid her hand down his arm and laced her fingers with his. "Together?"

Slowly, his grip around her tightened to a firm, reassuring squeeze. "Yes."

Her breaths came easier at his words. The knowledge that she would know her place in the world for at least a little while longer was more comforting than he knew.

"Thank you," she whispered, withdrawing her hand from his.

The warmth of his lips on the top of her head drew a smile. So tender, and yet so powerful, so dangerous to all but her. He said nothing as he hastily dressed and left the room, and his heavy footsteps pounded the stairs.

TWELVE

I t was late afternoon as Henry oversaw the pyre and tossed three silvers upon the ground beside it. Miniscule snowflakes fell from dark clouds overhead, melting before they even reached the ground.

"I won't tell anyone." The redheaded innkeeper stooped to collect the coins as his lips quivered. "I'll tell them I never saw where you went."

"I don't care what you tell them," Henry sighed, picking the nobleman's blood from beneath his fingernails. He glanced at the small, square window on the second floor of the building, his heart fluttering at the thought of Annora, then hardening as he remembered the pain that she was in.

Lord Caine's death had been slow and painful, but not enough.

Henry was many things, many *terrible* things, but he had never looked into his enemy's eyes as he snuffed out their life. He had killed before, but never in cold blood, never someone so helpless. He could have left Lord Caine weeping and bleeding on the tavern floor, rode away with Annora, and found a pocket of Aldland to live in peace. Perhaps he could have found her a cottage befitting a forest witch, and left her there to live out her days in quiet contentment as she wished. But that would not have been enough.

Lord Caine would have lived to stain another day with his existence.

Annora would have lived a long, comfortable, boring life in the arms of a handsome woodcutter.

Neither of those futures suited Henry.

He was many things, and selfish was most definitely one of them. Lord Caine had hurt Annora, *his* Annora, so he had to die. It was as simple as that, and Henry refused to think about the meaning of it any longer. For the time being, he would remain by her side, or between her thighs, whichever she found most agreeable.

Still, the deed had rattled him far more than he would allow himself to admit. His heart still beat as though he were sprinting, his fingers trembling even as he wore a mask of nonchalance. One more wrong to add to his ever-growing ledger.

"What should I do?" the innkeeper asked the flames as their light danced in the copper of his beard. "If they come looking for him?"

"I don't know. Tell them the truth. Tell them you cowered in the corner and watched while I killed their beloved overlord, that you did nothing to save him, nor the woman you watched brutally assaulted."

"They said she was a criminal—"

In an instant Henry's fingers dug into the flesh of the innkeeper's throat, knocking him off balance. The man's eyes widened as he stumbled back toward the pyre, as though the flames held a better chance of mercy than Henry did.

"She is a criminal," Henry snarled as the innkeeper struggled against his grip. "So am I, and I've killed men for far less than watching my woman tortured."

His woman? Was she? The words had sprung from him so naturally, but as they hung in the air between him and the sniveling wretch, he glanced over his shoulder to make sure she was not at the window, listening.

Henry's lip curled. Perhaps the innkeeper should die too, but Henry's capacity for hearing screams was at its limit. He released the man roughly, and sent him stumbling to the ground. "Did you have my wolf pelt cleaned last night, as I asked you?"

"Aye," the man whimpered, clutching the red skin around his neck. "I tried as best I could, but it still smells foul."

Perhaps it always would. Perhaps sitting wrapped in it for a decade had saturated the fur with the stench of his rotten core. Ten years ago, he had chests full of finery, more gold than he could ever hope to spend in a lifetime, titles, a castle to call home, countless admirers. Now he had nothing but a half-empty coin purse, a stinking wolf pelt, and, at least for a little while, he had Annora.

He sighed. "I'll take it anyway."

"Alright," the innkeeper nodded as he stood and hurried

back toward the building. He paused a couple of yards away from Henry. "Did you still want that cheese?"

A small gasp burst from Henry's chest, "Yes."

For the first time since Annora left the room that morning, his heart was buoyed. Though it made him uneasy even to think it, he liked her at least as much as he liked cheese, and that was rare.

When he returned to their room though, any sense of relief vanished. Annora lay propped in the bathtub as she had the previous night, but her eyes were pink and raw, her knuckles pale along the rim of the tub. She did not stir as he entered and sat the blade and folded wolf pelt on the edge of the bed.

"Who filled the bath for you?" he asked.

"I did."

She continued to astonish him. Small though she was, and injured, she had carted bucket after bucket of water up and down the stairs by herself. He could not help but smile at her ferocity. A woodland cottage was far too humble for her. She deserved nothing less than a castle.

"It's done," he told her, sitting on the bed and setting the plate of crumbling white cheese beside him. "Lord Caine is gone."

Her eyes fluttered shut, and a tear slipped down to the rosy swell of her cheek.

"Don't cry for him," Henry said.

She scowled. "I'm not."

"Good."

"I keep wondering what would've happened had you

gone down in my stead. Would you have been able to fight them off?"

"You did fight them," he said. "You almost severed the guard's finger completely."

"I kicked Lord Caine in the balls too," she whispered, as her lip curved into the slightest arc. The smile quickly fell. "Where can we go, Henry? Surely when it's discovered he's dead, people will hunt for us."

"They may," Henry shrugged, taking a nugget of cheese and popping it into his mouth. It crumbled on his tongue, spreading a cool, creaminess throughout his mouth.

She scowled. "How can you be so calm?"

"Because in all the world, I have only four things. I have my fur, I have a few coins, I have a plate of surprisingly fine cheese, and I have you, Annie. Everything that's important to me is here with me and the men who might've taken any of it are dead, so yes, I'm calm."

It was a lie. His heart fluttered against his ribs as his mind grasped for a plan. They had threatened him with death for simply injuring Lady Blackmere. Killing a nobleman would mean nothing less than a slow death, possibly for the pair of them. He turned to Annora, and let the sight of her salve his burning blood.

Her gaze trailed the length of his torso, slowly, methodically tracing every detail of him, as though committing him to memory, and when her eyes met his, heat crept along his jaw.

How was it possible for her to render him so utterly defenseless? In the arena he had been adored, admired, he had stood among rose petals and let praise and declarations of love rain down upon him, but it was nothing compared to when her eyes met his.

He stood from the bed, and stepped across the room dazzled by the light in her eyes as they followed his movements. "Let me see your back."

She yielded to his request, leaning forward and pressing her lips together to hold back whatever sound of suffering was begging for release. Henry mirrored her expression. The wounds were brutal. Crimson bruises streaked across her flesh, and a few of the blows had broken her skin.

Caine had definitely not died slowly enough.

Henry's jaw clenched. There was nothing he could do to help her pain, but he could give her comfort to try to drown it out. He took the small earthenware jug from the wash basin in the corner, and filled it with her cold bathwater.

"You didn't warm it first?" he asked.

"No, I thought the cold would feel better." She dipped her chin. "It's fine once you get used to it. There was never warm water for servants in Caer Duloon."

"Close your eyes," he said quietly.

She sighed through her nose as her shoulders slouched. "Are you hurt?"

"No." He let the water trickle from the lip of the jug onto her golden hair, starting at her crown and working his way down her waves. The skin on her back pebbled as cold rivers ran down it, following paths which only the previous night he had kissed. How their world had changed since then.

"So, none of it is your blood?"

"An insignificant amount." He set the jug down on the floor beside the tub, and began to work his fingers across her scalp. She sighed, wavering slightly as though her instinct was to lean back into him, but the pain prevented it. Though it went against his nature, doing something gentle with his hands after so much brutality, was as soothing to him as it was to her.

"What do we do?" she asked.

"Well, the first thing we need to do is ride to the nearest real town and buy you a comb. I'm certain there are birds nesting in here."

A chuckle shook her. "You could cut mine with the sword as I did yours."

"You would trust me with a blade to your neck?"

A thoughtful hum sounded at the back of her throat but she did not answer. Instead, she simply asked, "Which town should we run to?"

"I don't know. One where I wouldn't be recognized."

"You said yourself you don't look the same as you did. Would anyone really recognize you after so long?" she said, pressing her head back against his fingers, increasing the pressure on her scalp.

She was correct, though it hurt to admit. Henry the fugitive was a different man—at least outwardly—than The Dragon.

"Still," he said, threading her hair between his fingers and running though the few knots he could find. He would never admit it, but her hair was silken in his hands. "It would be good to find shelter where people could not simply hand us over if the guards came for us."

Annora chuckled. "Aye, well good luck with that. Most people would turn us in for a pint of ale."

The solution burned at the back of Henry's throat. In truth, there were few people in Aldland who could protect them, and even fewer who would. But with power, with authority, behind the walls of a castle, they might be safe. Desperation forced his answer. "Then we'll ride south, to the Champion's Guild."

"What?" She sat upright, twisting and sucking in a pained breath. "What good are make-believe warriors so far away?"

"They have a castle; one I know better than anyone else does. It was my home for most of my life," he shrugged, setting the jug back down. "I'll reclaim my titles and my gold. Lady Blackmere ensured there was no more Guild Master, no one to say no to me. It would be easy. I'll simply enter the castle, lay my claim, and take it from the inside."

"Simply?" A snort of laughter burst from Annora. "As easy as that, is it?"

"With you by my side? Yes." He pressed a kiss to the top of her head and stood, drying his hands on a thick white cloth, staining it with residual blood.

Annora lifted herself from the bath, water cascading down the curves of her body, like the Goddess herself emerging from the sea to cast her judgment upon him. The desire to lick each droplet from her soft skin ached in his chest, his tongue, and the roof of his mouth.

Her golden eyebrows stitched together, and her expression hardened. "And what about me? Once you're comfortably back in the Champion's Guild with your titles and riches, what happens to me?"

"There are servants, chambermaids. You could find work there."

"You want me to *serve* you?" Her expression hardened into sickened disbelief. "I'd rather die."

"No! Well, perhaps...only at first. Once I'm Guild Master, I'll make it so you never have to work. You can live in leisure by my side."

A bitter laugh burst from her. "And what a slow, agonizing death that would be."

"Death? It wouldn't be a death; it would be life. You would be provided for."

"I will *never* serve you, Henry Percille. You or anybody else." She shook her head in disgust, turning from him for a moment before whirring round to face him once more, her eyes newly alight with frustrated ire. "What do you want, Henry? Truly? If you want to ride down to Champion's Guild, drop to your knees and grovel, beg for forgiveness and titles before they arrest us, then I want no part of it."

Heat flooded his face at the very suggestion. "This isn't about redemption. I'm not ashamed of what I did to them and I don't want their forgiveness."

"So, it's about money? Fame? Glory?"

"No—"

"Then what do you want?"

"You!" The answer burned in the air between them, stealing the breath from his lungs as the hair on the back of his neck bristled. "I want *you*, Annora. I would gladly see this world burn if I knew I could keep you from the flames."

They were the truest words he had ever spoken, and they terrified him.

Her lips parted as the light from the tiny window gleamed in her eyes. "You hardly know me."

"I know enough."

She shook her head. "You've lost your mind."

"I know my heart."

"Do you? How can you when you barely know anything about the world? You've lived your life sheltered by prisons."

"And now I'm free, and I know I don't want to leave your side."

She froze for a moment. "And then what? When the world is ash and we are the only two left?"

He scoffed. "Then we'd fuck uninterrupted until we either tire of each other or waste away to nothing."

A cold laugh burst from her, as she stepped over the edge of the tub. "How bleak."

"Yet you can't deny it would be wonderful, just you and I."

"Can't I?"

His lip curled in frustration. "Oh, just say you want me too. We've played this game for days, pretending to hate each other."

She shook her head and crossed the room, away from him, wrapping herself in a drying cloth as she snickered. "You think I'm only pretending?"

A coil in Henry's jaw tightened. He had killed for her, spent the night pleasuring her, and she was even more of a harpy than when he had first met her in the cell. "You hate me?"

"At this moment, very much so. At this moment, I hate everyone and everything, including you."

"Fine." He pulled his shirt over his head and set to work unlacing his breeches. "Turn your back while I get into the tub. If you hate me, you don't get to see me."

An audacious smile spread across her lips but, with a shake of her head, she did as he asked. And that was somehow worse.

Henry's breath burned in his chest as he pulled down his breeches and raised a leg to step into the bath. As the frigid water touched his skin, his lungs emptied. "By the Goddess, it's colder than your heart."

"Aye, and soon to be polluted by your presence just the same."

As he lowered himself into the water, every inch of flesh it covered ached. He hissed, knuckles bone-white as he gripped the edge. By the time he was sitting, his temper had grown even fouler, but nothing prepared him for the sight of Annora, sitting on the edge of the bed, staring out of the little window at the gray sky beyond as she nibbled his cheese.

"Put that back," he hissed.

"No. I almost died for this cheese."

"And I killed for it. Put. It. Back."

She raised an eyebrow. "I thought you killed for me?"

Furiously scrubbing the blood from his forearms, Henry growled. "I lied, you wretched harpy."

A peel of laughter sounded from the bed, unjustly

wonderful and heartfelt. "I'm a harpy again, am I? What happened to calling me your Annie?"

"I changed my mind."

"Well, I much prefer harpy to Annie. Annie sounds like the sort of name a little girl might give a dairy cow. Calling me a harpy means I'm too much, too vicious, and too abrasive for your delicate self. I enjoy it."

"Put my cheese down," Henry barked.

Her chest shook with silent laughter. "Would you like me to spit it out?"

"Yes."

"Ridiculous man," she chuckled, stuffing two lumps of crumbly cheese into her cheeks and chewed.

Her defiance only served to make him want her harder. She burned in the core of him; an ache he could not escape, as much a part of him after only a few days than anyone he had known. Perhaps it was only an infatuation, perhaps she was simply the first drop of rain after ten years of drought, but even as she taunted him and stole his cheese, he desperately wanted to drown in her.

"They used to call *me* the Dragon, you know, back when I was a champion. But compared to you, I'm a beam of fucking sunlight." Cupping the bathwater in his hands he splashed it over his face and scrubbed, gasping from the icy cold.

Pink droplets fell from his beard and onto his thighs. His blood, Caine's blood, the guards' blood. It mattered not. They were all bad men who did not deserve to stand in her presence.

"Get dressed," he said, his voice as sharp and hard as

shattered obsidian. "The sooner we ride out, the more distance we can put between ourselves and whoever comes for us."

She stood, letting the cloth fall from her body as Henry's chest tightened. Her scars were dark and angry, and he longed to kill Lord Caine all over again.

"I don't want to go to the Champion's Guild," she said bluntly as silvery winter sunlight kissed her bare skin. "I don't want to fall on my knees at their feet and beg that they grant us mercy. And I've no intention of ever emptying another chamber pot."

"Annora—"

"I want to be free, Henry. I want to live on my own terms, comfortable and quiet. I don't want to fight or grovel or beg anymore."

He could bear the distance no longer. Standing from the bath, Henry stepped out and crossed the room toward her, trailing water across the floor. A soft gasp escaped her lips as he cupped her face in his hands. She stared back at him, hard-eyed, as he trailed his thumb across the plump cushion of her bottom lip, bristling even as she stepped toward him, pressing her soft body against his.

"We should part ways," she whispered, though whether it was a suggestion to him, or she was trying to convince herself it was not clear. Her eyelids fluttered shut as she leaned into his touch. "Nothing good can come of this. We're at odds over everything."

The thought of being without her sat uncomfortably in his chest, pushing out against his ribs. "If that's what you want."

"Goddess save me, it isn't." A crease deepened between her eyebrows as he traced the soft curve of her jaw with his fingertips, letting them trail down her throat. Her breath shuddered from her as she lifted her chin, bending to his touch. "But if we were to set the world alight, we'll only burn together."

"Perhaps that's how it should be."

"Perhaps."

"Come with me then. At least as far south as Blackmere. You don't have to decide anything now. I'll get you beyond the reach of Caer Duloon, and if you want then we can go on, or... or I'll give you a horse and whatever coins I have left and you can carve your own path if you want to."

Her eyes opened at his words and her lips parted. But whatever she was about to say was silenced by the clatter of horse hooves, riding toward the inn.

THIRTEEN

Every tightly reined breath was a hurricane to Annora's ears as she and Henry peered through the tiny square window. She balanced on tip-toe, squinting as the riders drew nearer and came into focus. There were five guards in total, all clad in Caer Duloon's midnight blue.

"Shit," she hissed. "Well, so much for our escape."

"We're still going," Henry sighed, tugging his blood-stained shirt over his head and stuffing the bottom of it unceremoniously into his unlaced breeches.

"But the guards—"

"Will be dealt with." He stalked from the window, snatching his blade from the bed and tucking his stinking wolf pelt beneath his arm. "Put your shoes on."

She stiffened at his command. Annora had spent her life serving, following orders, and his tone left a sour taste in the back of her throat. Back in Caer Duloon, she had often imagined shuffling through the cold stone corridors as an old woman, drawing her final breath as she attempted to lift a full chamber pot from beneath a noble lord's bed. She would die surrounded by filth and shattered clay.

But now she was cut loose, simultaneously free yet with limited options; she could go out alone, face the unknown, and try to make a comfortable life for herself, or she could follow him—the man prowling about the room preparing to kill again. Straight back to another castle, straight back to groveling and cleaning away the filth of people who had decided they were more important than her.

She should not have wanted to follow him half as much as she did, but he affected her more than she allowed herself to admit. With a sigh, she relented.

Shoving her blistered feet into her leather slippers, she dragged a breath through her teeth. "What's the plan?"

The corner of Henry's lips tilted. "Escape."

Oh, how she hated him. "Well, I need a weapon."

"What for?"

"To defend myself."

His smile spread, cutting across his face like a scythe. "Do you even know how to wield a sword?"

"Of course I do, it's not hard."

He arched an eyebrow and let the heavy silence speak for him.

"We haven't time for this," she hissed, the heat of her blood prickling beneath the surface of her skin. "I might not have had training, but I guarantee I've been in more real fights than you."

He strode across the room toward her, stopping at the foot of the bed where his crumbling white cheese sat on a tin plate. Thrusting it into her hands he said, "Carry this instead. Wait here until I tell you to."

Every curse she could think of spun through her mind as she stared, vision blurring with panic and anger. He would leave her defenseless, helpless, nothing more than a serving girl carrying his food while he fought on—

Her thoughts were silenced as his lips pressed to hers, his kiss fervent yet endlessly soft and tender. His knuckle pressed up against her chin, tilting her face toward him. Whatever spell he had perfected in that cold, lonely dungeon, he worked it though her with his kiss, binding her to him in a dark, unbreakable tangle. When he pulled away, her lips sought his for a moment longer, before she opened her eyes and remembered she was supposed to hate him.

"*I* am your weapon," he said, his voice close and quiet and just for her. "Point me toward your enemies, and I'll see that you never walk in their shadow again."

She scoffed as her heart fluttered. The man was as absurd as he was handsome, lust-drunk after only one night together. "How do I know you won't leave me again?"

Any trace of his smile vanished, replaced by a sincere and stern longing. "Annora, if I were alone, I would still fight them, but I would have no intention of surviving the encounter. Last night I'd fully intended to die by Caine's blade—" His throat flexed as though the confession choked him. "There's only one reason I did not get out of bed and ride out to meet him today, and it was not cowardice or fear."

Beneath them the drone of male voices filled the tavern, the scrape of wooden furniture on stone floors, the yelps of the innkeeper as they interrogated him. Henry turned his back on her, his feet padding on the floorboards as her heart thundered.

"Henry!" she called, the sudden sharpness of her tone betraying the cold indifference she had strived for.

He paused by the door, blade drawn, eyes dark with the anticipation of battle, and perhaps with the same need which coursed through her.

There was much she wanted to say; that she was grateful he came to her rescue and wrought vengeance on those who had hurt her, that he felt good and right despite her insistence, and that she could not see herself anywhere else but beside him, but she would let none of it out.

Instead, she simply settled on, "Don't die."

He chuckled and opened the door, disappearing down the corridor and leaving her alone in the room awaiting his signal.

Sucking in a deep breath she tightened her grip on the cheese plate and glanced out of the window. Thick coils of black smoke snaked through the sky from the pyre below, demanding further tribute. And he would feed them, she was certain of it. The Dragon might have been filled with promises and posturing, but he had been sincere about that.

At least for the moment, that man, that confounding, irritable, irredeemable man, was smitten enough to condemn the rest of the world to flames. For her.

Annora pressed her knuckles to her lips, lest her smile run loose, but the shrill clang of steel-on-steel tore through her thoughts as battle raged below. Her breath solidified in her chest as an agonized, curdled scream erupted from the tavern. Only when the fighting continued did she find her breath came easier. The sounds of battle meant Henry yet lived.

Not that she should care.

With a huff, she silenced her concern, shoving two chunks of cheese into her mouth and chewing them spitefully. Henry was spoiled and cruel, he had abandoned her once already, and insulted her with every second breath. Better he died by the sword as champions so often pantomimed. Perhaps he and the guards would all kill each other and she could make her way... well, somewhere.

"Ann—Annora!"

Her blood ran cold at the sound of her name bellowed through the tavern. She darted across the room before she was even fully certain it was Henry who called for her, slippered feet thundering down the wooden staircase. Every heartbeat was a battering ram against her breast as the carnage below came into view; upturned tables, bodies, blood. But they were insignificant. All that mattered were the two men still moving; one in midnight blue standing with his back to her, the other on his back on top of a table, feet kicking out in desperation as they grappled with a blade.

There was no time to think, no time to formulate a plan. Annora charged toward them, summoning every shred of anger, frustration and pain and putting them into her swing. The tin cheese plate struck the guard above the ear, sending jarring pain shooting through her forearm, but the blow was so silent she wondered at first if she had hurt him at all.

A moment later the tavern was filled with a harrowing

scream as blood oozed down the side of his head, and then cut suddenly short by a gargle as Henry cut the guard's throat with his own blade.

The world tilted around her as Henry climbed down from the table, once again blood-soaked. Annora's breaths choked her. Her legs faltered beneath her. The guard lay dying at her feet, clinging desperately to the hem of her skirt.

"My cheese..." Henry said, gazing down at the swelling crimson pool which was swallowing the morsels. "What a waste."

A hiccup of laughter burst from Annora, relief clouding her senses. Henry was alive, they both were, though the cost of that miracle had been paid in blood. So much of it.

"Look at me," Henry commanded, his eyes piercing blue against the spray of crimson across his face. Rough fingers pressed firmly against the burning skin of her cheeks. "Pay this wretch no heed. We have to go."

The guard on the ground grew silent, his grip on her skirts loosening as the life ebbed from his body.

"Goddess forgive us," Annora whispered. "No one else will."

Henry's brow creased as he ushered her away from the body. Three more guards lay lifeless in their path. "I'm curious what you thought they would do to us if we didn't kill them?"

He was right, and she focused on that thought, snuffing the flicker of conscience inside her chest.

"Those bastards," Henry whispered. His wolf pelt lay bloodied on the floor, a blade twisted inside it. As he untangled steel from fur, he frowned at a two-inch-long gash down the center of it.

"I know how to sew," she heard herself say, but her voice was growing distant to her own ears. "Goddess, what'll we do now?"

"Annora," Henry said, his voice uncharacteristically gentle. He reached out and brushed her cheek with the heel of his hand. "Caine and his men whipped you simply for breaking out of the cell. I refuse to even consider what they would've done after discovering their lord out there on the pyre."

"I know."

"I don't care about their lives. I care about yours, and as a result of that, I'm finding I increasingly care about mine." He glanced down, taking her hands in his. "Now come on. We have to go."

Turning, he pulled her after him, treading a trail of blood through the inn, but at the sight of the fire burning in the hearth, Annora paused, anchoring Henry to the spot.

"What is it?" he asked, his voice sharpened by urgency.

"The innkeeper," Annora said. "Where is he?"

He seemed to understand even before she did. The innkeeper who had allowed her to be ambushed, the innkeeper who had stood back and watched while Caine and his men tortured her. The innkeeper who would no doubt tell everyone the direction she and Henry fled in.

"He ran upstairs, hiding in his rooms."

Henry's blue eyes fixed on her, piercing, unfairly beautiful, and cold. He released her hand, brushing the tips of his fingers against the hilt of the blade at his hip. One word from her, and he would do the deed for her, she had no doubt of that.

But it was not his battle.

Annora needed the solace of vengeance. She hurried to the back of the bar, pulling bottles of spirits from the shelves, taking all but the honeyed wine and ale which would not burn, and doused every table and chair, until the air stung her nostrils. Henry stood in the doorway, keeping watch, glancing over his shoulder at her as she hurled the remaining bottles at the wall, taking catharsis from the music of shattering glass and clay.

And when there were no bottles left to break, she took a half-burned log from the fireplace with a pair of iron tongs, and held it to the inn's blood-speckled curtain. Almost at once the fire consumed them, flames licking the ceiling of the tavern as she tossed the burning log beneath an alcohol-soaked table.

"It's done," she said, more to herself than to Henry as she met him at the doorway and slipped her hand back into his. "If nothing else it'll distract him while we run."

The stench of smoke tangled with the copper tang of blood. Cold wind whipped around them as they ran from the inn, feet pounding the dirt path leading toward the stables.

"Can you ride bareback?" Henry huffed as the horses tossed their heads and snorted.

"I—" Annora swallowed as a wave of nausea rolled through her stomach. "I'll try. I don't know that I can ride at all."

"Now's as good a time as any to learn." He clicked his

tongue against his teeth as he unlatched a stall door and was met immediately by the slow, hollow sound of hooves as the horse walked obediently toward him.

Annora had spent her life surrounded by people on horseback, but the beasts had never seemed larger, nor more deadly than they did then. The horse was a dappled gray behemoth, its black mane strewn with golden stands of hay. Enormous velvety nostrils flared as she reached out to broker peace.

"Get on," Henry said, bending his knees and forming a stirrup with his palms.

"He's too big."

"*She's* a mare, and she's the size she needs to be to carry you for days. Get on."

What choice did she have? Stomach churning, she placed her foot upon his hands and pulled herself up onto the horse's back, groaning as the searing memory of the riding crop's bitter bite snarled across her skin. Henry remained by her side as the horse shifted beneath her, and Annora fought to keep her balance, bunching her skirt around her knees.

"Sit tall," he told her, one hand cupping the soft curve of her calf as he unhooked a bridle from beside the stable door with the other. "Try not to bounce around too much."

Breathless, and with her pulse thrumming in her throat, Annora found herself chuckling. "I'm sure that's the first time in your life you've said that."

A wicked grin spread beneath his blood-spattered beard as he placed the bridle on the horse's head. As soon as he removed his hand from her leg to fasten the buckles, she craved the heat of his touch.

His gaze slid back to her as soon as his task was finished. "Hold on tight with your thighs. Having spent a night between them, I know you'll have no problems with that part."

Handing her the reins, his fingers lingered on hers, warm and rough, and capable of so many terrible and wonderful things. They grazed the back of her hand, stroking along the ridges of her tendons, sending a shiver through her body. And nothing mattered but that; not the chaos they had left behind, nor the unknown lying ahead. The only thing in all the world she cared about was his hand on hers, grounding her, reassuring her.

"Thank you, my harpy," he said. "You saved my life."

Annora forced herself to swallow, to breathe as her chest tightened. "Then we're even, Dragon. At least in that."

A triad of creases spread from the outer corner of each of his eyes as he smiled up at her. "What a pair we make."

"Aye."

"I'm almost glad I didn't leave you behind in that cell."

"Almost?" She laughed as tears welled in her eyes, blurring her vision and taking him from her. She wiped them on the back of her hand, blinking so he came back into focus. Her blood-stained champion, the man she could not stop herself from wanting.

He released a labored breath and stepped away. "We must go. Once the innkeeper's done putting out your fire, he'll no doubt tell Caer Duloon's guards which direction we flee in."

He turned and hurried through the stables, unlatching every door as he went, freeing the horses who waited, watching the flames so intently they showed the whites of their eyes. The beasts wasted no time in escaping, hurrying from the black smoke pouring from the tavern, and out to the frozen moorlands where they were free to graze.

A moment later Henry emerged from a stable stall with a large bay mare. He attempted to mount the beast with the confidence of a man whose body had once permitted his every whim. A frustrated growl sounded in his throat as he slid back to the ground and searched for an easier way.

"Not a word," Henry muttered as he placed one foot on the cross beam of a stall door and pulled himself up.

"You did it more gracefully than I," she reassured him, heart pounding as her horse grew restless and turned a slow circle.

The earth seemed to shift with the horse's movement, a mere twitch of her muscles sending spikes of panic through Annora's heart. She gripped the beast tight with her thighs, her knuckles paling to snowy peaks around the reins.

They set out slowly, Annora leading the way as Henry followed close behind. They rode west, chasing the sun as it hung above the mountains, every yard they put between themselves and the inn helping Annora's breath flow a little easier.

They were free, and the world lay ahead.

FOURTEEN

T he mountains were lifeless.

Winter nights brought an eerie sort of silence; a deathly quiet Henry had once enjoyed. In the cell, it had meant his tormentors were occupied elsewhere and he was free to sleep and dream. At the Champion's Guild, silence had given him time to reflect, to envision the battles lying ahead of him and the outcome he craved. It had also given him a chance to watch and to listen, to discover who posed the greatest threat in the arena, what their weaknesses were.

But as Annora rode ahead of him, the silence did nothing but amplify her discomfort. There were no frog songs or chirruping insects to disguise the rattle of her shivering lips, or the curses she muttered under her breath as the already frigid temperatures plummeted toward deathly cold.

Frozen, humid air soaked through their clothes, leaving their skin flushed pink and throbbing. Steaming breath rose in coiling clouds from their horses' muzzles as they picked their way through the hills, far slower than he was comfortable with.

As the night crept on and darkness swallowed them entirely, Henry was more certain than ever that Annora would be the death of him, one way or another.

The guards of Caer Duloon would come for them, there was no doubt about that. It was simply a matter of whether the guards would catch up to them before the cold claimed them.

"I need to stop," Annora grumbled, pulling back on her horse's reins and patting the beast's gray neck. She was a terrible rider, but a kind one, and that could very well be their undoing. If not for the dried blood caked beneath his fingernails and spattering Annora's dress, nor the frost forming on the rocky ground, Henry could have mistaken their escape for a leisurely evening ride.

"I'm cold," she grumbled. "I'm hungry, the horse is probably feeling far worse than I. And I feel as though I've spent the day being kicked in the backside."

"You'll feel far worse tomorrow." Henry groaned as he leaned forward and swung his aching leg over his horse's rear before sliding down from her back. Before the cell, he could have ridden for days, his young limbs reinvigorated after only a short rest. The pinch in the base of his spine and the stiffness in his legs told him he was definitely no longer that man. Holding his breath so he did not grunt too loudly, Henry made his way to Annora's side.

"How long will it take to get to the Champion's Guild?" she asked.

"At this pace? We'll be halfway there by midsummer."

Her glower was sharper than any blade as she slid clumsily down from her mount, her legs giving way beneath her. Henry darted forward, catching her a moment too late, only managing to hold her arms aloft and deny her any chance to break her fall with her hands. Annora gasped as she landed hard on the ground.

"Are you hurt?" he asked.

"Get off me," she spat, wriggling free of his hold before turning her leg to the side to inspect the damage. Her wounds were invisible in the weak moonlight, but her thunderous expression was not. "Why'd you do that? I didn't need your help."

In truth, he did not know. Some part of him, some underused and frankly deeply unsettling facet of himself had simply sought to help her. It had seemed the right thing to do, the gentlemanly thing. In the darkness his nose crinkled into a silent, cringing snarl.

"You'll live," he grumbled, taking both horses by the reins and leading them away, leaving her in a heap on the ground. "We need to find shelter, and food and water for the horses."

It was easier said than done. The mountains offered little in terms of comfort or grazing. Annora cursed with every second step, wrapping her arms around her body to preserve what warmth she could. Tightening his grip on the horse's reins as he led them, Henry fought off the urge to pull her to him and offer her comfort.

Caring for Annora left him vulnerable, dulled his edges. If not for her, he would have ridden out from the inn that morning and died honorably cleansing the world of noble vermin. He would not be scurrying for his life across some Goddess forsaken mountain range.

He stumbled as a bone-deep chill slithered through his body, filling his head with fog. The effect lasted only a moment, but as he checked behind him to ensure Annora had not noticed, his heart flooded with dread. If he succumbed to illness, he could not fight with everything he had. He would let her down. He would lead her to danger.

Shaking off the sensation, he doubled down and marched harder.

By the time they came across a small stream, he was foul-tempered, cold, and half-starved, and he was by far the cheerier member of the party. Tough mountain grass grew close to the flowing water, and the stubborn northern horses refused to walk any further. And neither would the stubborn northern woman.

"I'll just die here," Annora muttered as she gathered her skirt around her knees and prepared to sit upon the bare rock.

Under any other circumstances, Henry would have threatened to let her do that, but he barely had the energy to stand. Traipsing toward her, he was about to say that he would gladly join her, when an abyssal black hole in the mountainside caught his eye.

"Come with me," he said, begging his aching legs to carry him a little further.

"You're joking," Annora grumbled as she stepped after him into the pitch dark of the cave's mouth. "There could be anything in here."

"And we'll freeze if we stay out there."

Stepping into the total blackness and finding the way with his hands, Henry tentatively searched the wall of the cave. Rough, wet rock grazed his palms as he explored with slow, uneasy steps. His eyes strained for a glimmer of light. As the moon peered from behind a cloud, the cave's maw glowed gray-blue, framing Annora's silhouette. Her fists rested on her broad hips as she glanced over her shoulder to the landscape behind.

"Have you fallen down a hole yet?" she asked.

"I'm sure you'd love that. Are you coming in?"

A reluctant sigh sounded in the dark, followed by shuffling footsteps, a whispered curse, and the heavy slap of hands against rock.

"Shit," Annora hissed.

Henry darted toward the sound of her voice, scuffing the soles of his boots on the uneven stone.

Her voice sounded again in the dark, "There's some kind of animal—"

Instinct lit a flame in his heart as he dropped to the ground beside her, shielding her from whatever savage beast threatened her. But the fur beneath his hands was cold and lifeless, and it was rock, not muscle and bone which lay beneath.

"It's a pelt," he sighed as his pulse roared in his ears.

Even in the dark, Annora's glare seared against his skin, and he bathed in the glow of it.

"Thank the Goddess," she muttered, relief lifting the shadow from her voice. "Now I don't need to borrow your rancid one."

"I wouldn't have let you anyway," Henry retorted as he lifted the clean pelt and threw it toward her. The dry clatter of wood sounded between them. Feeling around through the darkness, his fingers spidered over dry wood, cold steel and jagged flint. "This must be a hunter's cave. They've left supplies for a campfire."

"What if he comes back?" she asked as Henry set to work building a fire. She chuckled, "I suppose then it'll be a dead hunter's cave then, won't it?"

He struck the flint against the steel, sending a shower of sparks down onto the wood. Each glowing speck of hope was born and died in the same heartbeat. He knew without doubt that there was little skill to the task; the squires had lit his fires at the Champion's Guild, and even a boorish lout like Brandon the Bear had been able to do it when they were on the road traveling to tournaments. Yet, try as he might, the flame did not catch. He struck the flint a dozen times to no avail. "The wood is... I don't know. Deficient. Either that or the flint."

"Give it here." Annora took the tools from him, admonishing him with a frustrated huff. A moment later she had sparks, and after a while those sparks spread, glowing and smoldering on the wood. She appeared from the darkness bathed in a red glow as the wood caught light. "What kind of a dragon can't make fire?"

Retorts flitted through his head; a dragon who was so cold his hands shook, one who was so distracted by the harpy perched in the darkness he could not concentrate for fear of his throat being torn out.

But he found himself simply sitting and marveling as

she pursed her lips and blew gently, as though feeding the flame with a silent, lingering kiss. The amber glow danced across her hair, the flyaway frizz surrounding it transformed into a golden aura.

Her eyes were black in the firelight, and yet he still recalled every detail of their hazel hue; the greens and browns and vibrant oranges which held him so transfixed. He scowled, trying to remember the precise moment he had noted their color, but he could not. The knowledge had simply seeped into him and become as necessary as air.

"Thank you," he said.

"I've spent my life making fires for pampered, useless men," she said, gazing intently at the growing blaze. "What's one more?"

"At least you're good for something."

She raised her eyes to glare at him. A bubble of laughter swelled in his throat as the flames glimmered in the dark pits of her pupils. He had faced the finest fighters in Aldland in the ring, battled for his life against guards and lords, but never had he met with anyone who looked at him with such ferocity.

"How are your wounds?" he said, his mouth still tipped into an uncontrollable grin.

"Agonizing. Which is about half as painful as spending another moment by your side." Satisfied with her little fire, she stood and cast her eyes around the cave. "It doesn't look like the hunters left any food."

Throwing the sandy-colored wolf pelt over her shoulders she gazed down at him expectantly, more regal than any queen.

"What?" Henry asked.

"We need food."

"Yes?"

Her eyes hardened. "You know how to hunt, don't you?"

"Do I look like I know how to hunt?"

With a frustrated growl she turned on her heel and rubbed her hands over her eyes. "So, you're purely ornamental."

A chuckle shook his chest. "At least I'm a pretty ornament."

She cast a disdainful scowl his way, but could not hide the flicker of a smile which crossed her lips. "Well, I don't know how to hunt either, so I suppose we're going hungry. We should bring the horses inside so they don't run off."

"Let them run off. We'd probably make better progress without those knock-kneed nags." He released a contented sigh as he reclined by the fire, the heat sapping the cold from his bones. Yet Annora walked away from the flames back to the cave's mouth, chewing the edge of her fingernail.

"Sit with me," he said, the request leaving him as a command.

"Hold on."

He followed her gaze toward the entrance of the cave, to where another pelt sat rolled high, intended to block out the cold and hide the light of the fire from the world outside. Annora had to stand on the tips of her toes to reach it, gasping and grunting as her fingers worked loose the leather ties keeping it fastened.

A smile spread across Henry's lips as her body

stretched, her every glorious curve accentuated by the damp dress clinging faithfully to her frame.

"You could help me," she muttered as she managed to loosen one of the ties.

"I'm rather enjoying the view."

"If I pluck out your eyes, will you help me then?"

With a chuckle, Henry stood and made his way over to her. Even muttering curses beneath her breath, and reeking of horse and wet wool, she was as intoxicating and sweet as honeyed wine.

As he towered above her, untangling the ties with ease, his body brushed against hers, every fiber of his being clinging to the warmth and comfort of being so close to her. She stepped back into him, igniting a fire in the pit of his belly as the pelt unfurled and covered the cave's opening.

Henry's breath snagged in his throat at the sensation of her curves pressed flush with his. She rested her head against his chest with disarming familiarity, seeking comfort from him. Comfort that for whatever reason, he was honored to give. Whatever she had done to him over the past few days, he barely recognized himself.

"We should go back to the fire and warm ourselves," he said.

She said nothing, but wedged a finger at the edge of the makeshift door, pulling it away from the stone.

He held her as she stared through the tiny gap into the blackness beyond their sanctuary, as though looking away from the dark for too long physically pained her. Over the past couple of days, Henry had grown accustomed to that very same feeling, but it was her light he craved.

"You're trembling, Annora. Sit."

She sighed and withdrew her hand. "Perhaps the fire was a mistake. What if Caine's guards have already seen it and kill us while we sleep?"

"I won't let them."

A bitter laugh burst from her. "Henry, you can't fight forever—"

"But I will. Whether they send five or five-thousand to track us down, I'll fight them. For you."

She turned around to face him, her eyes meeting his and her lips parting as though she had forgotten him and was startled. If not for her insistence that she hated him, he could have sworn she admired him, if only in that moment. A gnawing need to press his lips to hers spread agony through his core.

"Annora, I would do anything for you if you only asked it."

"You don't mean it," she said.

Henry's brow furrowed. "Have I not fought for you? Have I not killed for you?"

"Yes...but—"

Her argument died midair as she gazed up at him, her eyes glassy in the firelight.

With a shuddering breath, she raised onto the tips of her toes toward him, her fingers sliding around the back of his head to grip his hair, pulling him down to meet her lips. Her kiss sent lightning shooting through his veins, straight through his heart, and all the way down to his toes which curled inside his boots.

Annora was the sweetest poison, one he could not be

without. And as she pressed her body to his, snaking one arm around his waist and pinning them together with surprising strength, Henry was sure of only one thing. That her poison made her immune to his, and the concoction they created together was more potent than anything he had ever known.

Her soft shoulders were cool beneath his hands as he gripped them, her lip quivering as he tugged it between his teeth, coaxing a broken moan from her. She was cold, and he found himself duty bound to warm her.

That morning, he had promised to pleasure her in the bathtub before Lord Caine had stolen that from them, but Caine was no more.

Henry's hands trailed down over the swell of her breasts, grazing her hard nipples through the damp, cold wool of her dress. She whimpered against his lips as he teased her with his thumbs, stroking firm circles as her kisses deepened.

"I'm yours, my harpy," Henry whispered against her lips as she gripped his backside, squeezing and kneading his soft flesh. She might never truly love him, but he cared not. He would gladly let her use him every day until he died. She could take everything she needed from him, squeeze every drop from his spirit and he would consider it a life well spent.

"Lie down by the fire with me," he told her. "Take your clothes off."

"Are you commanding me?"

"No. I'm begging."

With a knowing smile, she walked toward the flames,

shedding cold, wet wool in favor of her soft, magnificent body. She laid her clothes out to dry by the fire and issued a challenge with her slow, intoxicating walk. To follow her was to become ensnared.

Angry red lines streaked across her skin, each one surrounded by storm clouds of purple. After his own whipping, he had moped for days, weeping silent tears whenever he stole a moment of solitude. But not Annora. She stood strong, defiant; her pain pushed aside, bathed in golden light. Every inch of him ached for her, craved her, and every splinter of his spirit wished he had made her torturers suffer more.

Pulling off his own clothes, he followed her to the fire and dropped to his knees, landing on the soft fur on the ground. He awaited her, her humble servant, a worshiper at her altar, overcome with need and relief and the want which now simmered in his blood. Before she had a chance to lie down, he pulled her to him, pressing his face to the soft swell of flesh beneath her navel and breathing in the scent of her.

I adore you, he thought, *if you never adore me in return then so be it.*

A shiver coursed through him as she stroked her fingers through his hair, toying with the curling ends she had severed with his blade.

"What would you have me do for you?" he asked, his voice merely a breathless growl as he gazed up at her.

In answer she lowered herself onto his lap, wrapping her arms around his shoulders and laughing as they fought to keep their balance. He ignored the pain in his thighs as she tried to find a comfortable position for her aching legs. It didn't matter. He would gladly sit in the middle of the fire if it earned him her happiness.

His cock stood firm, pressed between their bellies as their smiles faded, and their lips found each other once more. Her fingertips traced the curves of his chest, sending shivers tickling though his core, a touch-starved man at a feast of sensation.

Words fell from him like confetti carried by a shivering breeze. "Goddess, I wish I could put into words how it feels to be touched after so long alone."

She sighed and shook her head. "Perhaps that's why you claim to be so infatuated with me so soon."

"Perhaps..." His breath caught as she stroked her palm over the soft mound of his stomach. "Although I think it more likely that in you, I have truly met my match."

"Such pretty words. You hardly know me."

"I know that you hate apples, and that you like how I eat your quim." He grinned as she rolled her eyes. "I know you've spent your life as imprisoned as I, and now we're finally free. Given the opportunity, I know I'm the last man in Aldland you would want to have escaped with."

A crease ran between her eyebrows as a huff of dismissive laughter escaped her. "That's not always true. Sometimes you're tolerable, but I've known men like you all my life. Full of sweet promises and all starry-eyed when faced with a pair of tits. But I'm a chambermaid, and you a champion. If you'd have met me ten years prior, you would've called me wench, had me take your filth away and not cared if it spilled on my wrist as I carried it."

"No..."

"Aye, because as far as men like you are concerned, people like me are born only to serve you. To make your life more comfortable."

He raised his hand to brush back her hair, tucking it securely behind her ear so that he might see her face fully.

"Believe me, my bitter, glorious, intoxicating harpy, since the first moment I met you, there hasn't been a single second where I considered myself comfortable. Frustrated? Yes. Agonized, tortured, desperate... all of those too. It would be far more comfortable to curl up beside a rabid hedgehog than wooing you has been."

Her eyes were thunder, but she gently bit her lower lip in a weak attempt to hide her delight. "Is this what you call flattery?"

He dipped his head to kiss the smooth skin at the curve of her jaw. "Well... are you flattered?"

The music of laughter pouring from her was all his heart needed. He smiled against her throat before letting his teeth graze her sensitive flesh. Her laughter turned to a broken sigh, sending flutters of pleasure between his thighs.

Reining in a sigh of his own, he said, "Let me know you then. Tell me something I should know."

She tightened her grip around him as her throat undulated beneath his mouth. "Such as?"

"Anything. Where were you born?"

"North," she said quietly. "A farm close to a tiny village further north than you have ever traveled. I doubt you'd know it."

"Does it have a name?"

"Brightoak."

He thanked her with a slow kiss, his lips caressing the soft dimple at the base of her throat.

She lifted her head, pressing closer to him, silently demanding more. "My parents sold me to Lord Caine in my eighteenth summer. Said I was too plain to be married off to anyone worthwhile, too soft and lazy to be useful on the farm, and too coarse to keep for comfort."

Henry's eyebrows dipped as he raised his head to look at her. Yes, she was abrasive; wonderfully, refreshingly so, but that she was ever considered plain or lazy was as absurd to him as not wanting her around.

He held her gaze and asked, "Would you like me to kill your parents?"

A snort of laughter burst from her as the corners of her eyes creased. "You would, wouldn't you?"

"Anything... I'd do anything you ask, Annora. I'm yours, completely, recklessly. Yours to accept or abandon."

She tilted her head to the side, her eyes darting across his features as her smile faded. "Would you give up this foolish plan to go to the Champion's Guild?"

A sigh pushed them apart as Henry slowly shook his head. "Annora..."

"We have an entire world to hide in, you and I. We could get lost, alone together where no one would ever find us."

"Or we can live a glorious life in the comfort of a well-supplied castle. I'll be the Guild Master and you... I don't know... Guild Mistress. Or we'll do away with the champions all together and simply be lord and lady. If you asked it of me, I'd raze all of Aldland and make you queen."

"Oh, Henry, for fuck's sake." With a frustrated growl she stood from his lap, tugging the fur out from beneath him.

"What?" Henry lifted his backside to aid her, yet she still scowled at him as she pulled it free and threw it around her shoulders.

"I don't want to be a lady or a queen, and I certainly don't want a castle and servants tending to me. I don't want to keep fighting and running. You're going to get us killed if you go to the Champion's Guild."

"Don't be so dramatic," Henry muttered, lamenting the loss of her warmth but refusing to cover his naked body. "The champions follow who they're told to. They even followed that lout Brandon for a time."

"I. Don't. Want. To. Go. I don't want anything more to do with those types of people. Can't you see that?" She pulled away the fur, revealing her bruised skin, as though he could ever forget the sight. Tears shone in her eyes, but they were not from sorrow or fear. Her face was a picture of fury. "Look at me. I still feel it. Every strike of Lord Caine's riding crop. I still feel it as keenly as though he's still beating me." Her lips trembled as she pointed to his own scars, her voice growing louder and more desperate. "You know how badly it hurts, but the promise of riches and glory makes you forget. Rich men in castles did this to us, and now you want to run to a whole swarm of them and hope they don't just run us through."

"Annora..."

"I know, I know, *don't be so dramatic,*" Annora scoffed. "Well, if any harm befalls me, you can be content with the knowledge that it's because you dragged me along with you."

"I grew up with the champions. They're my family."

She stared at him a moment, a deep crease forming between her eyebrows. "Tell me something about you then, Henry. How many times did you betray them? How many of the people you grew up with were glad to see you thrown in a cell?"

"More than I dare to count," he spat, the words lashing the air between them. Admitting it aloud hurt far more than thinking it for the past decade, the truth of it burning like a brand on his very spirit.

"So, they trusted you, again and again, and you betrayed them."

"Yes."

"And now you ask me to follow you, to trust that you aren't leading us to our deaths. But I can't trust you, Henry. How can I? Everyone who trusts you gets hurt."

His lips parted as she turned her back on him, but there was no argument he could present. She was right. His face burned as she walked away. "I only asked you to come with me as far as Blackmere before we parted ways."

"Well, perhaps that would be for the best," she said, setting the fur down on the rocks on the opposite side of the fire from him. "Perhaps then we'll truly be free."

Her words spread to the core of him like the deepest frost as he stared into the flames, the images of those he had betrayed haunting him as they always did. Ten years ago, he had been a monster, his mind set only on victory, on besting the man his own mind had twisted into an enemy. He glanced down at the black crescents of blood caked beneath his fingernails and his heart hardened.

"I'll be glad to be rid of you," he muttered, unconvincingly beneath his breath, unable to even pretend to hate her any longer. Castles, titles, riches... they meant nothing if she was miserable.

Ten years in a cell, and he was still every part the monster.

But he was frustratingly, and undeniably her monster.

CHAPTER
FIFTEEN

T he fur and fire kept the cave warm, but Annora was far from comfortable. She lay with her back to Henry, the campfire cracking and popping between them, answering the call of the burning ache raging inside her.

She wanted him, wanted his hands on her, his mouth, his cock. She wanted the comfort of his words and the way he gazed upon her.

Most of all, she wanted him close.

But he was wrong for her, she knew that with absolute certainty, and she would not apologize for saying so. Better to push him away than to find herself completely besotted and unable to be without him.

Annora tightened her arms around herself and closed her eyes. Pain radiated everywhere, from her blistered toes to the dull throb at the crown of her head. She ached inside and out, but she would not give in. No matter how she craved him, no matter how her body betrayed her, or clung to the fading memories of sensation; his lips on her throat, his hands about her waist, his big, irresistible, infuriating body pressed tight against hers.

She would not think of it. Not a moment longer.

It was a mere trifle that the heat of every one of the Dragon's kisses were burned into her flesh like a white-hot branding iron. She endured the heat.

And yet, despite her exhaustion, sleep evaded her. The firelight flickered above the enlarged shadow of her body on the jagged stone walls of the cave. The hollow clunk of Henry adding more wood to the fire told her he had taken on the burden of lookout, but there seemed little sense in them both staying awake. She rolled over, commanding herself not to look at him. She would not let herself fall into his trap.

His clothes were laid out beside hers, drying on the warm rocks, so he reclined, still naked, the light dancing over his frame. Every curve of his body made her chest ache harder, the sight of his large, hairy body igniting some inconvenient primal urge in the pit of her stomach.

But he was still an insufferable ass. And she certainly would not look.

Annora cleared her throat and tried to keep her eyes above his shoulders.

"I can't sleep," she said. "I'll keep watch if you want to try to rest."

He shook his head. "I don't sleep much. Not since..." He dipped his head and let loose a heavy sigh, twirling a bent splinter of wood between his thumb and forefinger. "The guards liked to keep me awake in the cell. They threw freezing water on me whenever they caught me sleeping. Eventually my exhaustion won out and I learned to sleep in scraps."

Pity sat heavy on her chest as she pulled herself up to sit cross-legged. She sucked in a breath as the pain of her wounds flared across her skin. "I'm sorry."

His eyes met hers across the flames, fanning the desire to move closer in the pit of her belly. He shook his head. "No need. I'm happy to keep watch whilst you try to rest."

She should try, she knew. Sleep aided all kinds of pain, and she was in so much of it she could have closed her eyes for eternity, but the most ferocious ache of all sat inside her chest, beating with a rhythm which drove her to him.

"You seemed to be sleeping well enough in the tavern this morning..." she said with a frown. "Or was it yesterday?"

He paused a moment, his gaze losing focus as though surrendering himself to the memory. "You're right. I did, didn't I?" A small laugh shook his chest. "You had your arms around me, and I slept well."

Annora's heart squeezed. The man sat across from her was everything she knew she should hate, and yet somehow, he was everything she wanted. A man who thought little of ending a life if it meant he could protect her. A man raised with selfish notions of pleasure, which he had set aside to learn about hers. Henry was a man born to comfort and luxury, with servants and admirers to perform any task for him he wished, but now he sat in a cave, naked, sleepless, and muddied, with only her comfort in mind.

And she knew with sudden certainty that he would not

lead her to the Champion's Guild if he suspected she would be in danger. He had done so much to ensure her safety.

"Perhaps if I sit close to you, you'll be able to sleep?" she suggested.

"Perhaps."

She stood, picking up the pelt from the floor and walked around to him. He kept his eyes on the flames, as if raising his gaze to behold her hurt him as much as their distance hurt her. And yet, when she sat beside him, he melted against her. His body softened as she lay her head on his shoulder, and he tentatively wrapped an arm around her waist.

"If you need to go then I won't try to stop you," he whispered softly. "But, Annora, I don't want to be without you—"

She reached out and took his hand, threading her fingers through his and rendering him silent. The arm around her waist tightened.

"Say, if the Champion's Guild burned down, where would we go?"

"Are you planning to burn it down?"

"I've a mind to." She shrugged playfully. "But pretend with me for a moment. If we could not go there, then where would we run to?"

Henry sat silent and still. He tilted his head, resting his cheek against her hair, untangling their fingers so he could follow the paths of the creases on her palm. His touch was unbearably gentle, and yet she drew from it, filling her heart with a warmth she never knew she could crave so intently.

"I suppose we'd ride out in any direction we chose."

She chuckled. "And if we chose different directions?"

"Then if you'd allow it, I'd turn back around and walk your path beside you. We'd find your dismal little woodland cottage, and I would be your woodcutter." He traced the lines of the veins in her wrist with his fingertips.

A shiver traveled through her body. There was so much tenderness in his touch that she almost doubted he was the same man she knew. His hands were capable of such terrible, brutal acts, yet they caressed her with such gentle affection. But laced with that tenderness was promise; if she remained by his side, he would lavish such delicious attention on the rest of her for as long as they lived. She swallowed the knot in her throat and tried to appear as though she was not tempted. "Do you even know how to chop wood?"

"I'd learn. I'll learn everything I need to be a man worthy of you. And when I fail at a task, I'll hide myself between your thighs and make you forget you were ever cross with me."

There was no fighting the smile which spread across her lips as the fantasy played out in her mind. He would be unbearable to live with in every sense of the word, and yet, she could not picture a more perfect future. To awaken every morning beside him, knowing he was hers.

With a start, she realized that was not her fantasy. It had never been her fantasy. Annora had always longed to live alone, unbound by anyone, serving only herself. But now... Goddess. Was she truly so changed after only a few days?

"Tell me of the cottage," she said, hoping his vision of the future contrasted with hers. "What does it look like?"

"Hm," he chuckled. "I've only ever been to one such place and it was awful, but there was a little waterfall outside, a pool for bathing, and a stream. Most of the stones were covered in moss, but we could clean that away—"

"No, I'd keep the moss. It would help keep me concealed, and further convince everyone that a witch lived within. If I can coax poisonous toadstools to sprout from between the stones, all the better."

He released a long-suffering sigh. "Very well, but I insist we keep a fire in the hearth no matter the season. After this is over, I never want to be cold again."

She grimaced. "Isn't this my cottage? What if I get too hot?"

"Then I'll strip you of your clothes and tease you until your skin pebbles."

A grin tightened her cheeks. "I suppose I can agree to that. Tell me, what's your favorite color?"

"Red," he said without hesitation. "Yours?"

"Green. They don't go together, sadly."

He lifted his head from hers, pressing his lips to her crown. "Nonsense. We'll surround our home in holly so that it prickles anyone who comes too close."

As she laughed, the words *our home* echoed in her mind, both a warning and a promise. She raised her head and turned to face him. He mirrored her gesture with perfect symmetry, until their lips were mere inches from each other.

"Could you be happy there?" she asked. "I know it's far from the life you imagined for yourself.

He sat for a long time, his eyes darting over her features,

his fingers resting on the pulse in her wrist. At last, a corner of his mouth lifted. "With you? Yes. I think I could be. And you?"

"It sounds like a fine life," she said, unable to keep her eyes from him, and unable to pretend otherwise. "To live with a handsome champion, no matter how frustrating he may be."

There was a sorrow in his smile, and a muscle in his cheek danced before he parted his lips to speak. "I'm no longer a champion, Annora. Just a man; a broken, flawed, ridiculous man, who has given his heart entirely to someone else and no longer recognizes himself, and yet I've never felt more certain that this is who I'm supposed to be." In the firelight, his eyes were a myriad of shades of blue, tangled with bursts of white and gold, his abyssal pupils blown wide in the dim light. "It has been a long time since I had a friend. A long time since I laughed with someone, or got to be playful. But with you..." he chuckled quietly. "I find myself craving your company, even if it's only for you to tell me how awful I am."

"You're not awful," she said. "Not truly."

"My harpy, you flatter me."

"Aye. Perhaps it's only in the hopes that you'll kiss me again, should I ask it of you."

The corner of his lips dimpled as he gave her a slanted smile. "I'll kiss you whenever you want. Wherever you want." His eyes dropped to her lips, sending a flutter through her chest. "I know the Guild holds nothing for me anymore."

Relief washed over her, sapping the tension from her body as she gazed upon him. "Are you sure?"

He nodded. "It was the only place in my life I've ever been happy, though those moments were few and far between as I got older. It seemed like the logical place for me to return to. But now... knowing it would make you miserable... I can't bring myself to take you there." His eyebrows dipped as though his words sounded as strange to his ears as they did to hers. "I'm no longer a champion, I know that. I haven't the strength for it, nor the inclination toward returning to that life of discipline. I don't want the Guild, or titles or a castle. I want... Goddess, please put a dagger through my heart and shut me up," he chuckled and clawed his fingers through his own hair. "I want a quiet life. I want you. I want to be wicked with you, and to pleasure you until your screams ring through the forest. And that's all."

His words hung between them, slowly sapping the air from her lungs. "And if you tire of me?" she asked, fighting against the knot tightening in her throat. "Once the chase ends and the world returns to normal. When you realize I'm a chambermaid who has seen nine more summers than you and that every tavern in Aldland is filled with beautiful maidens who would love nothing more than to bed you. What becomes of me then?"

He chuckled, his sorrow melting away as he raised her hand to his lips. "Every beautiful person in Aldland could line up outside this cave begging to sate my cock, and I would not lift that fur from the door because I'm here with you."

"More pretty words."

He kissed the back of her hand before turning it over and kissing her palm. "It's only the truth, Annora. I've sat alone with nothing but my thoughts for ten years. I know my mind, and I know my heart, and both want you. Only you."

Her heart beat like the wings of a honeybee as she sought out his kiss, pulling the soft cushion of his lower lip between her teeth as her fingers tangled at the back of his head. All her life she had fought to be strong, to assure herself she could walk the world alone and did not need anyone else, but Henry... no. She did not need Henry. Not at all.

"What of marriage?" he asked, his breath blowing hot against her lips.

"An unnecessary and outdated ritual," she said.

"I quite agree."

She swallowed hard. "The whole purpose of binding hands together at the service is so the couple can find each other in the afterlife, but surely—"

"If it's meant to be, they'll find each other."

"Aye." She chuckled and hoped it disguised the way her voice faltered, carried from her only with shallow, unsatisfying breaths. "And I'm sure by the time they die, most lovers are glad to be rid of each other."

He frowned a little, trailing his fingers along the underside of her wrist. "I don't think so. I've only been in love once—and it's quite a new and unexpected feeling—but I can't imagine ever wanting to be rid of you, even after a hundred years of being told I'm awful and foolish."

Her heart thundered against her ribs; a desperate animal caged against its will. But she alone held the key, and the thought of relinquishing that, especially to this man she barely knew. It was folly. "You are foolish."

"Maybe so," he said. "Maybe I know nothing. Maybe I'm nothing more than a man who has spent his life behind stone walls, but you broke me out of them. You, Annora. You make me want to surrender everything I used to believe I needed, and that is the power you wield."

She could hold back no longer. Surrendering to temptation, she pushed him down onto the rocks, crawling on top of him, parting her thighs to straddle his broad hips. He raised his head and kissed a path down her throat, to her breasts, sucking her nipples and desperately squeezing the soft flesh of her belly in his large, rough hand, as though he had been denied the feeling of her for centuries.

"Goddess, I missed you," he whispered against her chest as his dark eyelashes fluttered against his cheek. He breathed in deeply against her skin, before licking the underside of her breast as it hung above him.

He was absurd, needy and unfairly handsome, and yet, she understood the sentiment completely. The hours spent in misery, traveling, bickering, pretending to hate him, had been torture, and she had missed him too. If that made her ridiculous too, then so be it.

"Do you want it?" she asked, lifting her hips to tease his cock with the wet heat of her core.

"I *need* it," he hissed, lifting his head and pulling in his belly so he could watch. "I need you more than air."

"Beg, then," she demanded, reaching beneath her to stroke one finger slowly up the length of his cock. He twitched beneath her touch, baring his teeth as a tingle intensified low in her stomach. "I remember a lot of talk in the tavern. I remember you saying you wanted to leave me in the morning with nothing more than a memory I could frig myself to."

"I couldn't leave," he whispered.

"Why?"

"Because—oh Goddess." He screwed his eyes tight as she used the head of his cock to circle her clitoris, sending darts of pleasure through her own body and his.

Her toes curled against the rocks as she gazed down upon him. "Because?"

"Nothing in my life has ever felt as good as you." His broad chest expanded as he dragged in a deep lungful of air. "I'm yours, Annora. Take all the pleasure you need from me. Use me, break me, do what you will. I'll just crawl back on my knees for more."

Her lips parted around a silent gasp. All her life men had pushed her, demanding her obedience, expecting her to be less than she was. And yet Henry, as brattish and spoiled and filled with his own self-importance as he was, was willing to supplicate to her. And that excited her more than anything ever had.

He groaned as she slid her thumb through the silken beads of fluid leaking from the head of his cock, loving the way his big body quivered at her touch. She stroked her hand over the cushion of his stomach, gently squeezing his supple flesh. He was still by far the largest and most impressive man she had ever met, and he was hers to do with as she pleased.

"Earn me," she said.

He pressed his teeth to his lower lip as he reached between her thighs, a shuddering breath escaping as his hand joined hers, surrounding his erection but unmoving. She would give him nothing until she was satisfied, and from the way his pupils flooded out the blue of his eyes, he was only too keen to play her game.

"How would you have me pleasure you, harpy mine?" he asked, the firelight gleaming on his skin. "My fingers? Or would you prefer my mouth?"

"Your mouth, since there are far too many words coming from it."

A dangerous chuckle rattled from him as he withdrew his hands and firmly held her thighs. "Lie down then."

"No," she said, standing and relishing the look of confusion and longing on his face. Taking a step, she planted her feet at either side of his head. "This way I know you'll shut up."

Beneath her, his breath quickened, his chest rising and falling in either anticipation or fear. Opposing sides of her hoped for both. His hands wrapped around her thighs, pulling her down toward him as she sank to her knees, then leaned forward so she was on all fours, her quim pressed to his mouth.

And Goddess, how she had missed the feeling of his mouth on her; the fervent rhythm of his licks as he sought her pleasure, so keen to prove himself, to silence her with bliss, believing he had won even as he sent her tumbling toward ecstasy. He was either the most foolish man alive or —and from his appreciative moans from beneath her she had begun to suspect—the wiliest.

The muscles in her stomach tightened as her pleasure built, drawing a choked groan from her throat. How dare he feel so good. How dare it be that man who had ensnared her so completely. And yet, now that he was part of her life, she could not imagine letting him go. Her brute, her champion, the thorn in her side, and the air in her lungs.

Yes, she could love this man.

As though sensing her mounting pleasure and the lowering of her defenses, he wrapped his arms around her hips pulling her down harder, his muffled cries echoing around the cave as he pushed his tongue into her, then dragged it leisurely around her folds, circling her clitoris with agonizing slowness. She reached beneath her, gripping his hair, desperately bucking her hips to demand he quicken his pace, but he refused. He was hers to command, but he was also a brat, and clearly, he loved to tilt the balance of power. Slow, torturous, delicious and unbearable.

"Henry... oh Goddess curse you," she gasped, her fingertips pale against the rocky floor of the cave. She threw her head back, screwed her eyes shut and moaned, surrendering completely to the sensation of him.

He rewarded her by thrusting his tongue into her again, slower, deeper, dragging a cry from her lips.

His mouth drove her higher, until stars burst behind her eyelids, holding her teetering on the edge of ecstasy but refusing to let her climax take flight. The bastard only slowed his pace, kissing her tenderly, savoring every inch of her drawing out her pleasure and her frustration.

Annora's cries rang around the cave as she pressed her palm to her forehead, her skin burning beneath her hand. Liquid fire coursed through her veins, prickling, unendurable, soothed for a moment by an icy wind which blasted from the cave's entrance.

Her eyes shot open at the thud of a footstep, and were greeted by the sight of a man, a scout from Caer Duloon, standing wide-eyed not two feet from her. Fear tangled with pleasure as Henry continued beneath her, oblivious, his tongue seeking to expel her spirit from her body, while the man at the cave entrance reached for the knife at his hip.

Instinct drove her as she gripped the closest thing to a weapon she could find; a half-burned tree branch from the fire, and swung it with all the strength she could muster.

Sparks showered onto the cave floor as the air filled with his screams, and he ran, stumbling, swatting the thighs of his breeches.

The muscles in her belly tightened as Henry's head shifted. "What was that?" he said, muffled against her.

"A scout, I think. They've found us." She brushed her hair back from her face and began to lift herself from him.

His arms around her hips tightened. "Is he gone?"

"I set him on fire."

His laughter blew against her. "Are you close?"

She nodded, unable to wipe the grin from her lips even as her heart beat with a fearful rhythm. "I was."

Without warning his mouth was on her again, licking her as though his life depended on her climax, sending pleasure spearing through her body. When the next cry escaped her lips, she clamped her hand over her mouth, keeping her eyes on the fur at the cave entrance.

Closer and closer he drove her, hard, fast, crumbling her composure, draining her fears of what lurked beyond the curtain. It did not matter.

If all that remained of their lives was that moment, then it would be well spent and the best death she could imagine. To die with Henry Percille's tongue thrusting into her cunt was a fine death.

The deep, primal force at her core tightened and pulsed as she came, a sob tearing from her throat as his tongue lapped against her. Beat after beat of ecstasy throbbed against his lips, until she was convinced he had set a new rhythm for her heart to follow, and that the pleasure would never end.

At last, he relented and allowed her to stand, her shaking legs barely able to hold her as she took up the still-smoldering branch from the floor of the cave. Without a word, Henry took up his blade and stalked, naked toward the cave's mouth.

"Was it just one?" he asked, his voice little more than a low growl.

She filled her lungs for what felt like the first time in a thousand years. "Aye. Just one that I saw."

"Did he get an eyeful before you set him alight?"

"Aye."

"Poor lad. What a confusing day for him."

Goddess, curse that man. No matter the situation, he could plant a smile on her lips. As he disappeared behind their makeshift door, her heart squeezed, yearning to follow him into the abyss beyond.

Her heart no longer perched on the edge of its cage, hesitating, fearful that it could not yet fly. For as likely as Henry was to push her from the precipice, she knew without doubt that he would leap after her too, show her how easy it was to soar. And if she faltered, he would cushion her fall.

Hiding her smile behind her hand, Annora sighed. She was truly lost, and she could fight it no longer.

CHAPTER
SIXTEEN

Sleepless, famished, and soaked to the bone, Henry and Annora fled the cave. Charging into the unknown together, summoning what little strength they had remaining as they hurtled along the uneven path. The horses were gone—no doubt stolen by the scout or simply out on their own enjoying their new found freedom. Their absence increased their value tenfold.

"I told you we should've brought them into the cave with us," Annora said, her voice carried on heavy, panicked breaths. "Where are we going?"

"I don't know," Henry admitted. The reserves of his strength were so depleted that every word he spoke took the effort of an entire round in the melee.

It had been a decade since Henry had anything close to resembling purpose. Glory, greatness, revenge; each one of them had been a powerful driving force at some point in his life, leading him toward a multitude of great and terrible acts. But now, he had a new purpose, one as unfamiliar and unsettling as the land unfurling around them. One he dared not admit, even to himself.

Men like Henry did not deserve love, of that he was sure. But he would crawl to the end of the world if it led Annora from harm.

Dawn broke, and still Henry refused to stop. The blisters on his feet, the chill running though his body, the ache in his bones meant nothing. Annora would be safe. He could not give her everything she deserved, but he could ensure that she was unharmed. He would push himself to breaking to keep her from the guards.

For once, she did not protest. She simply walked beside him, her face set with determination. When the time came for her to sit and rest, he remained standing, eyes scanning the surrounding hills for signs of the guards, even as his body trembled with fatigue.

It was near dusk the next day when a town came into view and his legs all but gave out beneath him. Pinpricks of light glittered against the dark blue backdrop of the world, each one the answer to a prayer he dared not speak aloud. The sight of it alone was enough to unsteady him.

He leaned against a lichen-spotted boulder as a torrent of heat and ice churned beneath his skin, and for a moment the air around him grew dense and barely breathable. As soon as it began it ended, and he refused to let Annora see he was anything less than as strong as she needed him to be.

A town meant an inn or a tavern, and that meant hot food and a dry bed for the night. It was risky, but she needed it, and truth be told, so did he. As the world tilted and blurred around him again, he was sure that was all he needed. A short rest and he would be back to full strength.

They made it to the town as night fell and rain began to pelt the cobbled road. The streets were mercifully empty, save for a singing drunkard outside the tavern. Henry tightened his grip on the hilt of his blade as he and Annora passed.

"Going for a drink are you, bonny girl?" the man leered, his words slurred and filling the air around him with an acrid cloud. "Give us a smile."

Ordinarily, it would take little effort to end the drunk's miserable life, but Henry held back, telling himself that they did not need the attention.

"This is my thirty-ninth winter," Annora sighed. "Yes, I'm going for a drink. And no, I won't smile for you."

The drunkard chuckled, stumbling toward them. Instinctively, Henry stepped forward, holding her back behind his left arm as his right unsheathed the blade by an inch.

"Back," he spat. "If you touch her, I'll cleave your vile head from your shoulders and shit down your neck."

The threat sat in the air as the rain pelted them, until at last the drunkard laughed, stumbling against the wall of the tavern and bracing himself with a four-fingered hand. "Easy friend, I meant nothing by it."

"I'm sure."

The man hiccupped, his cheeks billowing a moment as if to spew his guts. "I was just about to ask if you wanted company."

"No," Annora said.

"Absolutely fucking not," Henry added.

Holding up his hands, the drunk grinned, though his eyes were closed. "Alright. Just mind how you go. Place is crawling with guardsmen from Caer Duloon."

The news struck Henry's chest like a lance of ice. He clenched his jaw and sought Annora's hand in the darkness. She locked her fingers to his with a ferocious grip.

"Why are they here?" she asked.

"They're looking for someone." The drunk squinted, wrinkling his nose in confusion. "Uh. What did they say? Man with yellow hair, woman with black hair... or something. Escaped prisoners. They've been murdering anyone who gets in their way."

"Well, that's terrifying. You can't trust anyone these days," Annora said, pitching her voice a little higher and more innocent than her usual tone. "And the guards think they're here, in this town?"

"I don't think they know. They're just riding to all the nearby towns warning people. Best be careful."

"We will," Annora said, squeezing Henry's hand. "Come on, love. Probably better not to linger if there are killers on the loose."

Love. She had called him love, and though he knew it was only an act, his foolish heart soared.

She was a marvel. The casual lies which dripped from her tongue could rival any stage performer. Despite her hunger, fatigue, and the cold which had long since seeped into her bones, she was a picture of innocence and fear for the rampant killers. Just when he thought he could not adore her any more than he already did.

As he and Annora turned to walk away from the tavern, the world around them continued spinning around him and the fog descended on him once more. Henry gripped his head to make it stop, willing himself to remain strong. But beneath his palm his skin was burning.

They still had the long night ahead of them; hungry, exhausted, cold, and soaked to the skin. He could not falter.

Annora was silent until they reached the outskirts of the village, following the tracks of cartwheels on the rain-battered road. "We need to find shelter for the night."

It was a simple statement, and a sensible one, but failure sat heavy in Henry's chest as they left the lights and comfort behind.

"Forgive me," he said, the words as unfamiliar to him as the far side of the world. "I know I don't deserve it, but I'm truly sorry."

In the darkness she was only a tightly-bundled silhouette, creating what warmth she could by wrapping the wet wolf pelt around her. His own pelt sat heavy and water-logged on his shoulders, a constant reminder of the cell, of his crimes, and the mercy he had not deserved. A shiver ran deep through his very marrow, cold despair sinking into his spirit.

"Ten years ago, I competed in the Grand Tourney at Caer Duloon," he chuckled as a fuzzy, cloying sensation gathered at the back of his head. "It's strange to think you were there in the castle while I was a free man. I should have found you then. I had gold enough to buy any house you wanted, and could have swept you away to a life of comfort and bliss. Not this."

They walked past the tall, black columns of trees, sparse at first, then denser as the forest grew thicker around them. The leaves had long since fallen, leaving behind skeletal limbs which loomed overhead, doing nothing to block the rainfall. A sodden carpet of brown leaves lay underfoot, churning as they made their way.

Annora's voice was rough and hushed when she replied at last. "I would've told you to stay away from me, called you a poser and laughed at you."

"You did that anyway," Henry laughed despite himself, but the levity was short-lived. The dizziness, the cloying, stifling feeling within his skull, the accursed cold. His strength was definitely failing, and Annora was far from safe. Reaching out into the dark he searched for her hand but his fingers only curled around air. "Annora, if we die tonight—"

"We aren't going to die," she said, the sharpness in her tone sudden and unexpected in the still blackness. "Stop that. Just keep walking. The only way we'll die is if you continue to act like an ass in public."

"An ass?" Henry frowned at the accusation, shaking away the cloudy sensation in his mind. "How so?"

"Threatening the man outside the tavern. If he'd called the guards..." She huffed in the darkness. "But you don't care, do you? As long as you can prove yourself and appear to be big and strong and push people around, you don't think about what could happen."

Heat spread across his cheeks and prickled down his neck. "I was protecting you—"

"Goddess, your arrogance will get us killed," she laughed bitterly. "I don't need protecting."

"I know..." The argument died in his chest as the world continued to spin around him, and he focused all his attention on staying upright.

Annora's footsteps grew distant, and he was left alone in the dark.

"I'll do it anyway," he muttered, more to himself than to her.

Fear and shame descended on him which he had not felt since those first days at the Champion's Guild, when he was a boy of ten, orphaned, alone, no money, no family, but a name he was duty-bound to live up to. The first night he had been so afraid in that loud, drafty castle.

But how enormous the champions had seemed then, somehow more than human; larger, more ferocious, and far more beautiful than anyone he had ever laid eyes on. He soon forgot his fear, replacing it with ambition, tenacity, destiny. He was the strongest and most skilled, and no more likely to give up and accept defeat than a hunting hound on the trail of blood.

But that man was no more.

The Dragon was broken beyond repair, and Annora had unknowingly taken the pieces and helped him begin the arduous, often thankless, task of molding him into something else entirely. Something both softer and more deadly. For the first time in his life, he craved softness.

He craved her.

And he would destroy anyone who tried to keep her from him.

"Annora..." He said her name because it felt good to say it, because the night was dark and filled with uncertainty, and she was the only true thing he knew.

Pain shot through his knees, followed by icy cold and the gritty texture of tiny stones digging into his skin. He was on the ground before he knew he was falling, his aching body drained of all strength.

"Shit," Annora hissed, rushing toward him. In the dark her hands pressed to his shoulders, his chest, and finally cupped his face. "What's wrong? What is it?"

Her thumb caressed the curve of his cheek, an anchor keeping him from slipping into the abyss.

"Goddess, you're burning up," she whispered. "We need to get off the road. Can you do that?"

It was an absurd question. He was Henry Percille, a champion, the Dragon. He could do anything he set his mind to.

But his limbs were tempered steel, his starved, exhausted body no more movable than the ancient gnarled trees surrounding them. The effort of trying to stand was too much. He crumbled to the ground, pelted by rain as Annora called out his name.

"Henry, please," she said, the terror in her voice shattering his heart.

I just need a moment. I'll be strong again for you in a moment. He wanted to say it. He wanted to offer her reassurance and comfort, but the words remained on his tongue as his eyes closed. The only word he could speak was "Annora."

P ain behind his eyes woke him. The world was still shrouded in darkness, but he was warm, pressed to the earth by heavy limbs, his own breath cool and wet on his lips. He did not need a physician to tell him he was unwell. His body could not decide whether it was too hot or too cold, and a painful bloated feeling behind his nose made it harder to breathe. Even the dark hurt his eyes.

It was painful to move his arms, but he sucked in a lungful of air and forced his hands to explore. Wet fur above him, warm soft skin beside him, and damp pine needles beneath. He was naked and so was Annora, and they were pressed together on the forest floor, hidden beneath their soggy wolf pelts.

"Shh," she soothed him, stroking her hands through his hair. When she spoke again it was with a whisper. "They're on the road close by. We need to be quiet."

She was right. Men shouted out in the darkness beyond their warm sanctuary, though mercifully there were no braying hounds to seek them out. Unless the Goddess's sense of humor was truly dark, it seemed unlikely they would be found.

Henry lay in silence, listening, his heart rate racing despite his bone-deep fatigue. As the shouts grew distant, he found he could breathe easier.

"What happened?" he whispered when he was sure they were safe. "Where are we?"

"Not far from where you fell," she whispered in response, her fingers still tracing the outline of his face, plotting a course along the curve of his cheekbone, across his brow and down to the tip of his nose. At her touch, a pleasant shiver traveled through his worn-out body and she held him closer. "I found a tree for us to shelter beneath. I needed to get you warm. Your skin was like ice."

Speaking drained him, but so many questions burned at the back of his mind. "Did I walk here?"

She chuckled a little. "No, I dragged you, and yes, you're heavy."

"And my clothes?"

"With mine, in a pile behind me. We're warmer without."

A chuckle rose in his aching chest. "Oh, yes, I'm sure that's why you stripped me naked. Not the fact you can't keep your hands off me."

He did not need sight to know she scowled.

With a gentle sigh, she grumbled. "I should've left you on the road for them to find."

"And yet, here we are..."

"Aye," she whispered, brushing her lips against his, sending a flutter through his body which confirmed he yet lived. "Here we are."

She hooked her leg around his thigh, pressing her hips tight against him. Despite his exhaustion and the sickness that raged beneath the surface of his skin, his belly tightened at the sensation of her so close. Even then, worn down and his spirit close to breaking, his heart fluttered at her touch.

"I'm sorry," she whispered. "For what I said."

He tried to shake his head, to tell her that she was right

to say what she had, but every movement was torture. So instead, he melted against her, drawing comfort from the woman he adored.

"Get some sleep," she told him, tracing the edge of his hairline with her fingertips and pushing back loose strands of his hair from his forehead. "I'll keep you warm."

Pulling him closer, she rested her chin on top of his head and wrapped her arms around his shoulders.

His desire for her clashed with his desperate need to sleep forever. Never in his life had he been more certain that he was no longer the man he once was. Henry the champion could march for days on an empty stomach. Henry the champion could perform acts of impossible strength after many sleepless nights. And Henry the champion certainly never cuddled.

But now he lay cradled in the arms of a woman far stronger than he. Even before he truly knew her, Henry's instinct had told him that Annora could best him in every way which mattered, and he had been right.

"Thank you," he whispered against her throat.

"I won't let any harm come to you."

And in the safety of her arms, he let himself stop fighting.

CHAPTER

SEVENTEEN

A nnora held Henry throughout the night, dozing but never truly sleeping. Sweat poured from him as he muttered her name, clinging to her even as their bodies sweltered. Before long, the heat beneath the wolf pelts became stifling as a fever burned through him, and when morning came, he did not awaken.

Searing heat radiated from his body as he murmured and groaned softly in his sleep. A shining film of sweat coated brow and pooled in the valley of his pulsing throat.

"Henry...?" Annora said quietly, jostling his shoulder. His eyelids opened, but barely, before fluttering back down. She tried again, firmer and more desperate. "Wake up, you ridiculous man."

Nothing.

Every labored breath he drew rattled in his chest before wheezing back out.

"Henry? We need to go." She stroked a finger down the length of his nose, pressed kisses to his eyelids, and traced the outline of his lips, but he remained the same; sleeping and burning. There was no waking him.

It took all Annora's strength to push the lead-weight of his arm off her and wriggle out from beneath their furs, and with every passing second her heart beat harder.

The forest was mercifully still, save for the chattering of jackdaws and the rustle of small animals searching for food beneath the carpet of soggy brown leaves. Annora waited still and silent, listening and watching for the guards of Caer Duloon. When she was satisfied that she and Henry were alone, she set about attempting to make him more comfortable. Though the rain had stopped, the boughs of the trees clung to silver droplets of water. They beaded on the points of the pine needles and on the edges of stubborn brown leaves that had refused to fall.

Carefully, Annora collected all the droplets she could hold in the center of her cupped palm, and crouched back down beside Henry.

"What do I do?" she whispered as she lifted his head and carefully tilted her hand so he could drink. The water droplets only landed on his lips before running down into his beard.

With every heartbeat, a deep, cold dread settled over her. Whatever sickness had pounced upon him, it was brutal. An irrational fear that he would never wake clawed at her chest.

She was miles from anywhere, a wanted fugitive, and dangerously attached to the sleeping man by her feet. Her belly was hollow, and the back of her throat stung with acidic hunger. And her heartbeat was only growing shallower and faster as she lingered. She had to do something. Pulling on her damp wool dress, she grimaced as the cold, heavy material clung tight to her body.

With trembling hands, she smoothed back her hair and pulled it into a loose braid. One thing she could make sense of, one thing she could control. But her fingers shook too much to tie it off. It unraveled slowly as she paced their makeshift camp.

Henry was there, and yet he was not. It could be days before his fever broke, days where they could die of thirst, or cold, or hunger. The man who had fought champions, slain guards and lords, and kicked down castle gates like they were made of parchment, was reduced to a lifeless heap on the forest floor. Though undoubtedly a champion at heart, after ten years sat stagnant, he was completely oblivious to his body's limitations. Henry had pushed himself too far and Annora was alone. The world seemed enormous and daunting without the reassurance of his looming, insufferable presence.

Stretching, Annora tested her limbs and found them trembling and sore, but she had strength remaining. Decades of hard work in the castle, spending every day walking through cold corridors and carrying heavy loads up spiraling stairs had toughened her.

That meant two choices lay before her; to stay by his side and hope he was fit to travel before it was too late for both of them. That was out of the question. All that remained was to leave him, naked and feverish on the forest floor, and find someone who could help him... someone who *would* help him.

It was a futile hope. She knew that with all certainty. And yet, as she knelt by his side, smoothing her hand over his burning cheek, it was the only path she could take.

"I don't know if you'll hear me in your dreams," she said, despising the tremble in her voice. "I'm going to go and try to find help. I'll walk until midday and if I don't find anyone, I'll come back here...Alright?"

Dreadful silence answered.

"Don't die..." She swallowed hard, yet the knot in her throat only tightened. "Don't you dare die."

The fever had taken him so suddenly half of her had wondered if he was only pretending to torment her further. But in the pale morning light his skin was slick and ashen, and the veins in his eyelids were stark red against their pale lavender canvas.

There were so many things she had told herself she despised about Henry, like the obnoxious curve of his smile, which she now longed for and craved more than anything. She had insisted she detested the cold, hard blue of his eyes which she could remember with perfect clarity, even as they were hidden behind his twitching lids.

"I'm coming back," she said. "I'll bring help."

Her certainty was a lie, but she needed it, even if he did not hear. She *would* find help. He *would* come back to her.

Goddess, but caring for someone else was painful.

She swallowed against the barricade in her throat and forced herself to draw breath. "And if you get well again, I'll admit that—well, maybe. I'll admit that I think I could..." She shook her head and squeezed her eyes shut. "I could fall for you. I could love you, and we could live together in that little cottage and forget the world. You can be my woods-man, and I your hag, or your harpy or whatever foul name you wish to call me. I'll even go to the rotten Champion's Guild if you want. But you can't die. You mustn't." She blinked hard as her vision blurred and stung, and she focused her attention on untangling a long brown pine needle caught in his black hair. "I forbid it, you ass."

She leaned forward, pressing her lips to the center of his forehead, breathing in the salt and earth scent of his skin. As the days went by, he was beginning to smell less like an odious wretch, and more and more like comfort and home.

"I'm coming back." Another kiss, this one on his lips which parted as if welcoming her. A pang of relief struck her heart as he released a heavy sigh, though he remained asleep.

Covering him with the pelts but leaving his head exposed, she took his blade from the pile of clothes beside him and hurried back to the path they had followed the previous night.

Carefully, she took five branches to make the shape of a star and left it by a crooked tree at the edge of the path so she could find her way back to him. When she was satisfied, she summoned every last bit of strength she had, and began to walk.

Every step was agony, but she was used to pain, every beat of her heart driving her on. The village they had passed through might have been the closest thing to civilization, but there was also a fair chance that it was swarming with guards, and people not quite so forgetful as the drunk, who would realize who she was and turn her in for a reward.

That left only one option; through the woods.

The wet wool of her skirt swished and clung to her legs as she marched on, her determination dwindling as the hours rolled by. The further she traveled, the more convinced she was that leaving Henry behind had been a mistake.

Not only had she left him to the mercy of anyone who might pass by him, but also the animals. No doubt there were wolves and bears in the woods... the thought of them turned her blood cold. Though she hardly dared think it, she cared for him more than she could ever admit aloud, and seeing him crumble so fast and so completely had rattled her. And Goddess, how she missed his arrogance.

The weak winter sun was high overhead, and there was no sign of a town or village. She stopped and smoothed back her hair, despair sitting heavy on her chest as she fought to draw breath.

"Go back to him," she whispered to herself. "Make sure he's alright and then try another direction."

She sent a silent prayer that he would be recovered on her return. She pictured his smug face, laughing at her for worrying, for even considering that rain and sleepless nights could fell such an ox of a man.

She even prayed that Henry had been listening to her confession. That he had heard her say she could perhaps fall for him, and that he would laugh at it when she found him. And she could be smug, as it was not true.

At least, the 'perhaps' part had been a lie.

Truth be told, she had lost her balance on the precipice. She was already falling, and part of her yet doubted he

189

would be there at the bottom waiting to catch her. It had been too short a span, too hard and fast. No matter how many sweet things he whispered to her, once the haze of lust lifted, he would rescind his affections. Men always did.

The clatter of horse hooves snatched her from her thoughts, and sent her heart racing. Instinct begged her to hide, but whoever the rider was, they could be her only chance to bring Henry the help he needed. Curling her fingers into fists, she remained on the road. If they would help, she would gladly take it. If they refused, she would drag them from their horse and have the beast carry Henry to someone who would help.

When the horse finally came into view, the sight was not at all what she expected. The rider was a woman, sitting atop a sleek black mount, dressed in a black wool riding cape which covered her warm, well-made clothing. Two copper braids snaked down her shoulders.

As she approached her eyes passed over Annora, her brows dipping only slightly before she said quizzically, "Good afternoon..."

"I need help," Annora said, as though it was not completely apparent.

"Are you hurt?"

"No." It was a lie, but she could manage her own pain. The whip marks still throbbed, and every inch of her exhausted body ached. Once Henry was safe, she would seek help for her wounds. Not before. "My husband—" she snapped her lips shut.

The word had slipped from her tongue, only to trip her. How easy it had sounded, how perfectly, absurdly natural.

"What's the matter?" The woman on the horse slid her hand beneath her cloak, and the slick whisper of metal inched from leather carried through the air. She was wary, her eyes darting across the bare trees.

Annora followed her gaze, but the forest was still. "I... I don't know," she frowned as she turned back to the jittery rider, before remembering the unsheathed sword in her own cold-numbed hand. "We've been traveling for days. He collapsed last night and I can't wake him."

The woman had no reason to trust her, and yet she gathered the horse's reins in one hand and shuffled forward in the saddle. "Here, get behind me and hold on. You look exhausted."

It would be easy to take the horse, to rob the woman of her warm clothes and the blade at her hip. The urge to do so persisted at the back of Annora's mind as she climbed into the saddle, perching awkwardly as she clung to the rider's soft, round waist. With a sigh, Annora closed her eyes, basking in the tingling sense of relief which flooded her bloodless toes. "Thank you."

The redhead cast a glance over her shoulder before clicking her tongue against her teeth and nudging the horse's side with the toe of her brown leather riding boots. "Is he far away?"

"Aye," Annora said. "I don't know how long I was walking for. A few hours at least."

The woman in front said nothing. No words of comfort, no empty promises that they would get to him soon. Just soothing silence broken only by the steady hollow thump of horse hooves.

As they rode, Annora's eyelids grew heavy. Both her body and mind craved sleep, but it evaded her, driven out by visions of him. Silently she cursed him, and herself.

"Do you think you can help him?" Annora asked, shattering the silence.

"I'll try," the woman said. "I'll do everything I can."

"We haven't much money to pay for a doctor."

"Don't worry about that." The woman turned her head to stare into the trees beside them. Her green eyes darted across the spaces between as her pale eyebrows dipped and grew heavy. After a moment she parted her lips to whisper, "We must be careful of bandits in these woods."

That explained the rider's eagerness to unsheathe her blade, but it did nothing to assuage Annora's fears for Henry.

"Where are you from?" the woman asked.

"Caer Duloon," Annora said, before realizing her mistake. There was every chance that this woman was on the lookout for the fugitives.

"Caer Duloon?" the woman repeated. "So have you heard what happened to Lord Caine?"

"Aye," Annora said, hoping the tremble in her voice was not as obvious as it was in her own ears. "A tragedy to be sure."

A thoughtful hum sounded at the back of the woman's throat. "Oh yes, I'm sure. Terrible. Anyway, the weather. Quite damp today, is it not?"

Annora stared at the back of the rider's head for a moment, before clarity broke through her confusion. She chuckled. "I take it you bear no love for him?"

"None whatsoever," the woman said. "Now, I'd never say I was glad to hear of such misfortune befalling him. But I'd also... well...I should stop speaking."

Annora chuckled, though to let her guard down entirely around the woman, however friendly she may seem, would have been foolish. "Well, we only passed through Caer Duloon to get here. I'm from the Marshlands originally."

"Ah," the rider turned a little to smile. "My husband is too. He shouldn't be far behind us and I'm sure he'd love to talk to you all about it once your man is out of danger. No wonder I haven't seen you before."

"Do you know everyone?"

"I try to," the woman said. "I spent far too long feeling like a stranger in my own village." She twisted in the saddle to show her face. "I'm Natalie, by the way."

"Annora."

With a smile, the rider turned her attention back to the path ahead. Relief surged in Annora's chest. To have found help from someone who could not have cared less for Lord Caine, and someone with the means and willingness to help Henry. It seemed fortune had finally smiled upon them.

EIGHTEEN

The air was a thousand searing pokers against Henry's skin.

His heavy eyelids parted long enough to glimpse the sparse tree branches sliding across the thick gray sky. The light ached, like having thumbs pressed into his eye sockets, so he shut his eyes, and retreated to the darkness.

Thunder rumbled as he slipped back into an uncomfortable sleep, his skin too hot, too tight, his muscles aching and weary. His thoughts lost coherence, and nonsensical images came to him in vivid flashes; Annora admitting she could fall for him, the sensation of being thrown onto a cart, gleeful whispers of his execution and of gold.

"Annora..." he whispered, seeking out the comfort of her touch, enduring the ache in his shoulder and bicep as he reached into the frigid air. But instead of tenderness there was only the shock of another hand swatting his away.

194

Lifting his head, Henry squinted in the piercing light. "Annora?"

"He's waking up," a harsh male voice grumbled beside him. "What do I do?"

"Hit him until he passes out," a woman suggested. "Or tie him to the cart so he can't escape."

Indignation flared across Henry's chest as he took stock of his surroundings. He lay in the back of a cart, and the thunder was nothing but the groaning wooden wheels beneath him. A man walked beside him while a woman sat up front, barking orders to the beast which pulled them.

He raised his gaze to the sky, enduring the pain long enough to know that they were no longer in the forest, but rumbling past weather-beaten stone houses, their crooked roofs bowed as if to watch him roll by.

A moment later and the bite of rope winding tight around his wrists roused him from slipping back into sleep.

"Who are you?" Henry asked. His throat was thick and raw with pain, his voice a barely understandable rasp even to himself.

"Shut up," the man at his side growled as he tethered Henry's arms to the wooden planks at the side of the cart. "If you start screaming, I'll slit your throat and deliver you to the guards dead."

A disdainful chuckle swelled in Henry's throat, but it pained him too much to let it go. He could barely speak, let alone scream. But his heart could not rest easy. Forcing his eyes open again, he searched the cart, fighting the urge to give up and slip back into sleep. The wolf pelts were still over him, covering his otherwise naked body.

"Is it just me?" he asked.

"Aye," the man growled. "Seems your friend abandoned you to die in the woods."

A strange sort of relief tangled with the pain of that. It seemed only right that Annora had abandoned him to save herself, and had he been able to, he would have told her to do so.

But then... he was sure he had heard her voice. She had promised to return to him, admitted she could love him.

Perhaps it had only been a dream, his fevered mind giving him what he desperately craved. He supposed it did not matter. Whatever the truth, his captors had not found Annora, and that was all that counted.

Despite his predicament, Henry's heart beat steadily. Annora was safe and far away.

"At least we'll get the reward for you," the man said.

"How do you know I'm the one they're looking for?" he asked.

The woman at the front of the cart spoke first. "They're looking for a large man, black of hair, bearded. That sounds like you. And we found you in the woods with a bloodied Caer Duloon guard's uniform beside you. It was hardly alchemy."

The man at Henry's side sneered. "You could always pay us more than the guards are offering and we might let you escape."

"And where exactly do you suppose I'm keeping the gold?" Henry asked, his voice weak and trembling from the effort of raising his head to glance at the shape of his naked body beneath the furs. "And would you really want it?"

"Gold? Ha—they're only paying one silver for you."

That hurt more than it had any right to. That his life had been reduced to the value of a single silver coin, and that no doubt Annora's had been set at the same. As far as Henry was concerned, he was worth a hundred gold, and Annora several thousand times more than that.

Closing his eyes once more, Henry pressed his head back against the wooden base of the cart and when he dreamed, he dreamed of her.

CHAPTER

NINETEEN

Annora's heart lunged against her ribs as she scanned the empty forest; her every breath hard-won against the weight in her chest.

"Are you sure this is the right place?" Natalie said as she dismounted. The worry in her features, and her poor attempt at hiding it, were clear, even though she kept her distance.

"I'm certain," Annora replied, placing her hand around the base of her throat as though she could help manipulate the flow of air to her lungs. "He was here."

"Perhaps he got up and tried to find you?"

It was possible, but as Annora searched for traces of him around the tall evergreen she had left him beneath, that possibility grew ever more distant. The pine needles had been disturbed, not only by her dragging him beneath the tree in the night, but there was also a long streaking trail leading outward.

"Someone took him," she said.

"Maybe someone saw he was hurt and tried to help?" Natalie offered.

There was no point in correcting her with grim suspicions. If Annora admitted that she and Henry were wanted criminals, there was every chance her new friend might flee, or change her mind about her loyalty and love for Lord Caine and turn her in for the bounty.

But there was no time to lose.

"There's a village, not far from here," Annora said, hurrying back to climb onto Natalie's horse. "They probably took him there." As she took up the reins, she cast a look back at the redhead who still stood among the trees, and at the realization dawning on her features. "I'm sorry, Natalie."

Natalie's lips parted as Annora commanded the horse with a tap of her heels. "Wait—don't—"

"I'll leave the horse in the village, I promise." Annora called over her shoulder, before pushing aside her fear and urging the horse to go faster.

Gripping the saddle with her thighs, and keeping the reins loose, she rode, her heart thundering to the rhythm of the horse's cantering hoofbeats.

It was entirely possible the guards would arrest her too, but she could not leave him. She would not. She had made a promise to return to him, and as she rode, she realized, the thought of being without him was somehow worse than anything.

They could arrest her, throw her in a cell, drag her to the gallows and cut her life short, but to spend her days knowing that ridiculous man died alone, afraid and unable to fight back; that would be a torture she could not endure.

As trees grew sparse and the village came into view, fear knotted in her throat, preventing her breaths from flowing freely, but still she rode on. Her knuckles paled against the leather straps of the reins as she pulled back on them, slowing her steed.

Annora had no plan, but her heart drove her on, her pulse throbbing in her ears and drowning out the sounds of life from the village.

A young woman stood on the front step of a small, stone house, shaking out a worn, blue woven hearth rug. A child ran along the roadside at Annora's heels, staring wide-eyed at the horse and its bloodied, bedraggled rider. Outside the tavern, a man in a brown apron wiped the windows with a cloth. Ordinary people went about their lives as though the world was not in ruins.

Annora dismounted, her trembling legs barely holding her upright as she clung to the saddle and willed herself to be strong. Curling her fingers around the hilt of the blade, she folded her skirt around it and pressed it to her thigh as she walked across the village square, her eyes scanning each of the narrow branching streets. In the night it had seemed so small, and yet to Annora it was endless, a hopeless maze, and Henry was lost within.

Movement in the periphery of her vision caused her heart to lunge. Hope and fear surged through her, a tangled maelstrom which quickly turned to terror. Two guards were heading toward her, dressed in forest green surcoats.

In an instant she was running, her blistered feet

pounding against the cobbled street. Puddles of rain water splashed up her aching calves as her breath came in ragged bursts.

The guardsmen shouted behind her, commanding her to stop, but she ran on, darting down the nearest side street. A strong hand clasped her arm, but she wrenched free, gaining another few steps before they were on her again.

"No!" she screamed, twisting round to face them, her hair plastered to her face as she fought with all her remaining strength.

It was not enough.

They were too strong and she was outnumbered. The blade clattered on the cobbles, pounced upon immediately by another guard, who was followed closely by a rickety wooden cart.

"Is that her?" the approaching guard said to the others, speaking over her as though she barely existed.

Inevitability crushed her as she stood, pinned and helpless. Of course, she and Henry could not kill a lord and escape to an idyllic life. Of course. It was absurd that she ever considered it.

"Think so," the guard at her back said in answer to the first.

"Aye, well we've got her friend here too."

Those words hurt more than the bite of their ironclad fingers against her frozen skin, more than Lord Caine's riding crop, or the ache deep in her bones. She had failed, and now she and Henry would die.

One of the guards spoke. "Send for the lord and lady and ask what we're to do with them."

As the cart drew nearer, Annora's heart skipped at the sight of a hand tethered to the side. "Henry?"

Darting forward, she pulled free of the guard's hold and hoisted herself onto the cart. Henry lay still, but for the flex of his throat and the rise and fall of his chest as she climbed onto him. He lay naked beneath the furs, yet even the parts of him exposed to the cruel winter air still burned.

"Henry..." she whispered as the guards gathered around them.

His lips parted as he pulled in a breath. "Annora?"

A guard's strong, armored hand gripped her wrist but, as she pressed her brow to Henry's, nothing else held meaning. Just him and her, and the moment she had wrenched from the hands of their captors. Slowly, his eyes opened, a fraction, just enough that he could see her.

"You came back?" he said, his voice faint, leeched of strength by sickness.

"Of course I came back."

She wrapped her free arm around his shoulders, holding his head off the floor of the cart as she pressed her lips to his, sinking in the sensation of him, holding on to what could be her last moment of comfort and relief and... Goddess she dared not admit it even to herself. But into that kiss she poured her love, and he—despite his sickness—matched her passion.

Yes, she had come back for him. She could not be without him after all. And while she would not tell him, she could not help but show him.

When she pulled back, her heart was racing. Her vision of him was blurred by tears she refused to let fall.

"Send for the lord and lady," one of the guards called out once more.

"That won't be necessary, guardsman," a deep male voice said, rendering the guards silent.

Annora raised her head and was faced by the sight of a giant striding toward them. His hair and beard were almost entirely gray, but for a few stubborn dark streaks, and his brow was furrowed with confusion and indignation. Henry was by far the largest man she had ever seen until then, but the mountainous stranger made even him seem waifish by comparison.

Annora's heart emptied as Natalie rode behind the man on an enormous bay carthorse.

"We meet again," the redhead sighed, her eyes hard and unforgiving as they met Annora's.

"Lord and Lady Blackmere," the guards said, bowing their heads.

At the sound of their name, Henry gasped, raising his head to look at them. "Blackmere..."

The name echoed in the back of Annora's mind, a memory barely paid any heed at the time. Blackmere. Henry had mentioned them, the lord and lady he had betrayed. The reason he was sent to rot in a cell.

Henry's strength ebbed as he wilted back down and lay still, his eyelids clamped shut but twitching, and his chest rising and falling rapidly. Instinctively, Annora shifted, covering his body with her own, shielding him from their view.

Though Natalie was naturally pale, at the sight of

Henry, she turned deathly white. The giant at her side withdrew his sword, stepping in front of his love.

A spark ignited in Annora's blood at the sight of the blade, and before anyone could react, she had her hand on a guard's dagger and had pulled it from the sheath at his hip. Lord of Blackmere or hired brute—whoever the enormous man was, she would not let him run his blade through Henry while he remained tied and helpless. Not while she still drew breath.

"Get back," she hissed. "Get away."

The large man's eyebrows arched in surprise.

The sigh of steel pulled from leather sounded all around her as the other guards withdrew their weapons, ready to defend the nobleman. In her heart, she knew there was no possibility of beating him, but if she and Henry were to die, she would fight with her last heartbeat.

"Easy," Lord Blackmere said, his dark brown eyes darting between her and the guards. "Someone needs to explain what's going on."

The disarmed guard spoke. "Guards from Caer Duloon are hunting these two."

"Why?"

"They broke out of the cells and killed Lord Caine and others besides. There's a reward out for their capture. We paid the people who brought him in and we were about to take them to the castle for you to deal with."

Lady Blackmere's eyes bore into Annora's, harsher than any northern winter. In the silence, her glower said everything she needed it to; Annora had betrayed her, repaid her kindness with deceit, and Annora was lucky that she and

Henry were not both skewered on the end of a guardsman's blade.

The flesh of Annora's back prickled as a voice in her head told her to stand her ground, to refuse to bow to the nobles or quake before their guards.

At last, the noblewoman climbed down from the horse and stepped toward the cart, carving a path through the guards to peer down at Henry's face, scrutinizing his features.

"Henry..." she whispered, barely audible above the rush of blood coursing through Annora's veins and pulsing in her ears. "The Goddess has a cruel sense of humor."

"He needs a doctor," Annora said. "Please help him."

Lady Blackmere turned to glance at Annora as though only just remembering she was there, and then at the blade in her hand poised to fight the guards. "Am I to trust you again?"

"That part was true. I swear it."

The crowd parted once more, allowing the enormous nobleman to stand by his lady's side. Though his features remained hard and fearsome, there was sorrow in his eyes, and a kindness completely at odds with his intimidating size and protective ferocity.

The nobleman's blade was lowered, but Annora's remained poised, every muscle in her body tense and ready to strike. Kind eyes or not, she would pluck them out to save Henry if she had to. They would not take him from her. If that meant they would die together, then so be it.

At last, the noblewoman pressed her thumb and middle finger to her eyelids, and sighed heavily before turning her back. "Take them to the castle. Let her ride with him if she wants to."

Relief washed over Annora as she sat back beside Henry's hip and the cart rumbled beneath them. Still, she kept her blade poised, glaring whenever guards came near.

Lord and Lady Blackmere rode behind the cart, the nobleman on his massive horse while Natalie rode on the mount Annora had stolen. They did not take their eyes from Henry as they rode, watching him with both suspicion and pity.

At the top of a steep cobbled street, the gloomy gray shadow of an ancient castle loomed above them.

"Do you know who we are to him?" Natalie asked at last, as they passed beneath a stone gate and began to climb the hill.

Annora nodded. "You're the ones who put him in the cell, who left him to rot for ten years because he tried to kill you."

The noblewoman turned her eyes from the cart at last, watching the quaint buildings of her village roll by. "Aye, that's part of it." She filled her lungs and gave a weary chuckle, shaking her head. "We'll send for a doctor. I don't know if they can do anything for him, but we'll try."

Gratitude sat behind the dam in Annora's throat. Kind or not, they were nobles, more likely to pay the doctor to slit Henry's throat than to make him well again.

"When we get inside, I'll show you where you can bathe and change clothes. Brandon will make sure nothing happens to him," the noblewoman said.

Annora scoffed, "Do you take me for a fool?" She edged

closer to Henry, placing her arm over his chest as she gripped the blade with her other hand. "He stays with me. If you wish for us to be parted, you'll have to kill one and leave the other alive."

The noblewoman's lips snapped shut.

Annora hardly recognized herself, but she had never been so certain of anything. She had lost Henry once, if only for a while. She would not lose him again.

As they rolled into the castle courtyard and more heavy wooden gates groaned shut behind them, the realization that Annora was once more imprisoned clawed at her. It reopened the wounds which streaked across her skin, reminding her of what she had sacrificed; a life free from castles and nobles and people who believed their names made them better than her.

She had sacrificed her freedom.

Henry's head rolled to the side. A warmth spread through her as he pressed his face to her outer thigh and groaned softly. Longing surged beneath her breast, as her fingers unfurled from the fist at her side, to run through the soft strands of his raven's wing hair. However foolish, her decision to remain by his side, to allow herself to be taken, was also right. She was exactly where she needed to be.

Lord Blackmere dismounted first, groaning as he swung his leg over his horse's back. "Send for the doctor," he told one of the guards. "Have her come here as soon as she can."

Annora tightened her grip on the hilt of her sword as he approached the cart, those kind eyes silently imploring her to remain still.

"Will you let me carry him inside?" the nobleman asked.

"I'll not leave him."

He bowed his head in agreement. "You can help carry him if it puts your mind at rest. But we need to get him inside where it's warm and the doctor can tend to him."

She knew he was right, and yet, setting foot inside the castle might have been as dangerous. A war raged in her heart; she could surrender and hope the strangers would take care of Henry, or fight with everything she had remaining, and hope, somehow, she could get them both to safety.

"I've known Henry for most of his life," Lord Blackmere said. "And I know it takes a lot to fell a man like him. I promise you no harm will come to him."

Perhaps it was the familiar lilt of his Marshland's accent, spoken in a deep, soothing voice which rolled from his broad chest like distant thunder, but she believed him.

Lady Blackmere, however, remained silent. The rosy glow of the setting sun illuminated the courtyard, though to Annora it might have been the light of an inferno closing in on her and the man she shielded.

"Can you promise the same?" Annora said to the lady, as her throat tightened. "Promise me he'll be safe."

Lady Blackmere dismounted, and gave a barely perceptible nod. "I swear it."

It was only a promise, but Annora clung to it. It was all she had.

❧

The doctor scraped an ominous, thick black substance around a mortar with a wooden pestle. She was an elderly woman, her long white hair tied in intricate braids which framed her round face.

Annora stood chewing the edge of her thumbnail, watching intently for any hint of wrongdoing, as she had done for an hour.

Lord Blackmere's rumbling voice came from the back of the room. "Will he be alright?"

"If he's strong—"

"He is," Annora interjected.

"Then he'll pull through," the doctor said, scraping the substance on the rim of the stone bowl.

"What is that?" Annora said.

In the back of her mind, the possibility that it was poison gnawed at her. She fought the urge to knock it from the woman's hands, fight the nobles and their guards, and burn the castle to ashes to protect him.

"Blackberries and honey," the doctor said, taking a carved wooden spoon and scraping it onto Henry's tongue.

Annora's brow creased in suspicion. "In winter?"

"Picked in the summer..." The woman countered, an amused smile pulling her narrow lips into a gentle curve. "Preserved for winter. Not as good as fresh, but we have to make do."

Henry's dark eyebrows slanted a moment, before he sealed his lips, worked the concoction around his mouth, and swallowed.

"He's a strong lad, he'll pull through," the doctor said,

handing Annora the mortar and spoon. "Keep him warm. Feed him blackberries and honey..." she glanced at the ceiling in thought. "Cabbage water and beetroot if you can. Whatever he'll take. And fresh water too. Ensure his thirst is sated."

Annora frowned, shaking her head. "That can't be all."

"What else would you have me do?"

"Wake him."

The woman chuckled as she stood. "Waking him would only prolong his sickness. He needs sleep." Her heavy hand rested on Annora's shoulder. "I know you love him, but let him rest."

The words stilled Annora long enough to allow the doctor to walk away from her and out of the door without further protest. It was absurd to even suggest that Annora loved Henry. She would simply allow him to rest because... well, because it was less effort than waking him. Nothing more.

She glanced down at her filthy hands, and at Henry's; large and nicely-shaped, but caked in dried blood and dirt. They were clasped safely in hers.

Try as she might, she could not remember taking his hand. Perhaps she had not let go of it since the moment she climbed into the cart beside him, binding her fate to his.

Lady Blackmere cleared her throat, snatching Annora from her thoughts.

"Will you be comfortable here?" Natalie said.

It was a strange question for a captor to ask. Compared to the dungeons of Caer Duloon, the bedchamber was palatial. In fact, compared to the tiny bare room she slept in before her imprisonment it was luxurious beyond anything she had ever known. Space to move around, soft woolen rugs covering the floorboards. The walls had been stripped of their decorations, but the bare stones were made homely by the fire crackling away in the large hearth.

Clearly the thought that she was capable and willing to burn their castle down to save Henry had not yet crossed the nobles' minds.

"Aye," Annora said.

"You'll be confined to this room for the time being, but there will be guards posted at the door who can bring you anything you need. I'll have supper and spare clothes sent for you. And water to bathe."

It occurred to Annora as Natalie's eyes scanned the room, that what she had taken for cold indifference was almost certainly pain. The noblewoman had taken measures to ensure that the man who had attacked her—and the woman who had lied and stolen her horse—were comfortable and safe. It was no wonder she could hardly stand to look at them.

"Bundle together your clothes, I'll see to it they're cleaned and mended, should you wish to keep them," Lady Blackmere said.

"That's kind of you, but our clothes are nothing but a memory of a place I'd rather forget."

The noblewoman stood in silence, her eyes darting across Annora's features. "Feel free to burn them then, if it helps."

"It will." Annora turned back to Henry, stroking her fingers across his burning brow.

It seemed nothing could disturb his sleep. Vulnerable and fighting back against the sickness ravaging through him, he was still as beautiful as when he was awake and arrogant.

Her gaze fell to the wolf pelt still bundled on top of him, reeking and soaked through, but important to him nonetheless.

"Wait!" Annora said, the sudden sharpness in her voice startling her as well as Lady Blackmere. She took the pelt from him and held it out toward the noblewoman. "Can you wash this?"

Insolent. It was audacious to even ask. Panic darted through Annora's heart, preparing her to be struck, but Lady Blackmere simply nodded and reached out to take the pelt.

"I'll have it cleaned and mended."

"Thank you, my lady. He's very fond of it."

The moment her hands gripped the fur, the noble lady froze. Her lips parted in silent surprise as she gazed down at it. "This is... I gave him this."

"He carried it with him wherever we went."

The noblewoman raised her eyes to glance at the sleeping, feverish man on the bed. Perhaps it was only a trick of the light, or Annora's hope of mercy, but her features seemed to soften.

"I'll have it taken care of," Lady Blackmere said, turning toward the door.

It would be more than a week before Annora saw either of the nobles again.

The days crawled by, agonizingly slow. Moments were measured only by Henry's labored breaths and the occasional glimmer of cruel hope as he stirred but still did not wake. It was hardest when night fell and the castle grew deathly quiet and all she could do was imagine a future where he never woke again. A future without him.

A future Annora did not want.

TWENTY

Footsteps tapped gently against wooden beams, rousing Henry from sleep. Breathing through his nose was impossible, and dull pain radiated from beneath his eye sockets, but he was awake, and famished, and far thirstier than he had ever been.

Opening his eyes, he expected a cell, but the sight which greeted him was altogether more homely. Instead of a simple prison cot, he lay on a soft bed, beneath a thick crimson sheet.

Faint amber firelight danced on the stone walls which were lined with iron brackets; the kind used to display weaponry, but which sat empty. There were no windows in the room, save for two arrow slits, narrow and black like the pupils of a cat. And above the windows, carved from stone, was a ram's head, a sigil he had half dreaded seeing again.

It had to be a dream and a cruel one at that. Of all the blighted shitholes in Aldland, he had been dragged back to Blackmere. Back to where his ill-luck began.

But he was comfortable and warm, and despite his pain, he seemed to be intact. Squinting, he could make out the shape of a person, bent double as they tended to the fire. A woven shawl hung about their shoulders, and the firelight flickered against long golden hair. Relief swooped through his chest.

"Annora..."

She started at the sound of her name, bolting upright and placing her palm on the stone mantel to steady herself. "Goddess, you're awake."

A thousand questions churned through his mind; where were they? How long had he slept? But the only word he could manage was "Water."

His throat stung as though he had spent the past month swallowing swords, and as Annora approached, he almost knocked the cup from her hands in his eagerness to satisfy his thirst. His fingers trembled, struggling to find their grip, until her hands slid beneath his supporting him.

"Thank you," he croaked, before he brought his lips to the cup and gulped the cold water. The bed dipped as she sat beside him, the comforting warmth of her body as necessary as the drink. "Thank you," he gasped again between swallows, his eyes still refusing to stay open for long.

"Easy," she whispered. "If you drink too much, you'll make yourself sick."

The shock of the cold water already churned in his gut, so he relinquished his hold on the cup and sat back against soft pillows while she set the cup aside.

"What's wrong with me?" he asked.

Her fingers curled around his hand, so soft and tender he could have cried.

"I don't know," she admitted. "A doctor came but there was little she could do for you. Your fever broke yesterday, but you've slept a lot these past few days."

Days. He had slept while she worried and waited, and that knowledge made his heart beat harder. What had she been through alone while he slept? Though he was still naked beneath the bedsheets, her clothes had changed. In place of her chambermaid's uniform, she was dressed in a loose white nightdress. Her hair, wet and bedraggled the last time he had seen her, was clean and spilled down her back in a golden wave of silk.

"Lord and Lady Blackmere have taken us in," she said. "Though I think we're more prisoners than guests."

His throat grew tight once more. Somehow, he had led Annora straight to the center of a spider's web, to the two people who hated him more than anyone. No matter what sickness still coursed through him, he would do what he could to protect her.

"They've been kind," she said, as though his thoughts were her own. "We're locked in here, but there are guards posted at the door who bring anything we need."

Kind to her perhaps, but the moment they knew he was awake, there was every chance that could change. And it would not be undeserved, at least not for him.

He squeezed her hand. "I led you to another prison cell."

She bowed toward him, pressing her lips to his temple. "There's nowhere else I want to be."

His fingers no longer trembled when he held her, and his thirst and hunger, and those who hated him were insignificant. There was only Annora, the soft sweetness of her body entirely at odds with her wonderfully granite spirit.

She brought her knees up onto the bed and lay against him, pressing her body close to his, burying her face against his neck. Pressing her palm to his chest, she whispered, "I missed you."

"Oh—" A choked sob wracked his chest as his fingers pressed to her soft upper arms, drawing comfort and security from her, as necessary as breath.

Ten years he went without touch, and yet, with her arms around him, he could not have imagined surviving for ten minutes without it. Without her.

She held him until his breaths returned to normal, until he was sure he would not slip back into abyssal, lonely dark. And then, in her arms, he slept peacefully. When he opened his eyes again, daylight shone through the narrow windows.

"How can I be tired after sleeping for almost a week?" he asked, stroking his fingers along the soft, pebbled skin of her arms.

"Because your body is healing," she said, hitching her leg over his hips as though holding him to the bed. Not that he ever wanted to leave.

Later that evening, a guard dressed in forest green came to the door with a tray, carrying a veritable feast.

"Lord Blackmere has prepared this for you," the guard

announced as he set it on a round oak table by the door. "He hopes you're on your way to recovery."

Feast was an understatement. A bowl of melted cheese and warm bread with a firm, golden crust to dip into it, roasted chicken with a little pot of salt and herbs to sprinkle on the meat. There were even honey cakes stuffed with elderberries, and fresh water and milk to drink.

"This looks suspiciously like a final meal," Henry muttered as his belly growled.

Annora shook her head as she pulled the cake apart with her fingers. "They've all been like this. And I haven't died of poisoning yet either. I think it's safe."

He ate because Annora ate, because if the food was poisoned or they were to be executed after their last bite, he would remain by her side no matter what.

"Lord Blackmere's a good cook," Annora said as she used a bread crust to scrape the remnants of the cheese from the edge of the pot. "You wouldn't see Caine dead in a kitchen."

"Brandon always cooked well. He used to awaken early at the Champion's Guild and help make breakfast for all of us."

She chewed thoughtfully before lying on her back and resting her hand on her belly. "What do you think they'll do to us?"

In truth, he did not know. If they were still the people he once knew, they did not have the heart for executions— they had spared his life once ten years ago when any other noble would have sent him to the headsman.

But he and Annora were still held captive by people

who rightfully despised him, and though he could be content confined with Annora for the rest of his life, there was little hope she would feel the same. Harpies did not do well in cages.

He took her hand in his, pressing her knuckle to his lips and hoped it gave her some comfort where his words could not.

When nightfall came, Annora sat by his hip and took a washcloth from a basin at their bedside.

"You don't have to do that," he said, his head growing clearer by the minute. "I can do it myself."

"I did this for days while you slept," she replied, ringing it out.

The water ran between her fingers and splashed happily back down to the basin, as though touching her was a blessing. When all the excess water was squeezed out, she turned back to him, pressing the cool damp cloth to his brow.

She sighed, letting her knuckles graze softly against his cheek. "One time I was doing this, just so. It made you smile and I thought you were coming back to me, but you didn't wake up."

He kept his eyes on her, leaning into her as she soothed him with a gentle touch, his hand resting on the curve of her thigh. Though exhaustion still snaked through his bones like a thousand binding vines, a more primal need cleared a path through the tangle. More than food and water or a week-long bath, he wanted her, he craved intimacy, and so it seemed did she. Her cloth traveled lower, to his neck, sending a shiver down his entire body and pebbling his skin.

"Are you hungry?" she asked, the light in her eyes so innocent that it was anything but. She knew exactly the power she held over him. "I can ask them to bring you something to eat."

"I'm hungry for you."

Her lips lifted into a smile as a soft chuckle shook her chest. "I think you should get your strength up first."

"You're strong enough for both of us."

She smiled but said nothing as she folded down the bedsheets, sliding the cloth over his chest.

His heart pounded to the pace only she could set as she cleaned him. Her finger glanced over his nipple, a fully intentional accident which she repeated again and again, until they were hard and aching, and his cock strained against the bedsheets. He sighed, melting against the pillows. He had only been awake for a matter of hours and already she insisted on torturing him in the most delicious ways.

She dipped the cloth into the water once more and wrung it out. His breath caught in his throat as she ran it over his stomach, the cool fabric and her gentle touch tickling, making him twitch and gasp. She stopped at his hips. A groan sounded in the back of his throat as he raised his arms and laced his hands behind his head.

"So excitable," she sighed. "I'm simply washing you."

"Wicked woman."

A smile curved her lips. "Would you want me to be anything less?"

"No. Nev—oh..." His heart leapt as her hand dipped below the covers, and wrapped the cool cloth around his aching cock. Slowly, gently, she began to wash him there. Perhaps they would be imprisoned in that room together for the rest of their lives. He hoped so. In fact, he could think of no better fate.

Nothing could compare to the bliss she bestowed on him, magnanimous torturer that she was. He would gladly give up every sunrise, every luxury, every moment of freedom if he could spend the rest of his life with her hands on him.

But it was her mouth which pulled a cry from him, her soft lips around the head of his cock, her tongue stroking the length of him. Hot and wet, sucking and licking until his thighs trembled and stars burst behind his eyelids.

Pleasure coiled quickly in the pit of his belly, too sudden, too intense. He cried out in ecstasy and agony, frustration and release, his hips lifting off the bed, thrusting into her mouth as he watched her take him.

She kissed a trail along his inner thighs when she was done, her lips tracing sprawling paths up to his belly where she laid her head.

The room turned around them for a minute while Henry caught his breath and the tingling pleasure between his thighs subsided. He ran his fingers through her hair, desperately clinging to those moments of bliss, but knowing all too well it could not last forever. Sooner or later, he would have to summon the courage to face Natalie and Brandon.

He swallowed down his worry, and stroked a hand down her hair and along her jaw. "What about you?"

She raised her head. Her cheeks were rosy pink, her

pupils dark and wide. "I thought you'd never ask. Perhaps almost dying has made you a better man."

"We'll see," he grinned as he pulled himself up to sit against the pillow, parting his legs and patting the bed between them. "Will you allow me to take charge this time?"

Raising an eyebrow, she regarded him a moment. "Are you sure you're ready? You don't need me to guide you?"

"I'm sure. Sit here. Put your back to me."

She did as he asked, the cool white fabric of her nightgown pressed to his chest and stomach as she leaned back against him. He pushed her golden mane from her neck and kissed her, his tongue lapping at her skin, her every gasp a mark of pride. His hands slid down her body, one of them to her breasts, teasing her nipples, the other squeezing her belly, skating around the upper rim of her navel through the fabric. So soft, so disarming.

"Part your legs," he said.

Again, she did as he asked, leaning her head on his shoulder as her arms came up to rest on the back of his neck. She was his completely, to worship and relish for as long as she permitted.

"What is the hold you have over me?" she whispered as he lowered the hand on her belly beneath her nightdress and through the patch of golden curls between her thighs. Her breath shivered as his fingers slid between her folds, teasing her, spreading her slickness. "I've been beside myself this week. I would have died for you if they'd tried to hurt you."

He grazed her neck with his teeth. "I know you,

Annora. I know that beneath it all, you're a woman who loves to be told how beautiful you are. You love to feel cherished and wanted and relish the knowledge that I'm all for you. And I know some part of you feels the same way for me."

She groaned in pleasure and the pantomime of disgust.

He growled against her ear. "Tell me to stop."

"Never."

"I'll stop if you wish it."

"Shut up."

He chuckled cruelly. "You're a goddess, Annora. You're *my* goddess, who loves to be loved, and loves to be told how good her pretty cunt tastes."

Her back arched as he circled her clitoris with his fingertips with one hand, still teasing her nipples through her nightgown with the other. She was perfect in her contradictions; her thorny armor hiding a body and heart both infinitely soft and lush beyond measure.

"Keep talking like that," she gasped. "Don't stop."

Already he was hard again, his cock wedged between the cleft of her backside, longing to claim her.

"After you come, I want you on top of me. I want you to ride me while we both use our hands to touch you. I want your ecstasy, to feel you pulse and squeeze my cock. And then I'll lick every drop from your cunt until I'm soaked in you."

"Yes," she whispered, turning her head to suck the skin of his neck, sending spikes of pleasure through him.

"Oh, Goddess Annora."

When her body tensed and trembled, he slowed his

movements, teasing her, bringing her to the edge and no further, relishing her protesting cries.

"Admit you're as addicted to me as I am to you," he whispered against her skin.

"Never."

"Tell me I'm the best you've had."

She turned her head to face him, flushed and thunderous and glorious. "Your skills in bed are balanced out by your awful nature. The only reason you're still alive is because the Goddess herself couldn't stand to be around you and sent you back."

Hiding his delight, he buried his head against her neck and pinched her nipple hard between his thumb and forefinger, both a punishment and reward. She hissed in a breath, grinding her body against his, seeking release.

"My delicious, wretched harpy," he whispered, sliding his fingers over her clitoris, circling her swollen flesh until she bucked her hips against him, crying out as her cunt pulsed against his hand. "That's it," he hissed, nipping the skin of her neck with his teeth. "Fuck, Annora, you're perfect."

He held her as her breaths returned to normal, still stroking, still coaxing weary moans from between her lips.

"You sat by me for days while I dreamed of you," he whispered softly. "I know your heart belongs to me."

Her fingers splayed across the back of his neck as her lips parted. "Fine." She drew in a shuddering breath. "You win."

As she sat up, pulling away from him, his heart plummeted, his body instinctively following her, eager fingers reaching out to brush the flimsy fabric of her nightdress.

A moment later she pulled off the garment, and his heart quickened at the sight. Though her back was still to him, she was everything he remembered and more; soft curves and creases, every inch of her deserving each moment of attention he could possibly lavish upon her.

Her wounds had healed but her scars remained, and because of that, he could never regret what he had done.

She reached behind and took his hand in hers and turned her head slightly, keeping him in the periphery of her vision.

"I admit it," she said. Her throat danced as she swallowed. "I'm yours."

The air prickled against his arms. He and Annora fell silent and still, both stripped bare and bathed in firelight, her golden hair tumbling over her shoulders. His mind turned circles, working to convince him that there was a mistake, that it was all a cruel trick played by the sickness which still ravaged him. But no matter how many times he told himself not to believe, no matter how long he sat waiting for the dream to shift, it remained.

Annora remained. Tangible, beautiful, glorious. His.

"I've never enjoyed the company of others," she said, turning a fraction more to face him. "But I find myself..." She frowned, as though the confession was as much a frustration as a relief. "When I'm not around you, I find myself wishing I was. For a while, I thought I'd lost you, and I couldn't bear it." Her grip on his hand tightened. "So, I feel as though I should tell you, and not simply so that you'll pleasure me. Not just some game. I mean it. If we die tomorrow, I'd want to die having told you the truth. You mean something to me. In fact, you mean everything to me."

Henry sat silent, unmoving, lest he interrupt her. Every word settled upon him, sinking beneath the surface of him.

"You're mine?" he asked, scarcely believing it.

"Aye," she nodded, able to look upon him at last. "And you're mine."

"I am," he whispered, barely able to catch his breath. "I've been yours from the very start."

"Even when you left me on the frozen moors?"

He chuckled, but the sound was muted by regret. "I was running from what I didn't understand. I always expected love would seep into my bones, but you plunged into my heart and remained there like a barbed blade."

A wide smile spread across her face, and in a heartbeat, he closed the gap between them, seeking out her lips, unwilling to endure another second without them. Her kiss was liquid fire down his spine, filling every inch of him with a heat far greater than simple lust. For the first time in his life, Henry Percille found himself wanted.

When she pulled away, he was left breathless.

"Don't think this means you can stop being wicked and obscene with me," she said, sinking her teeth into his lower lip. "If you start treating me like some forgotten, faithful housewife and not your wanton harpy, I'll go straight back to hating you."

"Harpies, like dragons, are impossible to tame," he grinned. "We'll soar together, and leave the world in embers behind us."

She laughed, and the sound of it was more glorious than anything he had heard. "Such pretty words."

"I mean them. All of them. But I may wish to be soft with you sometimes."

She gave an exasperated sigh, almost concealing the smile pulling at her lips. "Fine. You may have the first and fourteenth day of each month."

"Very good. And what day is it today?"

"The eighth, I believe."

That woman would be the end of him, he was certain, and a more perfect death he could not imagine. Truth be told, even when their passion blazed and they did things together which left him blushing for hours afterward, he was always soft for her. But he would pretend to be rough and indifferent if it made her happy.

"Well then," he said, letting his hand trace the valley of her spine to the back of her head, where he grasped a fistful of her hair and pulled her back to him. "Why don't we see if I can reach your heart in other ways?"

Her breasts heaved as her breath sharpened. Her eyes, black with desire, burned into him. "Wicked man."

"*Your* wicked man," he whispered, lowering his head until he whispered in her ear. "Always and completely yours."

TWENTY-ONE

S he turned, seeking his lips, unable to bear the distance any longer. His fist remained tangled in her hair, pulling, claiming her, sending a shiver down her spine which pooled deep in her core.

Relief made his touch all the sweeter. Relief that her heart was laid bare, relief that he felt the same way she did. But most of all, relief that he was back with her, that he was as obnoxiously large and vibrant, and as irritatingly intoxicating as before he fell ill.

He dipped his head, welcoming her kiss with a soft moan, heating her blood so it prickled the surface of her skin. He could pretend he was in charge all he liked, but she knew all too well that if she protested even a little, he would surrender to her as he always did. His cock pressed eagerly against the cheeks of her arse, his empty hand skating over her breasts and belly as though he could not decide what to lavish his attentions on first.

"Turn around," he growled, "I want to look at you."

Heart thrumming, she did as he asked, twisting around to straddle his broad hips. She sighed as he ran his hands along the sides of her thighs. There was so much strength in his hands, strength barely reigned as his thumbs skirted along her hips before dipping down to squeeze her backside. His touch earlier had left her wet and aching, and already desperate for release.

She gripped the base of his cock, leading him to her entrance, her lips parting as she sank onto him. Frissons of pleasure tingled along her spine as she took him, as his eyelids closed and his cavernous chest billowed with his shaking breaths.

"Mine," he growled, letting his hands slide back up to caress the curves of her belly. "My Annora."

The darkness in his voice sent a flutter straight to her core as she gazed down at him. "I'd stay here forever if it was up to me."

"I'd let you."

She smiled, pressing her teeth to her lower lip as she shifted her hips a little. He closed his eyes, lips parting as he whispered her name; a prayer and a plea.

"Remember back in the tavern, I asked you to pretend you loved me?" he said.

"Aye."

His throat danced as he swallowed. "How hard was it to pretend?"

She ran her hand over his chest. "It was far harder to pretend I hated you."

Leaning forward until her chest pressed to his, she

sought his lips once more. He kissed her softly, cautiously, his fingers trailing lightly along the sides of her breasts.

She rolled her hips, sending a tingle of pleasure down her spine as he pressed his head back against the pillow. He was beautiful; a brutal beast made of muscle, soft flesh, and scars who made her feel unlike any other. And he was hers.

The distance grew too much to bear, and in an instant her lips were back on his, claiming him. His kiss was hard, deep, as brutal as love and just as addictive. He raised his head toward her, demanding more as she lifted her hips, raising herself until only the tip of his cock remained inside her, before sliding back down and relishing his muffled groan against her lips.

He pushed his hands between them, seeking her pleasure, insisting on it, rubbing her clitoris with the pad of his thumb as he watched her ride him. All that man, all that strength and brutality, crumbling and quivering beneath her, blushing and gasping with each roll of her hips.

She was strong and more than capable without him, she knew that. But as he lay beneath her, watching her intently, whimpering at the slightest movement of her hips, sliding the heels of his feet against the bedsheet as though he could hardly bear the pleasure she bestowed upon him, she felt powerful.

His lips parted, releasing a sharp, desperate groan as he trembled and writhed, his face flushing scarlet in ecstasy.

"Annora!" he gasped. Her name was more beautiful on his lips than anything she had ever heard. "Annora..."

The muscles in his neck strained and reddened as his

orgasm pulsed through him, on and on until Annora was certain she had broken him.

"Ah, fuck... Goddess..." he panted at last, bringing one palm to his brow as he fought to catch his breath. "Forgive me."

"There's nothing to forgive," she said, caressing the curves of his chest as she let him rest.

His eyes fluttered shut for a moment as he pulled in a deep breath. "Lie beside me. Let me finish you off."

"How poetic," she sighed as she climbed off him and settled on the bed beside him so she was on her back.

His eyebrows arched as he rolled onto his side, pressing his body to hers. "You want poetry now?"

Slowly, his hands skated along the inside of her thighs as she parted them, making way for him. Tingles ran through her body, anticipation swelling in her core as she battled to keep her breath steady.

"No. I don't want poetry," she whispered as her hand joined his, guiding him down between her thighs.

"Then tell me, my harpy, what do you want?" He dragged a finger through her folds, spreading her wetness and his seed, drawing a low moan from her throat. "This?"

"Yes. You. I like it when you say obscene things to me."

He growled appreciatively in her ear, and the sound of it stole her breath. Her nipples tightened as he whispered in her ear. "Then I'll frig you and lick you senseless for the rest of your life if you'll let me. I'll dedicate my life to ensuring your exquisite cunt is constantly wet."

Goddess, those words, dripping from his tongue were almost enough to finish her. She dragged in a breath, relishing the coiling sensation deep in her core. "Keep going."

"I'll have you for every meal, spread on the table as I devour you and fuck you with my tongue." He pushed two fingers inside her, sending a frisson of pleasure rolling through her.

"Oh, Goddess, yes."

The sound of his fingers pumping into her was wet and obscene and glorious. She wrapped her arms around his shoulders, buried her face in the arc between his shoulder and his throat, clinging to him as he brought her closer.

"I'm yours, Annora. Yours to use for whatever pleasure you crave."

As she teetered on the edge of ecstasy, she sought his lips, her cries muffled against them as she came unraveled. A groan resonated through Henry's chest as she pulsed and throbbed against his hand.

"Good," he gasped as she released him from her kiss. "Goddess, you're beautiful."

Her heart skipped as she lay nestled in his arms, listening to the retreating thunder of his heart. A heart she knew was all for her.

And a heart which was still far from danger.

Beyond the chamber doors, nobles still waited to decide their fate, nobles he had crossed more than once.

"Is something wrong?" he asked, his voice soft and gentle as he stroked her thigh. "You look troubled."

She forced a smile, and wriggled closer to him. "No. I'm just glad you're back with me."

He shifted beside her, until he lay with his head on the pillow, gazing into her eyes. "I knew you'd miss me."

Ordinarily she would have argued, insisting she was glad of the peace, but not then. "I did."

"I couldn't have left you," Henry said, his voice growing muffled. "I'd have found a way back."

"I'd have dragged you from the Goddess's arms myself."

He raised his fingers, tracing her lips with such slow, relaxed tenderness, she half forgot they weren't alone, in some other life by their own cozy hearth.

"I adore your smile," he whispered.

"Everyone tells me I should do it more. That I should mask how I feel just to please them."

"Well, I'm glad you don't. You don't owe them that, and you're glorious whether you're scowling or smiling. But I am rather fond of earning your smiles."

Curse it all, that man knew how to make her heart flutter.

A moment later he snored softly beside her. A mountain of muscles and scars and devious intentions, and yet, somehow, despite her best efforts, the most precious thing in the world to her.

He slept soundly, as though Aldland was theirs to walk freely, as though there were no nobles or soldiers hunting them down. And she would not shatter the illusion for him.

For ten years, Henry Percille had paid the price for his wickedness. Now Annora intended to repay the rest of his debt.

Slowly, she untangled herself from his arms and dressed, wrapping herself in the thickest wool dress she could find. Blackmere nights were almost as brutally cold as Caer Duloon's, and as she slid open the hatch on the chamber door, her breath coiled out in a cloud of steam before she ever spoke.

"I need to speak with Lady Blackmere. It's urgent."

The guards posted at the door exchanged a glance. One of them, a tall man with a bright orange mustache, frowned. "She's in her room."

"Fetch her then. Tell her it's about Henry. It can't wait."

Shutting the hatch she drew a deep breath, turning to face the sleeping man once more, drinking in the sight of him as though it might be her last. His raven's wing hair, his dark eyelashes which fluttered as he slept, the curves of his body. She committed all of it to memory.

By the time the guards unlocked the door and beckoned her forth, her vision was blurred behind a veil of hot tears.

"This way," the guard muttered, closing the door behind her as she stepped into the corridor.

Lady Blackmere emerged from a distant chamber, dressed in a pale nightdress and wrapped in a crimson wool shawl, her bare feet padding along the floor. Her graying red hair was tousled from sleep, her features soft and puckered as though even the faint candlelight hurt her eyes.

"Is something wrong?" she asked as she drew close. "Is he getting worse?"

"No," Annora shook her head and glanced back at the bedchamber door. "He's recovered, I think. That's why I want to speak with you."

The noblewoman's expression grew rigid as she lowered the candle in her hand. "Very well."

Words tangled on Annora's tongue as she gripped the edges of her skirt. She had been free from Caer Duloon for less than two weeks and seen so little of the world. But what she had seen in that vast, harsh wild, was made bearable by the man who she could have sworn she once hated.

The man half of Aldland wanted dead.

Her jaw tightened as she met the noblewoman's eyes. "Lady Blackmere, I'm here to offer you my life in exchange for Henry's."

TWENTY-TWO

Before Henry was even fully awake, he knew he was alone. The moment his eyes opened, they shot to where his palm lay splayed on the empty mattress; the space where Annora should have been. But Annora was gone, and the bed was cold. Adrenaline pounded through his heart, chilling his blood.

They had taken her.

The bastards had taken her from him while he slept.

Untangling himself from the bedsheets, Henry climbed from the bed, his bare feet thundering clumsily on the floorboards as he hurtled toward the door.

"Where is she?" he bellowed, slamming his fist against the wooden door. "Let me out!"

Again and again, he pummeled the door, panic racing through his body, his only thoughts geared toward bringing her back to him. When his demands went unheeded, he threw his body against the wood, grunting as pain shot through his shoulder.

"OPEN THE DOOR!"

The air was knocked from Henry's lungs as the door swung toward him with enough force to send him stumbling back. Not since his days in the melee had he felt a blow like it, as though every bone in his body had suddenly shifted an inch closer together.

And the man behind the door, the behemoth bearing down on him, was all too familiar... Yet, entirely changed.

Though the years had unquestionably been gentle to Brandon the Bear, time had left its unmistakable mark. His hair was more silver than brown, and his face was softer, the creases around his eyes and mouth deepened by years of laughter. But as the old champion hefted Henry against the stone wall, those creases were canyons, his face screwed tight from the effort. Time had hardly dented his strength at all.

"Enough!" Brandon shouted, his deep voice at once a comfort and the cruelest torment as he held Henry against the wall. The heat of his broad, rough palms pressed into Henry's shoulders.

"Brandon..." Henry gasped as he fought to catch his breath. "Where is she? What have you—?"

"She's with Nat—with Lady Blackmere." The larger man pushed out a heavy breath, grounding himself as his grip on Henry's shoulder loosened a little. "She's alright."

Any other captor he would not have believed, but Brandon... Brandon had been many things to Henry; mentor, rival, friend, and enemy, but he had never lied. Placing his hand over Brandon's as he dragged in hard-won gulps of air, Henry nodded.

The grip on his shoulders loosened a little more as Brandon stepped back, his dark eyes lifting to the wall above Henry's head. "Put some clothes on."

A bubble of nervous laughter swelled in Henry's chest as he glanced down at his naked body. As champions they had dressed and undressed in front of each other a thousand times, but those days were long since passed.

Head spinning and arms throbbing from his assault on the door, Henry turned back toward the bed. "I don't know where my clothes are."

"No, well, you arrived naked. You can have some of mine."

Ten years ago, Henry would have balked at the idea, but as the Blackmere guards brought forth a plain oak chest filled with warm tunics and breeches, he was nothing but grateful.

As he dressed, old feelings of resentment beckoned at the back of Henry's mind; that he should despise Brandon, blame him for the years lost in the cell, hate him and Lady Blackmere because they had everything Henry had always wanted. But he could not. Henry was tired of hate.

And if nothing else, those ten years in a cell had brought him something he had only ever dared to dream of while he was a champion. They had brought him Annora.

"You look well, in spite of your illness" Brandon said, eyes still averted as Henry buckled the belt around his hips. "Married life has treated you kindly."

Henry's eyebrow arched. "I'm not married."

"Oh? Annora told Nat you were her husband."

An amused grin tugged at Henry's lips as he glanced at

himself in the mirror above the wash basin. "She did, did she?" He tucked information in the quiver of his mind; ammunition for the next time she sought to tease him.

His heart fluttered at the mere thought of her, and when his eyes finally returned to the mirror, he found that he was smiling. "Will you let me see her?"

"Aye," Brandon said, his voice and expression stern and grim. "They're waiting for you in the banquet hall. The guards and I will escort you down there."

At Brandon's word, one of the guards stepped forward, holding a set of black iron manacles.

The smile faded from Henry's lips, leaving a look of wide-eyed realization. He and Annora were still prisoners, and now that he was awake, it appeared they would stand trial. The instinct to fight roared inside his chest as he held out his hands, complying with the guard's command before he had even spoken it.

"Are you ready?" Brandon said as the locks clicked into place.

Henry could only nod, his words drowned out by the rampaging rhythm of his heart. Every muscle in his body prepared to fight, to run, but they had Annora and he would not leave her behind or risk her safety. Brandon had said she was unharmed, but the unspoken part of that was '*for now*'.

The people he had known ten years ago had been merciful, but time could splinter, turn soft hearts hard.

As a champion, Brandon had been known as the Bear, for his strength, size, and nature. But as gentle and lovable as bears appeared, it was never wise to grow comfortable around them. Beneath the fluff were teeth and claws easily capable of destruction.

"I'm ready," Henry said. "Take me to her."

He followed Brandon through the corridors of Blackmere castle, flanked by four guards whose every step was punctuated by the grind and clang of steel. For as much as Blackmere had shaped the course of his life, Henry had never once walked its ancient stone halls before. Once he had sought to control it, to become lord, to become someone worthy of his name, but now that he was there, he found it small, drab, and underwhelming.

"Lord Blackmere now, is it?" Henry asked as they began their descent of a spiraling stone staircase.

"Just Brandon will do."

"Well, it's good to see you, despite... everything." A nervous chuckle emerged from Henry's lips as his pulse quickened. "I'm happy you've done well in life."

Brandon turned, blocking the staircase with his hulking frame as the guards closed in behind. Henry's heart lunged against his ribs, trapped, unarmed, helpless.

"Don't think I've forgotten that you stabbed Natalie," Brandon growled with his fists curled by his thighs, unblinking as he stared at the center of Henry's chest as though he imagined pushing a blade slowly through his heart. "She might forgive you for it, but I won't. I sat by her bedside, measuring her breaths, fearing that every one might be her last." The Bear's lips tightened as he pressed his palm to the rough gray stone and pulled in a breath. "I can't say that I'm happy to see you, Henry."

"That's... entirely understandable."

"I gave you too many chances, I know that now."

"I ask only one more."

Brandon scowled. "What reason do we have to trust you? You stabbed Darius at Westgarden, you hit your squires Goddess knows how many times. You nearly took my eye in practice, tried to have me expelled from the Guild, tried to kill me at Caer Duloon. And Robert—" The larger man paused, his lips quaking in anger and heartbreak. "You had Robert murdered by those bandits—"

"Robert was a mistake," Henry blurted, his heartbeat pounding in his ears. "I never meant for him to die."

"But he did."

"That was foolishness on my part, not malice."

Finally, Brandon raised his eyes to meet Henry's, and the hurt in them hit him like a boulder flung from a trebuchet.

"I paid the bandits to take over the castle," Henry said, as his voice trembled. "It was meant to last a couple of minutes. They would charge in and overwhelm the guards, then I would fight them off and chase them out of the town. Lady Blackmere would reward me, and my valor would be sung of for centuries. I thought my coin could buy my glory and their loyalty—"

"Well, then you're a fool," Brandon spat with a shake of his head. "You gambled the lives of champions and towns-folk for false glory."

"I know."

"And you still killed Robert—"

"I *loved* Robert!" The words left Henry's lips before he could stop them, and hung in the air between them no matter how he wished he could take them back. But they were true, as painful and absurd as they were. "He was my friend too and dearer to me than you ever believed. And I've sat alone in a cell for ten years reliving the moment I saw the cross-bow's bolt pierce his skull. I dreamed of it over and over until I was certain there was no point in me living. Not until I met Annora. And I love—" The hairs on his arms and the back of his neck bristled as the words left his lips. But Goddess they were true, so painfully and desperately true. "I love her."

Brandon's expression softened as he drew back. He pushed out a breath and turned his eyes away from Henry once more. "Come on. They're waiting. We should be doing this in the hall."

The guards at Henry's back closed in, their steel chests brushing against his back as Brandon descended. Whatever awaited Henry at the bottom, he could approach it knowing that for the first time in his life, he had spoken the absolute truth of his heart. He loved Annora, even if she was not there to hear the words.

They continued their journey through the heart of the castle, until at last they approached an enormous wooden door, which two guards pulled apart as Brandon approached.

The sight beyond the doors knocked the air from Henry's lungs. Annora stood in the center of the banquet hall, dressed in a crimson gown, trimmed with green embroidery, more befitting of a noble lady than a chamber-maid. Her blonde mane spilled like spun sunlight down her back and she did not turn to look at him as he was ushered over the threshold. Her eyes were trained on the noble-woman sitting at the head of the hall.

The noblewoman who turned Henry's blood to ice with a glance in his direction.

As with Brandon, time had left its mark on Lady Natalie. The copper in her hair had faded, though it was not quite so silver as the Bear's. Once, long ago, Henry had taught her to fight, carved her into a champion and known her as the Lioness, but as she sat glowering at the woman he loved, she had never seemed more ferocious.

"My lady," Annora whispered, her voice wrung dry. "Please don't do this. I beg you."

Heat flared along Henry's throat as he approached. There were no marks on Annora that he could see and physically she seemed unharmed. But as he was brought to stand beside her, her panic was evident in her wide, pleading eyes, and the tremble of her lips, so subtle he might have missed it had he not committed them entirely to memory.

She did not tear her eyes from the noblewoman even to glance at him. "Lady Blackmere, please."

Natalie held up a hand, begging silence as Brandon approached her and bent to whisper in her ear. The hall was silent but for the clang of steel as the guards stepped back to their posts, and the erratic rush of Henry's breath as he stood waiting.

Still Annora refused to look at him, her eyes remaining fixed on Natalie and Brandon, her lips parted in a silent, desperate cry.

"Annora?" Henry whispered. "What is it? Look at me, please."

She remained stubborn and steadfast, unwilling or unable to even glance at him. Cold dread slithered through Henry's ribs as they stood awaiting judgment.

Finally, Natalie stood from her seat, and fixed her gaze on Henry. "It's been a long time."

"Yes," he said, hoping she did not hear the tremble in his voice. "I'm sure you hoped it would be much longer."

For a moment he could have sworn he saw a glimmer of a smile at the corner of her lips, but as soon as it began, it dissipated. She tilted her chin and addressed him bluntly. "You put me in a difficult position. Further to escaping the cells at Caer Duloon, I'm told that you killed Lord Caine," she said, her voice echoing around the great hall. "Along with his guards. And you burned down an inn."

A shrill ringing sound pierced Henry's skull as the accusation emptied his heart. There was no point refuting it, not if he was to save Annora. He would take the blame for it all. "Yes. That's true."

"No, it isn't," Annora said. "I burned the inn."

Damned woman. He stepped forward, raising his voice to draw the attention back to him. "I killed Caine slowly, and I'd do it again given the chance."

"You don't deny it?" Natalie asked, the shock evident in her voice.

Henry's jaw tightened. "No. And I don't feel any remorse for it either. In fact, I'd say on the long list of terrible things I've done, that one ranks among my favorites."

The noblewoman lowered her eyes. "After all this time. I had hoped you'd changed."

He was a dead man.

In his mind, Henry began to cling to the details, as though he could take them to the afterlife with him; the scent of Annora's hair as he had lain with her, the warmth of her skin, the way her fingers pressed to his chest, shielding his heart. He clung to the hard sensation of his feet on the cold stone floor, the cool, refreshing caress of the air as he pulled in a breath, the glittering dust dancing in a sunbeam pouring through the tall windows.

"Henry—" Annora hissed.

"I killed Lord Caine because he had Annora whipped with his riding crop whilst she was pinned and helpless. He told her he would whip her until she died, and he relished her agony. He said he would sew her lips shut so she could not scream, and that he would shatter her limbs so she could not escape." Henry balled his fists, preparing to be silenced, to be sentenced and dragged away. He would let them. He would march to his death without so much as a sigh if it could save her. He would not allow any doubt that he was the guilty party.

"You killed Lord Caine to save Annora?" Brandon asked.

"No. I cut his knees open to save her so he couldn't get away. Then I went back to kill him once she was safe, simply because he deserved to die." Henry turned his head, meeting Annora's gaze as she stared at him, forgetting where he was long enough for his heart to lift. "The bastard suffered till his final breath, and it was still not enough. And

I hope beyond hope that if I die today, I'll find the prick in the afterlife and beat the shit out of him there too." He directed his next comment toward Brandon, "Don't tell me you wouldn't have done the same for Lady Natalie."

The nobleman gave a long sigh, before shrugging his enormous shoulders. "I can't."

"I had no love for Lord Caine," Natalie said sharply. "But I'm duty bound by my position to uphold Aldland's laws. Regardless of his... odious nature, his guards won't stop hunting you. His niece has taken on the helm of Lady of Caer Duloon, and she's determined to see you answer for what you've done to her family."

"Kill me if you must then," Henry said. "Have me flogged in the streets. Have every one of your townspeople line up to carve the names of the dead into my flesh. But don't hurt Annora."

Annora's eyes were glassy as they scoured his face, her lips pressed into a firm line. "You don't need to do this," she whispered.

Brandon simply stared, his eyes narrowing a moment before he glanced at Natalie and then Annora. Henry's pulse beat in his throat. Never had he felt more vulnerable, as the eyes of everyone in the room bore into him, weighing the purity of his spirit. But Annora's was the only judgment he paid any heed to. The only opinion that mattered.

"Her life is worth a hundred of mine," Henry said. "Lord and Lady Blackmere, I beg you, don't cut it short. The world would be unbearably dark without her light."

Annora blinked twice before her eyebrows stitched into something resembling a scowl, but her ire was weakened by the heartbreak gleaming in her eyes. "Don't you dare," she whispered.

Even now, even faced with the possibility of death, his heart laid bare in the hands of people who despised him, she made him smile. His glorious, grumpy harpy.

And then, something happened which he did not anticipate. Lady Blackmere laughed quietly, shaking her head. She turned to Brandon as though he could offer the answers she sought, before raising her eyes to the window above their heads. "My predicament is this. The Lady of Caer Duloon wants you dead. The people of Blackmere know I have you in my custody and word will spread."

"So kill me publicly and sate their thirst for blood."

"Henry, Blackmere doesn't even have an executioner."

"Then I'll duel Brandon—"

"If you think I'm letting you hold a blade within fifty miles of this castle or my husband, then you're greatly mistaken," Natalie sighed. "You are asking me to kill you and spare Annora, but Annora has also offered me her life in place of yours."

Icy fear gripped Henry's heart as he stared at Annora. "What? No. I'll not let you die for me."

"Not death," Annora said. "I said I'd serve them every day for the rest of my life if it meant they would let you go."

Stunned silence fell over the banquet hall as Henry's mind grappled with her offer. That she would surrender her freedom, work until her body broke, trade his life for her servitude... It was out of the question.

"Ten years," Annora said. "You spent ten years forgotten in a dungeon. It's time you were free."

He whirled around to face Natalie and Brandon, panic ringing like a shrill, constant bell in his skull.

"You can't do this." He stepped forward, heart spiking at the sudden clatter of steel as the guards darted toward him. Even now, manacled, unarmed and begging for death, they did not trust him. They had no reason to. Time after time he had betrayed them, put glory and riches on a pedestal above the lives of people who trusted him, but now he had nothing. Nothing but her. "Please, Brandon, Natalie, I beg you, take me. Let her go."

"Oh, stop it," Annora hissed, her voice hard and sharp as broken glass. "Don't you see, you ridiculous man. Neither of us have to die. I'll buy your life with mine."

She moved to his side, cupping his burning face in her trembling hands, and at once his heart knew at least a little peace. With the slightest touch, she brought him comfort and solace, unworthy of her as he was.

He leaned into her touch, always in pursuit of more. "Annora, please let me do this for you. I need to know that you can be safe and happy, even if it costs my life."

"How can I be happy?" Tears glistened in her eyes as she stroked a thumb across the arc of his cheek. "If you died, I would never be happy again."

"You would. You will. Annora, you've said yourself the world is full of men like me."

"Stop." A crease ran between her brows as she glowered at him, as her tears edged ever closer to the precipice. "You know that's not true."

"But it is—"

"There's no one like you because there's no one that I've ever loved like I love you."

She stepped back, taking her hands off him and staring in wide-mouthed horror as though the words had sprung from her unbidden.

"It's alright," he said, quietly and only for her. "You don't have to say it."

Her golden eyebrows dipped as she pressed her fingertips to her lips and her gaze wandered beyond him. "No... Goddess, it's true." Her eyes scanned his face, following every feature, every line, as though seeing him for the first time. "I love you, and I don't want you to die."

Even if he had known the right words to say in that moment, he could not have said them. There was no air in his lungs with which to speak, no thoughts in his mind beyond the primal urge to run to her, protect her, to take her there on the banquet tables in front of Lord and Lady Blackmere. She was his. Completely. Openly.

His.

And whether alive or dead, he was hers.

TWENTY-THREE

T he silence in the bed chamber was disrupted only by the click of a key in its lock. Confinement once would have driven Annora out of her mind, but she was back with Henry, where the world made sense and her place within it was all too clear. Being locked away in the bedchamber was nothing but a comfort.

Henry stood, leaning against the stone wall, his hands still bound in iron manacles. The back of his head was pressed against the stone, and his blue eyes were fixed on one of the fading tapestries. There was nothing for them to do but wait for Lord and Lady Blackmere's decision.

"Well," Annora said, folding her arms over her chest. "Do you have anything to say?"

He had not uttered a word since her confession; Henry, the man she once had to silence by sitting on his face, who loved to prattle on and listen to the sound of his own voice, was apparently no longer capable of words. Standing against the wall, hands rigidly bound in front of him, he may as well have been one of the decorative, lifeless suits of armor lining the castle's corridors.

Frustration swelled in Annora's chest, hot and fierce, colliding with the cold dread that she had said too much, opened her heart too readily, and given it to the wrong man entirely.

"Forget I said it," she huffed, turning her back on him. "They're only words."

"Were they true?" he asked at last.

"No. They were just a ruse to appeal to the Blackmeres." She could not look at him as the lies tumbled from her lips, filling the air with bitterness and salt. "It was a trick. I hate you, in fact."

The gentle touch of his hand on her shoulder sent a bristling energy surging down her spine. She planted her feet firmly on the floor, determined not to turn, not to let him win her over with those blue eyes, or his revoltingly handsome face.

"Alright," he said, his voice a tightly reigned whisper, hot and dark against the back of her neck. Carefully he slipped his arms over the top of her head, so his cold iron manacles rested on the burning skin of her breast. "Well, let me say this then. *I* meant every word. I love you. I do. I love you whether you reciprocate it or not. I love you, and if the Blackmeres will allow it, I will gladly die to save you."

Her eyes closed as the skin of her neck tingled beneath his lips. "I don't give a shit about the Blackmeres. *I* won't allow it."

He chuckled softly, planting a kiss on the back of her

neck. "And I won't allow you to sell yourself to servitude for me."

"But we'd be together."

"And you'd be miserable," he said.

"I'd be more miserable if you were dead, you foolish man." Twisting around to face him, Annora scowled.

"Do you remember in the tavern, when I intended to ride back to Caer Duloon? I expected to die. And I told you then that all I wanted was for someone to remember me fondly... when I'm gone..." his voice wavered as he spoke, before he silenced himself with a cough. "I have that now."

Annora closed her eyes and pressed her back teeth together, trying to hold back, but her heart broke free regardless. "How can you be so selfish?"

"Selfish?"

"You said you didn't go back to Caer Duloon that morning in the tavern because you couldn't bear to leave me, after hardly knowing me. But now you do know me. Now you know that I love you, and now you've changed your mind and you do want to leave."

"I'm not leaving, I'm doing this to save you!"

"I would be unsalvageable, you fool," she cried. "If you do this, if you let them take you, I would be broken beyond repair. And that is why I hate you. I hate you because you barely think things through. I hate you because you made me love you. And I hate you because I don't hate you at all." She buried her head in her hands, shielding the burning tears in her eyes from his view. "Why did it have to be you? Of all the people in Aldland, why you? Why not some docile farmer or a sweet carpenter or blacksmith with strong, rough hands and the temperament of a rock?"

Henry chuckled softly and pulled her closer, bowing to press his forehead to hers. She collapsed into him, unable to even pretend his arms were not her home.

His breath quickened before he spoke. "Because my poison needs your sting, and your fire feeds on my fuel and burns bright."

Despite it all, despite the ache in her heart, her frustration and longing and bitter anger, she smiled. "We're as bad as each other, aren't we?"

"Completely."

There was no one else for her but him; she saw it as clear as the blue of his eyes. Even if there were a thousand people in Aldland she could be happy with, there were no others who made her feel so completely and utterly overwhelmed. Henry was strength and arrogance, but he was gentle and oh so devoted to her. Even as he faced death and she a life she swore she would never return to, he made her laugh, he made her smile and feel safe and warm and wholly necessary.

She was no chambermaid with him, but a harpy, ferocious and vicious and equally as deserving of legend as he.

"You infuriate me," she whispered.

"I know," he said. "I'll never stop. Not while I live."

She raised herself onto her tiptoes, her fist in his hair, pulling him down toward her. At the first touch of his lips, burning tears coursed down her cheeks. Every kiss they had shared until then had been fire, blazing bright between them, but that kiss was guarded. Not an inferno, but the warmth of a familiar hearth whose flames were slowly fading. It was a kiss goodbye.

"Stop it," she whispered, pulling away from him and trying again, stoking life back into him with the caress of her tongue.

He raised his head from her reach. "Stop what?"

"You think this is our last kiss."

His lips parted, but no sound came from them. No sharp-tongued ripostes, no infuriating arguments. Instead, he raised his arms up and over her head, withdrawing from her. In his mind the sentence had been served, his pyre already built.

Her heart splintered as the warmth of his body left her. "Henry—"

He shook his head, "I'll not let them take you—"

"Nor I you!"

The rattle of the key sounded again, the grating wheeze of the lock being slid from its chamber, the creak of the door. Their time was up.

Annora could not turn to see who entered the room; breaking eye contact would mean she admitted defeat, that he had won, that she would let him die for her. Turning would mean wasting time which would be better spent memorizing every detail of a face she might never see again.

His eyes burned into her with an intensity unlike anything she had ever known. "I love you," he said.

"I love you too." The words fell from her lips, natural, plain and wholly true. They winded her all the same. Even above the clatter of armor and marching footfalls, her panicked breaths were a roaring hurricane. And even as the guards surrounded them, she kept her eyes on him.

Henry, in all things, was her equal, unwilling to tear his eyes from her.

Her heart pounded to a frantic rhythm but it beat for him, so hard and urgent she was certain that it would break through her ribs in its attempt to reach him. Fear built a barricade in her lungs as one of the guards stepped out of the formation.

"Lady and Lord Blackmere have reached an agreement. You'll come with us back to the banquet hall."

"So soon," Henry said with a bitter chuckle.

Cold dread sat heavy on Annora's chest. If it took so little discussion to decide their fate, then it was entirely possible her gut had been right and their lives meant less than nothing to the nobles.

Following the guards back through the corridor, her vision darkened and shook as her pulse raced and every shallow breath was like inhaling scalding steam.

Her legs trembled beneath her as they descended the spiraling stone stairs, but through it all, through the panic, the dread, the hopelessness, were his hands, bound in iron but warm and sturdy and tight around hers.

Henry. Henry the champion, the Dragon, the prisoner, the killer.

Henry, the man she loved.

But he was not made of stone. As strong as he was, and for all the comfort he gave her, his breaths were shallow and quick, the same as hers. His grip, though comforting and unyielding, still trembled as hers did. He was afraid, and as they reached the banquet hall doors, he looked to her, as though somehow, despite her terror, she could offer him strength.

But the only words which came to her were the truth, the only thing which was certain. "I'm yours," she said. "No matter what."

He smiled softly and said, "The days I've spent with you, my harpy, are the best I've ever had."

"I know."

His smile widened to mirror her own, fading only when the enormous wooden doors parted to summon them.

Together, hand-in-hand, they faced their destiny.

Somehow, in the minutes they had been away, the banquet hall had grown impossibly large and foreboding, their footsteps echoing forever against the stones. And yet they stood in the same place; she knew by the crack in the flagstones she had stared at all morning as she begged the Blackmeres to spare Henry's life.

Her pulse thundered in her ears, as Henry's grip on her hands tightened.

Lady Blackmere broke the silence. "Thank you," she said, addressing the guards. "You may leave us."

There was a moment's hesitation, a silence heavier than any thunder, before the guards obeyed the noblewoman's request. One by one, the armored men filed from the banquet hall. The heavy wooden door clunked shut, and their footsteps faded.

Annora and Henry were left alone with the nobles.

In all her years in Caer Duloon, Annora had never once known Lord Caine to entertain anyone—let alone prisoners

—without his guards. Then again, Lord Caine had not been married to a man who looked as though he could carry a carthorse like it was a week-old kitten.

"Sit," Lady Blackmere said, a request, rather than a command.

Still, Annora's legs were rigid, fastened to the spot by a mixture of fear and suspicion. Something was amiss, she was certain of it.

But Henry, foolish as he was, acquiesced to the noblewoman's wishes, approaching the same banquet table she and her husband were sitting at. And Annora, as love-struck and fearful as she was, allowed her hand to remain in his.

Every step they took closer was like wading through sand, her feet heavy and reluctant, but her heart was unwilling to let Henry go alone. When they reached the table, they sat opposite the nobles, her hand still firmly clasped in his.

"We've considered your offers, and can confidently say we're not interested in either of them," Lady Blackmere said plainly, as her fingertips followed the ridges of her carved wooden armrest. "We have no intention of having you serve us, nor do we wish to see you executed."

"Oh—" Annora breathed, her throat clenching as relief surged through her. Henry's grip on her hand tightened still. The ache of his grip anchored her to the world as though he was afraid that she would leave him.

"But," Lord Blackmere continued. "We can't let you go free." His eyes remained fixed on Henry. "We'll need to assure Caer Duloon that you've been... dealt with, and *you* will need to uphold that."

"What do you mean?" Annora asked.

The air was as thick as a restless summer night as the two men faced each other.

"He means they need to believe we're dead," Henry said at last.

Lord Blackmere sat back in his seat. "Aye. That's about the sum of it."

"And we want you to remain close," Lady Blackmere added, before chuckling quietly to herself. "Not so close that we have to see you, mind. Just... close enough that we know you're causing no harm."

Retaliation bristled in Annora's chest, but was silenced by the caress of Henry's thumb as he circled her knuckle. "That seems fair."

"I'm surprised to hear you say so," the noblewoman said.

"I know what I did to you," Henry replied. "I sat in the dark for ten years thinking of little else. And I know you have no reason to trust me, but please believe that I would rather die than see Annora harmed. Whatever you need me to do, I'll do it."

The noblewoman's chest rose as she pulled in a breath. "I believe you. And I've seen firsthand the ferocity with which Annora is willing to defend you."

Annora's head spun as she tried to make sense of their words. "So, me and Henry would be dead to the world, hidden away with nothing to do but live out our remaining days quietly?"

"Aye." Lady Blackmere glanced at her husband. "The only question that remains is where to put you."

"Might I suggest a place?" Henry said, grimacing even as he spoke.

Lady Blackmere's eyes narrowed before lifting her chin. "Go on."

"Does anyone live in the cottage?"

"The cottage? You mean..." The noblewoman's lips turned to an incredulous smile. "You despised it, didn't you?"

Annora's brow furrowed. "What are you talking about?"

With a sigh, Henry turned to face her, running the pad of his thumb over the peaks of her knuckles. "The last time I was at Blackmere...when I..." he frowned, choosing his words carefully before abandoning his train of thought. "We had to take refuge in a cottage out in the woods a day's ride from here. A dreadful, ratty little ruin held up only by moss and the grace of the Goddess."

Annora's heart lifted at the thought of it, and it seemed he felt it too.

He could barely keep the smile from his lips as he muttered. "I think it would be perfect for you."

The Blackmeres glanced at each other, an unspoken hesitation passing between them. Annora's lungs ached as she awaited their decision, still expecting that at any moment she would awaken to discover she had fallen down the spiral stairs and hit her head.

After so many years of scrubbing chamber pots and bowing to the whims of nobles, she could have the simple life she had always dreamed of. A little cottage where no one would bother her. Freedom. And with the man she had tried so very hard to hate, but who had seeped into the very bones of her.

All that remained was for the nobles to agree.

Lord Blackmere sat forward. "That cottage means a lot to Nat and I. It's where we fell in love. We were married there."

"But it's falling down?" Annora interjected, her heart racing as she spoke out. "Henry said it's crumbling."

Lady Blackmere placed her hand on her husband's forearm. "Aye, it is. We haven't been there for years and even then, it needed repair."

In the corner of Annora's eye, Henry raised his face to the ceiling and gave a resigned sigh, but when his gaze fell back to Annora, he smiled. "We could... help."

"Aye," Annora said, hope making her heart beat harder. "I've spent my life cleaning and fixing and mending. I'm sure Henry's good for something too."

Lady Blackmere pressed her lips together, stifling a smile, but Lord Blackmere was not quite so adept at hiding his expressions.

The nobleman turned to his wife. "What do you think?"

Lady Blackmere pushed out a breath, before turning her gaze to Annora. Every heartbeat was the pounding of a battering ram, every breath tightly reined by the expectation of refusal. Annora stared back, unwavering despite the nervous tremble coursing through her body.

I love him, she thought. Her mind screamed it, as though somehow the noblewoman would hear her thoughts. *I know him and I love him and I choose him. Let us be.*

Beneath the table, Henry's fingers caressed the back of

her hand as if to reassure her that no matter what, they would remain together.

"Very well," Lady Blackmere said. "You may live in the cottage on the condition that your names are never even so much as whispered amongst my townsfolk. Brandon and I will ride down there to check on you every now and again."

Annora's heart soared. "Thank you. We won't let you down."

Though some part of her screamed warnings that it was too good to be true, she could not fight back the elation rising in her chest.

Lady Blackmere turned to speak to her again. "May we speak to Henry alone for a moment?"

Her joy dropped like a frozen stone in her belly, and uneasiness, cold and sickly, rose in its place. She looked to Henry for assurance.

"It's alright," he said.

His words meant little, but the calm in his eyes, the slackening grip on her hand, those she trusted.

"Alright." She stood, from her seat, ignoring the decades of conditioning telling her to bow to the nobles. Her back remained straight, her head high. In the morning, she would leave the castle with the man she loved and never set foot within a mile of one of the wretched things again.

It was all she had ever wanted, and everything she had told herself she did not need. And it would be home. For the first time in Annora's life, she was free.

TWENTY-FOUR

Annora had barely been gone a moment, but he missed her. Without her hand in his, the iron manacles around his wrists were unbearably cold and coarse. Without her beside him, he was uneasy and incomplete.

That harpy. She had ruined him entirely, and he worshiped her for it.

For the first time in all his years, he was hopelessly, helplessly besotted with someone other than himself, and curse it all, love compelled him to do things he dreaded. Such as spend the rest of his life in a dilapidated ruin of a cottage.

Love, it seemed, was equal parts torture and comfort.

"Annora adores you," Natalie said. "She put herself between you and the blades of my guards when you were brought in. She was ready to die fighting to save you."

Henry's heart squeezed at the thought, but he put up

his shield nonetheless. "Well, I'm not surprised. Women have always loved me."

"Aye," Brandon said with a sigh. "But Annora knows what you're truly like and by some miracle, it hasn't put her off."

Laughter rose inside Henry, bursting from him in a sudden, sharp bark. The older man chuckled, and for a moment, an illusion descended on the banquet hall. A tableau of what could have been. In another life, without the poison of ambition and envy, they could have been friends. No feuds, no cruelty, no Caer Duloon. But then he would not have met Annora, and he would not trade her for anything.

"Thank you," Henry said. "I know I don't deserve this."

Brandon nodded once. "Aye, well, we're also doing this for her. Don't let any harm come to her."

"I'd die first."

The older man's lips slanted into a smile which faded as soon as it appeared. "I believe you."

"What will you do for money?" Natalie asked.

"I hadn't thought that far," Henry replied with a shrug. "Truth be told, I fully expected to die today."

"You should've known better." Natalie shifted in her seat, tightening the wool shawl around her shoulders. "I'm sure you could help sow crops or till the fields."

"And I know you've a strong back suited to building," Brandon added.

Henry chuckled. "I'm not sure I have the temperament for it."

"Mercenary, then," Natalie said, her green eyes as dark

as the glass of a poison bottle in the dim light of the hall. "There are always bandits and outlaws to be dealt with, and I think it's rather fitting you help Blackmere be rid of them."

It seemed as logical and natural as anything else. Henry pushed out a slow breath and nodded. "That I can do."

"Very good." Natalie was the first to stand, pulling an iron key from her belt and unlocking the manacles around his wrists. "We'll send you on your way to the cottage tonight, during the guard rotation. There will be horses for you at the edge of the town."

"Thank you."

"We'll provide you with clothes and enough food and firewood to keep you warm until you're settled in. Do not let anyone see you leave. In the morning you'll be dead."

Henry nodded in understanding "Will you at least give me an exciting death?"

She considered it a moment, before her lips twitched into a smile and her eyes softened. "I'll tell them Annora died in a blaze of glory, fighting our guards until her last breath. She gave her all to defend the two of you. But everyone knows you were sick when we brought you in. I'll tell them it was touch and go from the offset, but then you were kicked in the head by a horse in the courtyard, and passed after the doctor saw you. We burned your body on a pyre at the lake, because it was beginning to stink, so unfortunately we can't send your remains to Caer Duloon."

"Ah."

There it was. His legacy. After a decade of training and competing to be a champion, another decade spent festering in a cell, Henry was dead to the world.

He laughed quietly. "Well, I suppose that's all I deserve."

"It is," Brandon shrugged as he stood beside his wife. "And I truly hope you make good use of your second life. I hope that you're happy—"

"No, you don't," Henry chuckled dismissively. Because how could he? How could the man who Henry had betrayed time and time again ever truly hope for his happiness? No, it was a pleasantry, nothing more.

But that time Brandon did not echo his laughter. "Yes. I do. I always hoped you'd do great things, and now I think you will."

The words hit Henry harder and more devastating than the headsman's ax ever could. All his life he had craved Brandon's approval, as a squire and a novice champion, and even when he was at the height of his success and despised the man.

As the Blackmeres made to walk away from the table, Henry's thoughts manifested on his lips.

"I can't be sorry for what I did to you," he said, closing his eyes and bracing himself for punishment. "Not truly. My actions sent me to the cell, and without that I would not have met Annora. But I am sorry that it was you. You didn't deserve any of it."

When he opened his eyes, Brandon was staring down at him. His broad chest rising and falling slowly as he pressed his lips together. For a moment Henry was a squire once more, about to be admonished for scuffing the champion's armor.

"So why did you?" the larger man asked. "Why did you do it?"

"You risked everything for something I barely believed in," Henry said. "All your titles, your reputation you'd worked so hard to build, even the Champion's Guild. And you got away with it. Time and time again, you loved and won while I hated and lost. I could never understand why you risked everything you had at the Guild for love."

"But now you do?"

"Yes. Goddess yes, if she asked me to, I'd burn the Guild to cinders."

"Aye, well... don't," Brandon said with a chuckle, clapping his hand on Henry's shoulder. "Just love her harder than you ever knew you were capable of and appreciate everything she does. I'll call it even."

"Aye, me too," Natalie said. "Treat her well. And stay away from the Guild."

Henry bowed his head. "Thank you for letting me keep my life. Both times."

Natalie and Brandon's footsteps faded across the banquet hall, and as the door groaned behind them, Henry remained.

He sat alone a moment, raising his hands to the table. In the pale light streaming through the windows, his palms were scrubbed cleaner than he had ever seen them. In years gone by, in the Guild and in the cell, they were rough, calloused, the dirt and blood so ingrained he thought they would never come clean. Hands which had done so many awful things, but were now learning tenderness. She had scrubbed them clean.

All his life, he had craved greatness, legacy, fame, glory, but Annora's light had dulled the sheen of it all. Greatness did not need fanfare or applause. Her smile, her laughter, her love, knowing she felt completely safe and content in his arms, knowing that she wanted him despite, *and because of* everything that he was; that was greatness. She was the world, and he would do whatever it took to keep up with her.

Henry Percille; the champion, the prisoner, the bane of all who knew him, was dead. The man who outlived him would be greater in every way.

～

Under the cover of the lapis night sky, Annora and Henry hurried toward the castle gate. Their breaths swirled around them in clouds of silver as their footsteps cracked the thin layer of frost coating the courtyard stones.

A voice in the back of Henry's head chided him and told him he had lost his senses. Ten years ago, he would have laughed at the idea of giving up everything to live in a pile of rubble for somebody else. But that was before he had met Annora. It was before he had found himself.

He and Annora hurried through the town, keeping to the shadows, each carrying a pack of clothes on their back. Annora walked beside him, her expression set in steely determination.

"You know where we're going?" she asked for the fourth time since they'd left the castle.

"Of course."

She tightened her grip on his hand, sending a cloud of butterflies somersaulting through his stomach. Even then, in the cursed hours of a winter night, with hardly anything to call his own, he was the richest man he had ever known.

They reached the outskirts of the town before dawn, finding two horses tethered to an outpost. The beasts were already saddled and one of them was loaded with a pack of firewood and a bundle of blankets.

In the darkness he placed his hands upon something soft and warm; silken fur beneath his fingertips, stitched to a thick woolen cape. Henry's heart squeezed as he unfurled it. His fur, a symbol of his imprisonment, of the mercy he had not deserved, and now, it would accompany him to his new life, mended, made better and stripped of the taint.

Annora stepped closer. "I only asked her to mend it and clean it for you. I didn't think she'd do that."

Blackmere castle sat on its hill, shrouded in darkness but for a light flickering in one window. Perhaps Natalie and Brandon had watched as they fled, perhaps they sat uneasy with their decision to let him go, but he would not betray what little trust they had placed in him. Nothing was worth the risk of losing Annora.

"Do you think they forgive you?" Annora asked as she pulled herself up onto the large chestnut mare.

"No," Henry said, as a glimmer of regret caught light in his chest. "Not yet."

He fastened their packs to the second horse and placed

the cloak around his shoulders. It fluttered around his ankles as he hopped up into the saddle behind Annora and took the reins.

"Let's go home," he whispered, the word sounding impossible, wonderful, and terrifying all at once. His heart melted as she leaned back against him, the warm honey scent of her hair tightening his belly. He wrapped his arm around her waist, letting his hand rest below her breast, relishing the warmth and comfort of her body against his. "I adore you."

Annora twisted in the saddle, her lips finding his in the darkness. Her kiss was a promise, a reassurance, that life was good and about to get better.

"And I you." She traced the curve of his jaw with her fingertips before turning back to face the rising sun.

And together, they rode toward the dawn.

TWENTY-FIVE

F rost glittered beneath the winter sun's chaste kiss as the world came to life around them. Spherical little birds hopped between the barren branches, singing their songs of love and war, and plucking red berries from the holly bushes.

"It's beautiful here," Annora whispered, leaning her head back on Henry's shoulder.

And it was, but not because of the little birds or the silver sparkles gleaming in the crystal waters of the nearby stream. No. It was beautiful because she was there with him.

"Wait until you see the cottage," he said, breathing in deeply against the top of her head. "It's perfectly abysmal. You're going to love it."

She chuckled against him. "Well, lucky for you I have a fondness for terrible, broken things."

"Like attracts like, I suppose."

She swatted his hand, but held it fast to her waist, warming his cold fingers with the heat of her body.

"Are you sure?" she asked.

"About what? Us? Yes."

She shook her head. "No, I know all too well that you're entirely, hopelessly besotted with me. But about this life; the quiet, the cottage. We could ride on. I doubt the Blackmeres would follow us but if they did, we could outrun them. We could still go south and you could still—"

"I don't want that," Henry said, lifting the golden curtain of her hair to place a kiss on the nape of her neck. Her gasping breath billowed from her lips in a silver cloud in the frosty air. "I want you. I want to make you happy in your wretched little hag's cottage."

"But your titles, your riches..."

"Worthless without your happiness."

She offered no further protest as they rode on through the seemingly endless emptiness around them, but she could swear he leaned into her a little more, tightened his grip on her hand a little harder. The silence between them was comforting and easy, broken only by birdsong, and the constant babble of the swollen stream up ahead.

"We're close," he told her.

He dismounted with a grunt, lessening the horse's load as the forest grew dense around them.

"Are you even any good at repairing cottages?" she asked.

He gazed up at her and grinned. "We'll see."

Her heart stumbled at the sight of him, and despite the

chill, her face grew warm. She would never tire of those blue eyes, nor the way he could snatch her breath from her lungs with a smile, or the brush of his fingertips against her calf.

"You're staring," he said.

"Aye, so are you."

He chuckled, glancing ahead before turning back to her a shade darker. "I suppose I am."

Perhaps it was infatuation, or love, or her desire for him which swelled and heightened with every passing moment, but Annora's heart thrummed faster than she had ever known it to.

He was hers, so in love with her that he had been willing to give his life to save her. He had been entirely right about her from the start; despite the steely demeanor she wore as armor, and despite knowing she could be strong without him, she loved to be cherished and wanted, and relished the knowledge that he was all for her. And she was all for him, there was no point in denying it any more.

"Well," Henry sighed, no longer staring up at her, but ahead. He brought the horses to a halt. "Here we are."

The sight before them stole Annora's breath.

The cottage was everything she had ever dreamed and more besides. She had wanted isolation, quiet, a house fit for a crone which would scare away travelers and children alike, and her perfect vision had only served as a starting point for nature to take over and heighten the fantasy.

Wilted brown plants hung flat against the crooked roof, tangled decaying vines clung to the windows, allowing light into the cottage only by the grace of winter. A canopy of skeletal trees stretched above; their stark fingers joined across the roof.

"Henry..."

"Do you love it?" he asked, the sincerity in his voice enough to bring tears to her eyes.

"I do."

"Then I do too."

She let him slide his hands at either side of her waist, placing her palms on his shoulders as he lifted her from the horse. She tore her eyes from the cottage to gaze down at him instead; so radiant, so utterly, brutally beautiful in the dappled light of the forest.

"How does it compare to the castles you hate so much?" he asked.

"It doesn't. It's a palace." She grinned and threaded her fingers with his, leading him toward the cottage. "And it's ours."

In the years since anyone had last set foot there, the forest had attempted to lay claim to it. Shriveled brown ferns curled their leaves toward it, as if desperate to touch the moss-ridden stones. It was every bit as daunting as she imagined, and it was perfect. It was home. She stood on the doorstep—*their doorstep*— and turned to face him,

"Then I suppose that makes you queen?" He tried to frown, but his lips betrayed him, unable to fight back his smile.

"I suppose it does."

"Well then..." He took a step toward her, driving her back against the wooden door as he braced his hands on the frame. "In that case, I am your most humble servant, my queen. And I plan to spend my life on my knees before you, granting your every obscene little wish."

A slow smile spread across her lips as she raised her hands to join his at the top of the doorframe. "Fortunately, we've no neighbors for miles. No one to hear you beg for release as I ravish you."

"That better be a promise."

Goddess, how she loved that man.

EPILOGUE

"You're a heartless bastard," the man growled from beneath Henry's boot. "They'll hang me if you don't let me go."

Henry sighed, staring at the point where the road disappeared over a hill. There was no sign of the guard and they were late. "No, they won't. Just be decent with them and pay back what you owe."

"How can I? You robbed m—"

"I didn't rob you. I *confiscated* your ill-gotten gains," Henry hissed, stepping off his prisoner and prowling in a frustrated circle around the wretch. He could let him go, but then he would not be paid, and the few scraps of silver and copper he had taken from the man were not enough to get he and Annora through the coming winter.

The mere thought of her sent a pang of longing through his chest. Bringing in his mark had only kept him from home for a night, but it was a night too long. The forest beckoned him to return, back to Annora and the comfortable life they shared. But before he returned to her, he first had to collect his payment.

"The guard said they'd be here by noon to get you," he muttered, more to himself than to the man lying on the ground. "What could be keeping them?"

His answer appeared on the horizon not long after. Two guards flanked a behemoth of a horse, ridden by the indomitable lord of Blackmere.

Two years ago, when Henry and Annora had first moved into the cottage, a visit from the nobles had struck dread into Henry's heart. Fears that their progress in turning the pile of stones into something resembling a home was not fast enough, or that he had pushed his luck a little too far in rifling through the pockets of his marks before turning them over to the guards. But time had worn that dread down to annoyance, then mild inconvenience, and finally, as the old Bear drew closer, to something decidedly warmer.

"Shit, that's the lord of the castle," the prisoner on the floor gasped. "They're hanging me for certain, I know it."

"Oh, do rein in your ego. He's not here for you. He's here for me." Henry rolled his eyes as he turned from the man and stepped out to greet Brandon, bowing low and waving his hand with a flourish. "Your majesty, it's been too long."

Brandon's hearty laugh echoed across the moor as he slowed his horse from a trot to a walk, and finally brought her to a halt before Henry. "Majesty now, is it? It's a damn sight better than the nicknames you came up with for me at the Guild."

Hot equine breath blew against Henry's palm as he reached out to touch the velvet softness of the beast's muzzle. "How's life at the castle?"

Detaching a coin bag from his belt, Brandon pressed it to Henry's palm, paying him for his work. "Wonderful, as always. And how about you and yours?"

"Better every day."

"Good. That's good. Do you think you'll marry her?"

Henry chuckled. "If she asked it of me, but there's no ritual that would strengthen what we already have."

Brandon smiled warmly, but his face hardened once more as the guards spurred on their horses, pursuing the prisoner who had managed to scurry away. The lord lifted his chin and called out, "Gentle with him. He's only a petty thief."

"You've never changed," Henry said with a smile as he shielded his eyes from the midday sun with his hand. "Always so soft-hearted."

"Not always. Just as long as you've known me," Brandon replied. "But you've changed. A lot."

"Have I?"

"Aye. I like this version far more."

Henry's heart skipped. The compliment drowned out the prisoner's cries for help as he was dragged by the guards. The thief's hands grasped the sleeves of Henry's gambeson coat, but his efforts barely swayed him.

"Please," the thief sobbed. "Don't kill me."

Brandon's lips tightened and his complexion paled as he shifted in the saddle. "We're not going to kill you. We'll take you back to Blackmere and you can repay all you took from those families. Then we'll decide what to do with you."

"I can't pay it back. He took it."

Ah, there was the dread after all. Henry sighed and bade goodbye to the meager scraps in his pocket as the prisoner pointed a trembling finger at him.

It seemed impossible for Brandon to grow any larger, and yet, as he straightened his back and stared down at Henry, he may as well have been as tall as the mountains themselves. The older man sat silent, arching a single gray eyebrow and awaiting the confession which brewed in Henry's chest.

Brandon was the first to break the silence. "Take the prisoner away," he said to his guards. "I'll deal with this one."

Every one of Henry's instincts told him to prepare to fight, but he no longer listened to them. Not where Brandon was concerned. The man had given him too many chances, risked too much to give Henry the life he now had. So, Henry simply watched the rippling dark clouds overhead, and awaited his admonishment.

"Nothing to say?" Brandon said, leaning his elbow on the pommel of his saddle as he patted his horse's neck. "No witty remarks or attempts to worm your way out of it?"

"No."

"Hm." Brandon lifted his eyes and glanced at the woods on the eastern horizon. "How are things? Are you struggling?"

"No," Henry snapped, offended by the very idea. "Annora and I are very happy and well taken care of. It's just… well, meat isn't cheap and I'm no hunter. It never hurts to have a little extra—"

Brandon held up his hand, requesting silence. "Annora's birthday is coming up, isn't it?"

Henry frowned. It was still almost half a year away, not that the nobleman would know. But as Brandon reached into a pouch hanging from his belt, and the light danced on shining yellow metal, Henry found himself unable to argue.

"You needn't do that," Henry said.

"Aye well, you overpaid your taxes last year." With a flick of his thumb, Brandon sent the coin spinning through the air.

Henry caught it against his chest. "I haven't paid tax in my life."

Brandon's eyebrows dipped for a moment, before an incredulous smile flickered across his lips. "Well, I've never had a head for numbers. You'll have to take it up with my wife if you have any questions. Until next time."

Henry stood silent as the nobleman rode away after his guards, leaving a cloud of dust in his wake. He watched until the man disappeared beyond the horizon, and only then did he glance at the money in his hand.

There was more than enough for he and Annora to feast through winter. Though it was past noon, there was time for him to reach Blackmere before the market closed. Being somewhat good certainly had its benefits, but as he raced toward the town, wickedness was still far more appealing.

∾

The holly berries had turned red and autumn spread like wildfire through the woods. Annora sat on a rickety stool outside her cottage, breathing in the sweet scent of crisp earth and woodsmoke. The waterfall was heavy and eager after days of rainfall, its constant roar a soothing accompaniment to the dance of falling leaves. The end of their second year at the cottage was coming to a close.

The chill in the air always brought back memories, some welcome, others not. Caer Duloon, and Lord Caine, still haunted her, but after two years, they were little more than phantoms from another life. She paid the memories little heed when they came.

All that mattered was the man striding toward her, leading a graying chestnut mare through the trees. The moment Henry's eyes met hers, a wide grin spread across his face and her heart answered with a joyous leap. Their time together had been kind to him, and he was larger, softer, and infinitely more beautiful than Annora could bear. And mercenary life suited him well, kept their cupboards full, and kept the Blackmeres happy.

The approaching cold no longer filled her with dread. Cold nights were their favorites, when they lay together beneath the bedsheets she had stitched, sharing warmth and pleasure. Winter meant warmed honeyed wine by the fire, the scent of smoke tangled in his hair, the heat of his mouth against her pebbled skin.

"Back already? I hardly noticed you were gone," she said, standing from her stool and stepping out to greet him.

A smile spread across his lips. No matter how many times he returned from the market, he never seemed to tire of her joke. "Aye, sadly I must return to this hovel and the crone who keeps me bound to it," he said, greeting her with a soft kiss to her temple, then stooping to press another to her lips. Quietly, and sincerely, he added, "I missed you."

"Goddess, so did I."

With a grin he pulled a cloth packet of sausage from his bag and handed them to her, before delving back in to retrieve a small wheel of sheep's cheese encased in gray wax. "I almost entered a blood feud with a washerwoman for this, so we must enjoy every bite."

She chuckled as she tucked it beneath her arm. "I appreciate you defending our family's honor, especially with such serious matters as cheese."

Henry paused, a slow smile lifting the corners of his mouth for a moment. "Our family?"

"Aye."

His expression softened, before he plunged his hand back inside the bag. "There is something else. Something I had planned to give you for your birthday, but I couldn't wait until then."

Annora laughed. "My birthday isn't for five months."

"I was *very* excited." He beamed at her as he placed a long, slender, cloth-wrapped package in her hand, this time bound in soft white silk. "Be careful. It's breakable if you drop it. The artisan assured me it was sturdy enough for our purpose, but..."

Annora's breath caught in her throat as she unwrapped the silk, and a cold hard item rolled onto her palm. Her heart skipped a beat as she beheld her gift; a glass cock, crafted with meticulous detail, down to the thick veins running along the shaft. The glass was crystal-clear and glimmering in the autumn sun. Alongside it was a vial of golden oil.

"Is this for the next time you leave me?" she asked.

He laughed. "Well, yes you can use it for that, but there's another part to it." A moment later he pulled what appeared to be a thick leather harness from the sack, pressing his teeth into his lower lip.

The realization of what he was asking fanned heat across her face. "You want me to wear it?"

"Aye," he said, his voice low and tinged with a darkness he rarely had cause to use anymore. "I want you to wear it and claim me. Fuck me until I sob into the pillow."

A shiver of excitement ran through her body as she stepped back toward the cottage, unable to take her eyes from him. "I don't need a cock to claim you, I know all too well you're completely mine."

"But that's less fun."

She chuckled, narrowing her eyes. "How did you afford this?"

Henry shrugged a heavy shoulder. "I've been saving for it."

"By which you mean you robbed people?"

"Only those I deposited with the guards. I'm not a complete monster."

As she backed through the threshold of the cottage door, she reached out with her empty hand to grip a fistful of his padded jacket, pulling him inside with her. "You are. But you're my monster."

His big, brawny body collided with hers, and in a heartbeat his lips and teeth were on her too. No matter how many quiet months passed without guards or nobles to bother them, Henry still kissed her like every moment was his last, like he still planned to ride out in the morning and face the grim end he had spent a decade imagining for himself. But he never would, they were far too happy and so revoltingly in love.

She pulled away, stroking back the loose locks of hair which had fallen over his eyes. "You're mine forever, aren't you?"

"Every part of me," he whispered, cupping her face in his hands, stroking the soft curve of her jaw with his thumbs. "Always."

"Good." She raised onto the tips of her toes, biting her lower lip. As he sighed against her, her heart fluttered, and she could stand the wait no longer. "Upstairs. I want you on your back so I can watch your face as I ruin you."

As always, her wish was his command. They hurried up the rickety wooden staircase, into the loft where their bed sat perched above the rest of the cottage. Henry sat breathless on the edge of the mattress, helping her out of her dress and into the harness, his neck and cheeks already flushed pink before she had even touched him. When she was ready, she undressed him slowly, kissing every newly bared inch of his body.

"I'll be gentle with you," she whispered as she nipped

the soft flesh above his navel with her teeth. "And I'll go slowly."

"Don't you dare," he hissed, twisting his fists in the bedsheets as he lifted his head to watch her. "I've thought about this for months."

"I thought this was supposed to be *my* gift?"

"It is," he grinned. "And I know the greatest gift I can give you is my complete and utter ruination, my glorious, radiant harpy."

With a chuckle she drew back, taking the vial of oil and coating her cock and fingers, before sliding her hands between his thick, muscled thighs. The instant her fingertip circled his hole, he bucked his hips from the bed, moaning at the slightest touch.

"It's a good thing we have no neighbors for miles," she purred, as she pushed her finger inside him, stretching and readying him. "You can be as loud as you need to be."

But the cry on his parted lips was silent as she pushed the glass cock into him, her quim pulsing at the sight of him, quivering, straining, the veins in his throat bulging as he took it to the hilt.

"Good," she sighed as his cheeks flared red. "Does it feel good?"

Slowly, she rolled her hips as he cried out in bliss.

"Oh, Goddess, yes," he moaned, one strong hand gripping the edge of the bed as he wrapped the other around his cock, stroking himself as he watched her.

She swatted his hand away, admonishing him with a tsk. "You're mine to do with as I please, Dragon."

His lips curled into a silent snarl, his gaze burning into

her as she pumped his cock in her fist. She moved slowly, letting his pleasure build until he shivered and gasped beneath her.

She ached for him, yearned for him, desperate to feel his touch, to chase her own release, but watching him come undone, watching that beast of a man tremble and whimper as she thrust into him, was too good to stop.

"I love you," he gasped. "Goddess help me, I love you so much."

"Come for me, my love. Show me how good this feels."

As she thrust into him, his eyebrows stitched together and he came undone with a cry, his seed spurting against her belly as his thighs trembled and his toes curled.

Perhaps it was their freedom or perhaps the isolation, but he had grown louder in their time together. And every cry she wrung from his lips, every startled gasp and wanton moan, was an ode to her, and to the sway she held over his heart.

"Good," she purred as the last of his spend rolled down the length of his cock. "Goddess, if you could only see yourself now, blushing and glistening so prettily."

The snarl returned as she slid into him once more, relishing the way he bit into his lip as he raised his head to watch her.

"You'll be the death of me, woman."

"Aye," she said. "And you'll take me down with you."

A moment later his hands were around her wrists, pulling her down until his lips brushed hers, sending a burst of heat through her veins. He whispered against her lips, "On your back. Now," sealing his command with a kiss which threatened to chase her own spirit from her body and replace it with his.

She slid the cock out of him, her lips parting at the feral moan which burst from him, her fingers trembling in anticipation as she fumbled with the buckles.

"My, my, Annora… have I rattled you?" he asked, lifting himself onto his elbows to watch her.

"I need you," she whispered. "Now."

He reached out a hand, stroking up the length of her thigh before slipping it between. Her breath caught in her chest as he dragged a finger through her folds, narrowing his eyes and releasing a breathy moan at the sensation of her.

Her toes curled against the floorboards as his fingers explored her.

"You're so wet," he whispered, pressing a kiss to her belly as he let his thumb circle the swollen bud of her clitoris. "And you fucked me so well, I think it only fair I do the same to you."

"Goddess, yes," she whispered, letting her head fall back as he pulled her nipple between his lips and flicked it with his tongue.

"But my cock is sated and your cock needs cleaning before I use it on you, and I don't know that I can make you wait that long."

That bastard. How she loved him. "You could always… oh," her grip tightened on his shoulders as he pushed a thick finger into her. "Put that insatiable tongue to good use."

He chuckled darkly, pulling her down onto the bed with him and rolling onto her so she was pinned beneath him. The crush of his big body was almost enough to send her careening over the edge of ecstasy, and as he moved to lower himself between her thighs, she held onto him tightly.

"What's the matter?" he asked.

"Stay on top of me. Pin me," was all she managed to say.

Her wish was his command. Keeping his torso on top of hers, he twisted, so the weight of his chest was on top of her belly, his lips on her clitoris, his nose against her entrance. She gasped as his broad palms spread her thighs, holding them apart as he began to kiss her, hard and fast, making her buck and strain helplessly against him.

"Is this what you wanted?" he asked, his lips brushing her sensitive flesh as he spoke. "To be helpless as I have my way with you?"

She nodded, screwing her eyes tight, lost in the sensation of his touch.

He lavished her with hard, deep kisses, and soft exploratory licks, driving her hard toward her climax. Though they had only been apart for one night, he savored her as though he had not tasted her in years, slowly dragging his tongue through her folds, plunging it into her with wild desperation.

She raked her nails along the beast's back as she came undone, and as she lay panting and flushed pink, he kept her pinned. The moment his tongue returned to her clitoris her body jolted against him, pleasure rippling through her.

"Henry—"

He laughed wickedly, refusing to take his mouth from her. She lay trapped beneath him, restrained, at the mercy of that monstrous man, and loving every moment of it. And all she could do was take it, ride wave after wave of pleasure as she climaxed against his mouth again and again. Unraveling, cursing his name and screaming it in ecstasy in the same breath.

"I hate you," she whispered, pressing her nails to his back and leaving angry red crescents.

"Liar," he growled, before fluttering the tip of his tongue beneath the hood of her clitoris.

She threw her head back against the mattress, gasping as her thighs trembled in his hands. "Oh, fuck, I don't. I love you. I love you."

He raised his head then, but granted her no relief, his fingers taking the place of his tongue, strumming her, teasing, torturing her in the most delicious way. "Have you had enough?"

"Never."

A low growl of approval rolled through his chest as he shifted, lifting himself off her and turning around to lay between her thighs. His cock was hard again, and his lips curled into a snarl as he dragged his length through her wet, swollen folds.

Every inch of her body tingled in anticipation as he teased her, until she could bear it no longer, digging her heels against his backside and pulling him down into her. Goddess, how she adored him; her Dragon, and his appetite for destruction, which was wholly and devoutly focused on her.

He pushed into her slowly, ensuring she felt every inch of him, burying himself to the hilt before withdrawing almost entirely, tormenting and teasing them both until they were red and breathless.

"What now?" he asked as she clawed at the red blush spreading across his chest. "Shall I fuck you hard?"

"Yes," she gasped, rubbing her clitoris, desperate for release. "Hard."

"Mm—" his eyes closed as he drove down into her and began to pump his hips faster.

The slap of their bodies colliding again and again accompanied her moans as her climax built beneath her fingertips. Every time he spent the night away from her, he liked to ride her hard and fast, pounding into her with untamed desperation, his fingertips digging into her soft flesh as though someone was coming to take her away from him.

She bucked her hips as a kick of pleasure jolted her, bringing her close.

"That's it," he growled, lifting her calf over his shoulder, pushing deeper into her so every thrust sent a shiver through her spine. "I want to feel your sweet cunt squeeze my cock."

She was already coming undone before he finished speaking. Her pleasure tore through her, barbed and burning hot, pulling a savage cry from her lips which he answered with his own. His fingers pressed against her ankle as he pushed his face against her calf, scarlet and gleaming with sweat, before he collapsed onto her.

His breath blew cool against the burning skin of her throat as he lay his heavy arm across her chest.

"Happy birthday, beloved harpy," he muttered against the pillow.

Annora chuckled and rolled over to face him. "*Your* beloved harpy," she said. "I'm always yours."

The corner of Henry's mouth curved into a smile as he pulled her closer, throwing his thigh over her hips so she could not escape. Not that all the guards in Aldland could have dragged her from him.

She was forever his harpy, and he her dragon, and they would always soar together.

he End.

ACKNOWLEDGMENTS

When I first started writing the Blackmere books, I never intended to give Henry his own book. I absolutely despised the little shit. But I'm so glad I did. Writing this story was so much fun, and I'm so grateful for the support I've received during the process.

As always, thank you Jake. Your love and support have meant the world always, but especially at points this past year where I didn't think I could get back up. I couldn't have done this without you.

Thank you to the wonderful Hags (my amazing friends who send me cheese when times are tough), and to Kenny, Ali, Renee, Kait, Agata, and Tanya for your support and friendship.

Thank you to Lauriel of LMO Editing for your edits and support, to Naj of Qamber Designs and Media for yet another stunning book cover, and to Jack Harbon for formatting and making this book beautiful.

Thanks to Emily, Kelly, and Janel for your proofreading, feedback, and encouragement.

And a special thank you to my Vixens for Life on Patreon: Emily H, LB F, Katie B, Melanie, Linda W, Janel A, Deanna S, Amanda F, and Stacie C. I can't even put into words how much your support means to me.

ABOUT MARIE LIPSCOMB

Marie specializes in writing romances with plus sized heroines and plus sized heroes. She is the author of the *Hearts of Blackmere* and *Vixens Rock* series as Marie Lipscomb, and also writes short, bonkers, high-heat romances including *No Getting Ogre You* and *Santa Claus is Going to Town On Me* under the pen name M.L. Eliza.

Originally from Bolton, UK, Marie now lives in North Carolina, USA. When she's not writing, she can usually be found playing the same three video games on a loop (*cough* Dragon Age)

Also by Marie Lipscomb

The *Hearts of Blackmere* Series

The Lady's Champion

The Champion's Desire

Forever His Champion

The *Vixens Rock* Series

Rhythm

Strings

Amped

Writing as M.L. Eliza

No Getting Ogre You

Santa Claus is Going to Town On Me

CPSIA information can be obtained
at www.ICGtesting.com
Printed in the USA
BVHW040157280422
635614BV00014B/330